GEMINI LOST

Mischievous Malamute Mystery Series Book 5

HARLEY CHRISTENSEN

To my mischievous crew—Mark, Max and Maui...

Thank you for bringing joy into my life
and filling my days with endless laughter...

PROLOGUE

Los Angeles

I finally got my California sunset but it didn't turn out quite the way I had envisioned.

As I was packing for the return trip to Phoenix, anticipating a long overdue reconciliation with my bed, I received an unexpected phone call from Officer Piedmont, aka Peedy, Kelly Decker's childhood friend. Prior to her untimely death, she had mentioned the discussion of a meet and greet between our pups once the case had been resolved. Now that he was the guardian of his best friend's canine companion, he wanted to honor her wishes.

Though he'd caught me off-guard with his proposition, I quickly agreed, knowing that it would not only do a world of good for Decker's pup but for Peedy, too, as they had both lost the most important human in their lives.

I was pleasantly surprised as he approached, boyishly cute in his t-shirt, board shorts and flip-flops—a tall, tanned drink of California, with sun-kissed curls barely tamed by the crop of his haircut and which only enhanced the aquamarine brilliance of the eyes staring back at me. A flash of white emerged as he broke into a massive grin, revealing dimples and a small scar that passed from his lower lip to the base of the cleft of his chin.

"From the description Decker gave me"—he immediately blushed, composing himself as he looked down—"of this big guy, you must be Arianna."

"Please, call me AJ," I replied, extending my hand, "and this is Nicoh."

He nodded and clasped my hands with his own, which were warm but firm. "Nice to meet you, AJ. Logan. And Mia."

The statuesque German Shepherd flipped her tail and cocked her head, giving her canine counterpart a thorough once-over. Nicoh murmured a low whoo-whoo, which I translated to "ooooh, she's pretty," before huffing out a breath as he swooshed his tail from side to side while dancing from one paw to the other.

"Mind your manners, buddy," I replied. "Mia will put you in your place if you don't behave."

Nicoh released another huff before bowing his head and leaning in so that Mia could sniff. She did, and after a wagging of tails, they took account of one another in typical canine fashion.

Of course, both of the humans blushed and I managed to awkwardly squawk out, "Don't worry. I don't think they'll be offended if we don't follow suit."

I winced at my choice of words but Logan chuckled easily, adding, "Yeah, I think a handshake should suffice. For now, at least." His eyes widened. "Err...what I meant was—"

I waved him off and we laughed. Now that each of us had put our foot into it, we had effectively broken the ice, if not melted it.

We walked up the beach, the dogs next to one another as Logan told me a bit about growing up in the valley, reminiscing about adventures with his best friend. It was easy to see how much they had cared about one another, fought for one another and loved one another.

"I'm curious, how did you get the nickname Peedy, anyway?"

I asked, though I'd assumed it was short for Piedmont, betting that he'd caught crap for it each time Decker had used it in front of his peers.

Logan tossed his head back and laughed. Hard. Before long, he had me laughing again, too.

"What?" I finally managed to snort out.

"It's not 'Peedy.' It's P.D., as in the initials 'P' and 'D'." He paused to chuckle again, after taking in my confused expression. "It stands for Piedmont and Decker. I called her the same thing. We always pretended we'd grow up to be detectives like our pops and form our own agency. Like Simon and Simon but without the whole sibling rivalry thing."

"I would imagine," I replied. "Close enough to the truth, though." Logan nodded. "You ever consider it? Leaving law enforcement, opening your own agency?"

Logan looked out at the ocean. "To be honest, I just don't think it would be the same without her...without D."

"I know it feels that way now, Logan. But, maybe you should keep your options—and that door—open. I think Decker would want you to."

"Maybe, someday." He shrugged before turning to me. "Why, are you offering to be my partner?"

I laughed. "I think I already have my hands full—between my photography business, my saucy best friend and...this guy." I waved a hand at Nicoh, who was acting about as goofy as I felt as he trotted to keep up with the beauty at his side.

"Well, it would be immensely useful, considering you clearly already have an impressive skill set under your belt," Logan teased.

I snorted. "It takes a considerable amount of patience, persistence and downright stubbornness—honed over years of dedication to mastering the craft."

He released a chuckle and nodded. "I would guess so."

We walked in comfortable silence for a few moments, until I shared what had been weighing on me.

"Seriously, Logan, at least take what I've said into consideration about hanging up a shingle. I think it suits you. And I think Decker would agree."

"You do the same, AJ, if you change your mind about hanging that shingle with me?" I smiled and nodded, becoming self-conscious when I noticed he was studying me. "Now I know why Decker chose you."

"Chose me?" I stopped, nearly tripping over my own feet in the process.

Logan grabbed my elbow to ensure I remained upright. "You remind me so much of her." He chuckled. "Except for the two left feet, that is."

"Thanks," I replied, brushing hair out of my eyes. "It's one of my handier skills—tripping over my own feet, that is. You never know when you'll need that one in pinch." Logan laughed, causing me to blush. Again. "You're right, I'm sure Decker typically had both feet firmly planted and always knew which direction she was traveling before she took the next step."

He nodded. "She was also an exceptional judge of character. The day before she was…killed, she wanted to make sure I passed along a message—a request—in the event something happened to her."

"An ominous bit of foreshadowing," I murmured, prodding Logan to continue. "This request…"

"She wants you to look into her mother's case," he replied, searching my eyes, his tone serious.

"Her mother's—what?" I stammered. "Why me?"

"Decker said the two of you shared something in common. Something…deeply personal."

"Death," I whispered, thinking of my parents, my sister, my friends.

"It not just death that connects you, AJ," he replied, holding my shoulders so that I was forced to face him. "It's the way they died."

"They were murdered," I replied. Logan nodded. "Where... how would I know where to start?" Panic washed over me, not wishing to let Decker or her faith in me down.

"With both feet firmly planted, confident that you know what direction you're taking before you take that step."

I looked down, frowning when I realized he was using my own words against me.

He tilted my chin until I met his eyes.

"And with your assistance?" I asked, disappointed when he shook his head. "Because you can't? Or won't?"

"Because I'm a cop," he replied, his tone sad but earnest. "I can, however, offer you a starting point."

"A lead?" My reply came out sounding far more hopeful than I felt. Before he could respond, I spouted out, "Why not take it to the Stanton's—or Anna? This is more their area of expertise."

"No, AJ, she wanted you." Logan released a breath before continuing, "Besides, there's a serious conflict of interest where they're concerned. As it is, there will be hell to pay when this comes out."

"I'm not sure I like the sound of that. Maybe you should just tell me about this lead Decker had."

"It's more than just a lead, AJ. Decker had a name."

"Okay..." I gestured for him to continue, even though I was still not convinced I wanted to know, regardless of how far this name, whoever's it was, took me.

"Terrence Edwards," he replied, ensuring he had my full attention before he added, "The man who changed Decker and her pop's lives forever.

"Until this moment, that bastard has gotten away with murder."

CHAPTER ONE

As luck would have it, my mouth was working about as well as my two left feet as I tripped, biting my tongue as Logan side-stepped, gripping my elbow as I huffed out my thanks.

He would have gotten a better reaction if he'd stripped down to his skivvies and danced the Cabbage Patch.

He'd landed a whopper on me. Wait—make that two. The first came in the form of Kelly Decker haunting me from beyond the grave, holding me solely accountable for bringing her mother's killer to justice.

Whopper numero dos, minus pickles, catsup and all the other tasty stuff, came in the form of the name of her mother's killer—who just happened to be the father of a friend and the soon to be father-in-law of another. And, did I mention, said killer happened to be a fairly…notorious Los Angeles criminal defense attorney?

A return trip to the Valley of the Sun was looking better by the minute.

Fortunately, Leah precluded any ill-timed responses from escaping my piehole as she raced up the beach, smartphone in hand.

Apparently, it's a difficult feat when you're chewing gum.

Let's just say, it didn't bode well for her. She was within inches of us when she toppled and the phone thwacked Logan in the shin as she face-planted in the sand.

I was sensing a theme here.

As she peered up at us, not in the least bit apologetic about encroaching upon whatever conversation we'd been engaged in, her expression turned sour. Before we could react, she spit out the fluorescent purple wad of chewing gum she'd managed to secure in her downfall.

"Sand," she growled—as if it warranted an explanation.

Noting our expressions—Logan's was confused, mine was more…constricted…she quickly added, "Ramirez needs you… pronto." She jabbed a finger at the phone, which had landed beyond her reach after she'd likely given Logan a nice knot.

"Tell him I'll call him back," I replied between gritted teeth. "I'm in the middle of something."

Leah snorted. "Yeah, told him it was possible that you were tied up playing tonsil tennis with Chippy here but he was insistent."

Logan had the good graces to keep quiet, though he was somewhere between amused and appalled. My cheeks grew warm and all I wanted to do was smush that gum—sand-coated or not— back into her mouth, along with the smartphone.

I was about ready to execute that fabulous idea when Leah quickly added, "By the way, he said if you balked, to tell you that your *father* just ambushed one of our state's congressmen."

Logan turned to me, his brow furrowed. "I thought Decker said your parents had been murdered—err…had recently passed."

Leah waved a hand, gave me an apologetic shrug and then proceeded to toss another gallon of accelerant on top of the heap.

"Sorry, I was referencing Martin, her bio pop. Ha, *pop…*

fitting, considering how he tends to flit in and out of things at the most inopportune moments." She glanced at me before adding, "He's been a bit of a nuisance lately."

Nuisance didn't even begin to cover the way Martin—or Ramirez, for that matter—had gotten into my craw as of late. It did spur me to redact my previous sentiment. Rather than return to Phoenix, I was starting to embrace the idea of joining Leah on the ground and burying my head in the sand, especially when I reached for the phone and noticed we'd been on speakerphone the entire time.

After shooting her my best evil eye, I disabled the speaker-mode and moved out of earshot of Logan and Leah before growling into the phone, "This isn't a good time. What do you want?"

"Such a pleasure talking to you, too, AJ. But this isn't a social chat." Ramirez's voice rumbled over the line.

Despite the weeks that had passed since we had last spoken, I noted that there was no love lost given the virtual icicles pegging me in the ear.

No more love lost, anyway.

"Congrats. You've moved up in the world." I worked hard to keep the snark out of my tone, but I'll admit it was a challenge.

"Excuse me?" came the response.

"Last time we…talked, you were a homicide detective. So unless someone's died, why are you calling me?"

There was an awkward pause.

"Hello? You called me, Ramirez. Spit it out. Like I said, it's not a good time."

"I was asked to contact you on the Congressman's behalf. Because of our previous…association…"

Association? I couldn't help but snort. "I think you've also had some sort of 'association' with his wife, if memory serves."

Another moment of silence ensued from the other end.

Just as I was about to hang up, he finally managed to ground out, "It was actually Serena's suggestion that we get you involved."

"*We*? Oh, my, my, my, how things have changed. Do tell— how I can help? And, just for the record, I can hardly wait to hear how Martin Singer plays into this fantasy."

"As Leah mentioned, the Congressman was ambushed when he got into his car. The assailant was waiting for him in the back seat."

"Oooh, what sharp little ears you have…glad you managed to confirm all of that, despite the fact her mouth was filled with sand," I replied, pausing to huff out a breath. "Still doesn't explain why anyone in your little band of do-gooders would claim Martin was involved."

"I didn't say any of us claimed he was involved. It's a possible conclusion I drew from the conversation the assailant had with the Congressman." Ramirez's nasty tone grated on my eardrum. Apparently, the detective was as short on patience as I was.

It served him right and I said as much.

"Good for you, you got your man. Go ahead and post a gold star on your fridge. But next time, leave me the hell out it," I snapped and was about to hang up when the naughty little AJ on my shoulder prompted me to add, "For future reference, Detective —whatever Martin Singer is involved in, fictional or not, has no bearing on me, as I've not laid eyes on the man in weeks. And while this little convo has been amusing, I really need to get back—"

"Wait, AJ—the Congressman asked for you." Ramirez's tone was urgent but it only exasperated me that much more.

I was, for lack of better phrasing…in a mood.

"Because you told him about my connection with Martin." I posed no question, though the sarcasm I leveled on him was thick and my index finger was still itching to press "End" on this ridiculous, intrusive conversation.

"No," I heard an audible sigh before he continued, "because when the assailant left the Congressman, he dropped a business card." He paused and if sensing my hand gesture, added, "It was yours."

CHAPTER TWO

I hated to ruin a great line, so I didn't. I simply told Ramirez I would be in touch once I got back to Phoenix and he begrudgingly agreed before I disconnected.

It took a bit of sidestepping, apologizing and all-around awkward maneuvering to break away from Logan. On one hand, I assured him I understood the seriousness of Decker's request and was committed to pursuing what she had entrusted me to. On the other, I was backhanding myself, as I knew the mention of Martin's name would probably result in an entirely different commitment.

He was, after all, family.

So, as we raced back to Phoenix, no thanks to Leah's lead foot, which became increasingly pronounced the more I whined, I allowed the other topic of dread to wash over me.

Ramirez.

Leah offered me none of her usual quips or proffered any advice, tugging at her hair as we drove much of the six hours from Los Angeles to Phoenix in solitude. She knew better than to intrude on my mental meanderings as of late, when my life had been crap from the moment I'd engaged in a battle to the death with Winslow Clark. And lived to tell about it. My reward was to have both Ramirez and Martin dump me the moment I came back to life, offering neither resolution nor absolution.

Let's just say, it was a bitter pill to swallow. And perhaps, on the flip side, I'd become a bit of one myself.

Leah had none-to-gently pointed that out prior to the L.A. trip, which was part of the reason I'd agreed it was probably best for me to get out of town to clear my mind.

Well, that hadn't turned out quite as planned.

As we crossed into Phoenix, I made a comment to that effect, only to have Leah volley one back, smugly reminding me about the scene she witnessed as she happened upon me with Logan on the beach.

I quickly reminded her that, after he was unable to locate me, Ramirez had elected to call her, causing her to inject herself into our afternoon out, which had solely been for the benefit of the dogs.

Right.

She'd rolled her eyes at that one.

Twice.

It wasn't a good look. Think brain freeze played at double the speed.

I had yet to tell her about Decker's request. I hadn't had time to process it yet myself. It was a decades-old crime that hadn't been solved by professionals. Why the heck would Decker place that burden on me?

I pushed my thoughts about Logan and Decker down as I contemplated the brief conversation I'd had with Ramirez, noting it had been almost accusatory.

I didn't doubt that Martin was involved, but was incensed that Ramirez thought I had knowledge of Martin's doings and was assisting him in some fashion.

The notion made my blood boil.

Men.

Idiots.

Both of them.

Ramirez, for being so bull-headed.

Martin, for being such a jackass.

How dare he insinuate himself into my life, only to bow out because I refused to give him what he wanted.

Yup. It all came down to the chips.

Damn them.

They were a constant source of anxiety. And pain.

I was so caught up in my thoughts that I hadn't heard Leah. She finally had to nudge me to the point I'd have bruises for the next two weeks.

"What?" My tone came off a bit more snappish than I'd intended.

"Geez, AJ, sorry to barge into the inner sanctum but your phone is ringing. It's Ramirez." She nodded at my phone, illuminated by the face of Dirty Harry—a little joke that she had decided to play with my phone months earlier.

I snatched it from the dashboard and released a snarl of frustration before accepting the call. "Are you tracking me, Ramirez, or what? I told you I'd call you when I got back to Phoenix but that didn't mean the second we'd entered the city limits."

He didn't respond though I could hear him breathing. I was about to impart a snide comment when Ramirez finally spoke.

"Actually, I was hoping to head you off before you made it all the way home. Can you meet me at the Starbucks at the Paradise Valley Mall?"

"Truth be told, I'm more of a Dutch Bros. Coffee type of gal these days—but then I guess you wouldn't know that, considering you haven't been around—"

"Huh, funny, me too," he interjected. "Err…Dutch Bros. guy, that is. You'll be happy to know they have one there, too, across from J.C. Penny, near Target, Costco and REI. Have Leah drop you there and I'll bring you home afterward."

He was about to hang up when I quickly added, "Why Paradise Valley?"

"It's where Congressman Fenton lives."

Without offering anything more, Ramirez disconnected.

I glanced at Leah. "What did you make of that?"

She shrugged. "Don't ask me. At least he's gotten on board with a better class of coffee."

I snorted. I wished that he could get on board with the fact that Martin was not an influence on me nor had become ingrained in my life.

Leah dropped me in front of Dutch Bros. It was late, and while there were people sitting in the sparse outdoor area, Ramirez was not among them.

Just then, I heard someone calling my name and swiveled. Ramirez waved at me from behind the front seat of a massive jet-black Dodge Ram truck.

I sauntered over as he propped the passenger side door open, hopping on the step and jumping in.

"New ride," I commented, assessing my surroundings while trying to avoid eye contact.

"Loaner, compliments of a drug house seizure."

"Nice," I shrugged, rubbing absently on the edge of the seat, noting the suppleness of the leather.

"AJ, I know this is not comfortable—"

"Not comfortable?" I snarked, my eyes flashing to him for the first time, sucking in a breath as I took him in again.

His silky waves had grown out but his green eyes were just as intense, as he sat casually in a maroon button-down shirt, jeans and boots.

Collecting my breath and my wits, I quickly added, "Why should this be...comfortable?"

Ramirez squinted and then nodded. "I understand."

"Do you? Understand?" I replied through gritted teeth.

"It doesn't have to be like this, you know," Ramirez responded.

I refused to meet his eyes, so I couldn't see what they revealed.

Perhaps I didn't want to.

"No, of course it doesn't. As long as I renounce my loyalties to Martin, whatever that entails, all will be cute puppies and rainbows. Isn't that about right?"

Ramirez sighed. "At the end of the day, you can't have it both ways, AJ."

"So you've said before," I replied. "But somehow, I never got to choose. You decided which way the wind blew…and out with it you went. Seems like you're the one who wants to have it both ways."

"Maybe," Ramirez replied slowly, "when it comes to things of a personal nature. But this is business, AJ. Police business. And I can only protect you so much where Martin is concerned."

"Protect me?" I asked, still working that piece of leather edging in an attempt not to face him. "Since when do I look like I need protection?"

"Let's talk holdouts, AJ."

"Excuse me?" This time I faced him and was surprised by what I saw.

Fear.

"You have something Martin wants, don't you?" He spoke so slowly, I could have pulled the words from his mouth like taffy.

I open my mouth. Shut it. I hadn't been prepared for the question. So few people knew about the chips—that I was the one who possessed them and the only one who knew where they were currently hidden.

Still unable to formulate the words necessary for a cohesive response, Ramirez took my silence as a cue to continue. "Leah told me you'd written him off and yet, you're suppressing evidence that could help him in his quest—whatever that may entail."

"That makes no sense. If Martin wants it and I'm keeping it from him, how could that be considered helping him?" I snorted.

"Because you're still not sure of his intentions and in the wrong hands, the information could be dangerous but in the right hands, who knows? Maybe you still think you can protect him, even if it's from himself."

"I'm still not sure where you drummed this up or got the crazy idea I had something Martin wanted but I assure you—"

Ramirez raised a hand. "Don't. The Congressman needs to speak with you. I simply wanted to prepare you for what he's about to say so that you can compose yourself. Chances are, you won't like it."

"Spoken like a true politician. So what—now you're serving as a mouthpiece for the Congressman?" I paused to catch my breath but was not interested in waiting for a response, as I continued my onslaught.

"Are you his heavy, too? Because, if this is a police vehicle and you're threatening a potential witness, I don't have a problem calling your superiors and telling them you've gone to the dark side and are using department property to facilitate crimes against humanity."

"Spoken like Martin's daughter," Ramirez replied, mimicking words and my tone.

If he'd intended to jar me, he'd gotten the desired effect.

"Go to hell, Ramirez. This whole thing is bigger than you and your stupid ego. You have no idea how far this reaches and how many people will be impacted if this information were to get out."

He smiled smugly. "No. But apparently you do." Before I could toss out some colorfully-phrased adjectives, he added,

"Buckle up. We don't want to keep the Congressman waiting. He doesn't like to wait."

Inwardly, I seethed. Ramirez knew that I didn't like to be kept waiting, either. One thing about the new and improved AJ that Ramirez didn't know—I hated to be kept in the dark twice as much.

CHAPTER THREE

After Ramirez informed me that the Congressman lived in Paradise Valley, I assumed that we were going to his home. Instead, we whipped through a business park. At this hour, the lot was nearly empty but Ramirez nestled into a parking spot that was a significant distance from the entrance of one of the buildings. When I noticed it was the only area not blanketed with light, I wondered if he'd selected it because it provided him with the cover of night.

He turned off the engine. "He's in suite C-232, on the second—"

I put up a hand. "I'm sure I can find it. You're not coming?"

Ramirez shrugged. "Wasn't invited."

I squinted at him but he continued staring out the windshield.

"Just go. The Congressman's waiting. I'll be here to take you home once you've finished your chat."

I opened my mouth. Then shut it.

There was really nothing more to say.

In some ways, I was thankful.

In others—maybe with a different...audience—I could have

used a pat on the back or an "atta, girl" as the butterflies danced in my stomach.

What was I walking into?

I made short work of the stairs and easily found the suite Ramirez had indicated. The lights were on and the main door was unlocked so I took it as an invitation to enter. I glanced around and while professional, the inside of the office was by no means lavish. It looked, for all intents and purposes, like a business office.

"Hello?" I called out, not wanting to spook anyone not expecting my arrival.

Congressman Bob Fenton rounded the reception desk, looking very much the youthful, cherubic way he had when I had last seen him at my friend Charlie's party with his lovely wife, Serena.

Gah! Once again, I was forced to remember the image of Ramirez's ex.

I managed to rein in the green monster, focusing on the Congressman. Instead of party clothes, however, this time the Congressman wore a simple navy polo and jeans. I had to smile when I took in his Chuck Taylor All-Star high-tops.

"I admire your choice of footwear, Congressman."

"Please call me Bob. It's so nice to see you again, Arianna." The Congressman smiled and extended a hand.

I took it and nodded. "Call me AJ."

"Appreciate you coming, AJ. I hope your drive back wasn't rushed?" When I tilted my head, he added, "Jonah told me you were in Los Angeles with Leah visiting friends. How is she, by the way? Doing freelance work, I hear?"

I nodded again, commenting that she was fine and that our trip was as well. Once the niceties were out of the way, Bob escorted me into a small office at the back of the space.

Noting the confusion on my face, he offered a brief explanation. "I have a formal office downtown, but these are the offices that house my former 'day job' so to speak."

"I'm sorry, but what did your former job entail?" I was a bit embarrassed I had to ask.

Leah's eyes would have rolled right out of her head.

He waved a hand, not the least bit offended. "Oh, estate planning, things of that nature. My business partner has taken over the bulk of the responsibility since I took office but I still have a seat at the table and a small space to call home, when I need some time…away."

I nodded but wasn't sure exactly what that meant—whether from home or the office of a public servant. After a few awkward moments of silence, he finally brought the horses back into the corral.

"Jonah told you I was approached." His voice was so quiet I barely made out the words.

I noted it was not a question.

"He called it an ambush," I replied, and though the Congressman nodded, his face turned the shade of a man who'd been sluffed a Scotch bonnet pepper.

"I was leaving my downtown office. It was late and I had waved the security guard off as he offered to walk me to my car. I was parked in a secure structure, just a couple of hundred feet away. What could go wrong, right?"

I shrugged. My luck had been less than fifty-fifty lately, so I probably wasn't the best person to ask.

"Anyway, everything was fine. I got into my car. Called Serena to tell her I was on my way. She reminded me to stop and grab a bottle of wine for dinner. She always stays up and eats dinner late with me just so we can have some time together. There's been so little of it lately."

It was benign commentary—filler, really—so I remained silent as he looked at his hands, blowing out a breath before he continued, "I had just pulled onto the freeway, and there he was, whispering in my ear. We were damn lucky I didn't hit the accelerator and crash into the car in the next lane."

"Did you recognize him?" I asked.

The Congressman shook his head. "He was sitting directly behind my headrest, so even when I tried to get a glimpse of him in the rearview, all I could see was the bill of his baseball cap."

"Smart," I murmured, to which he nodded. "What did he say? Or, more importantly, what did he want?"

"You know. It was so weird. At first, he was congenial. His voice was calm and he talked about the weather, almost like we were conversing in line at the grocery store."

"Did he direct you to drive anywhere?" I asked.

"No, and that's one of the funny things. My mind had gone on autopilot and I did the same thing I usually did, I headed in the direction of my home. The wine store was on the way."

It was an odd thing to mention but I prompted for him to continue.

"It wasn't until we were nearing my usual exit that his voice became more harried and his words started coming out so quick that I had a hard time making sense of what he was saying. Up until that point, I didn't feel as though he was going to harm me."

"But then?" I prodded.

"I wasn't so sure. He was almost frantic. I couldn't tell what he wanted…money, information, favors." Fenton shrugged.

"Maybe he wasn't there to get something from you but to impart some information?" I suggested, causing him to start.

"How did you know?"

I shrugged. "What did he tell you?"

"He didn't really 'tell' me anything." I cast him a doubtful look. He had called me here for a reason, after all. He caught it and huffed. "Look, it wasn't like some fortune cookie message, tied up into a nice succinct wrapper. It was more of a rant. And the less I understood, the more frustrated he got. It was like he thought I knew something I didn't and so when he was trying to expound…whatever…it was falling on deaf ears."

"He was agitated because you didn't know what he was talking about?" I confirmed.

I wasn't sure what it would yield me, though I was admittedly intrigued.

Fenton nodded. "Yeah. At least I think so. He kept talking about the rising of some consortium and how they would bring about the end of days. It sounded like a bunch of crazy, conspiracy theory rantings if you ask me."

My heart did a little skip. It did sound a bit like Martin when he was on a roll, but he wasn't one to get in a fervor or work himself up in a lather, unless…

"Did he make any references…to a person or a place? Or a name?"

Fenton sat for a moment, squinting as he tried to recall the conversation. Finally, he shook his head. "Not a name…a sign. An astrological sign."

I sucked in a breath. "Which one?" I managed to whisper.

"Gemini."

If the color had drained out of my face, he made no mention, continuing to ride that train of thought. "When he said it, I thought that perhaps he was one of those intuitive types, who had gotten caught up in the political scene and wanted to help me get my moons aligned or something like that." He paused to chuckle.

I didn't think so. Intuitive or not, most would not go to the extremes of ambushing a public official in his or her car, simply to read their zodiac sign. Still, I said nothing and let him continue.

"When I exited the freeway at the same point I usually did, he jumped out of the car at the first stop sign and disappeared into the shadows."

"You're kidding." It wasn't really a question but he shook his head. "Did anyone else see him? Anyone at the stoplight?"

"No. It was late. Traffic was light. I pulled into the parking lot of the wine store and called Serena. She immediately called Jonah, who agreed to meet me there. When he arrived, he checked out the car and found this."

He pulled a business card from his desk—now sheathed in a plastic sleeve—and started to hand it to me but I shook my head.

I could see Nicoh's smiling mug on the front from the way he'd held it. I'd seen the card enough to know whose it was.

Mine.

CHAPTER FOUR

"Jonah didn't say as much but I got the impression he thought you knew who the man was." Fenton might have said something prior to that but I think my mind had taken a brief sidebar, as I paused to curse Martin.

"How so?" I asked, my words coming out like molasses as my tongue stuck to the roof of my mouth.

"I don't know. He asked questions…vague ones…as though he was trying to lead me to the answer, without actually leading me, if you know what I mean."

I nodded, though I didn't. If anything, it felt as though the Congressman was the one on the fishing expedition. And in my experience, when my feelers perked up, it was best to take note and apologize later.

"Well, I don't know. Who it might have been, that is." I waved a hand, my voice a heck of a lot calmer and nonchalant than I was letting on. "I give dozens of cards out in a day, all over the city. Anyone could have passed one on, dropped it, tossed it, whatever. I also don't know anyone who has any psychic inclinations, political or otherwise. Though perhaps I wish I did." I chuckled lightly, watching Fenton's demeanor change as he shifted and narrowed his eyes ever so slightly.

Had I not been staring right at him I would have missed it, but it was there. What he played off as amusement flickered up, igniting as a mere hint of anger before burning out just as quickly. This guy was well-practiced. Or well-trained.

He met my gaze, his eyes bright and his tone firm but pleasant. "Ah, I see. Well, that's disappointing. I'm sorry I had Jonah bring you here."

"Had Jonah bring you here"? I bit my lip to keep from saying something I'd regret. Instead, I counted one-two-three as my mother had taught me and amped up my pearliest whites.

"Hey, it was worth a shot. I would've been happy to help, if I could've." I sounded about as fake a pink lawn flamingo. "Are you sure you don't want to file a report on this guy?"

He waved a hand. "What good would it do? He was just probably some palm-reading zealot, who felt he had an important message to impart. I'm sure it happens all the time."

I managed to take a page from Leah's book and couldn't seem to leave well enough alone. "The important message part, perhaps, though it's still weird he would have been able to get into your car without notice." Yup, I'd just stepped in it.

I noticed he stiffened, but figured I might as well keep mucking up my shoes. "I assume Detective Ramirez suggested you change the locks and have the alarm re-coded?"

Fenton nodded, studying me as he did. "Already handled."

"That was fast. How about your wife?"

"My wife?" He frowned, raising his shoulders in question.

"Did she have any suggestions?" I asked. "Or thoughts about the man's identity?"

For a moment he stared at me like I was the town idiot but then returned to his earlier, more casual demeanor. "That's why she got Jonah involved—she figured he could contact you directly."

"Huh, I thought Detective Ramirez found my business card *after* he arrived."

I'd kept my voice even, without a hint of accusation but there it was again—that flash of venom.

Gotcha.

"Well, again, thank you for coming. I'm sorry to have gotten you all the way here for nothing. Like you said, it was worth a shot." Fenton waved a hand toward the door.

I'd been effectively dismissed. I smirked but complied. If memory served, Leah had said he was one of the good guys. I wondered what had gotten in his craw as of late that had been compelling enough to shift his moral compass. Or who.

Ramirez was leaning against the front of his truck when I exited and said nothing as he watched me pass, yank open the passenger door, haul myself up into the seat and slam the door shut.

After a moment, he got into the driver's seat and the vehicle rumbled to life.

"That good, huh?" he finally said as we pulled out of the complex.

I shrugged, more annoyed than angry. "Nothing. At all. I just can't wrap my head around why you thought this had anything to do with Martin, simply because the guy dropped my business card." I shifted in my seat to face him. "Do you seriously believe Martin and I actually have the type of relationship where we swap deets?"

Noting the downturn of his mouth, I snorted before continuing, "Anyway, Fenton thinks it was a palm-reader or psychic type who wanted to share some important message based upon his sign or the placement of the moon."

"Really? He said that?" Ramirez glanced at me, doubtful.

"More or less, though don't quote me on it verbatim," I replied. "Regardless, I had nothing to offer him in return. He couldn't make any sense of what the man wanted. And definitely had nothing in the way of a description of the man. To be honest, I don't think our Congressman was in any real danger, though I understand how frightening the situation probably seemed at the time."

Ramirez stared at me, trying to gauge...something. But when he offered no immediate commentary, I decided to tackle something that had been bothering me.

"The Congressman said that he'd pulled over, called Serena, who in turn called you. He stayed put until you got there. Did you get the impression he was being truthful when you arrived? And after you'd had a chance to search his car?"

"Perhaps someone's forgotten who the cop is here," Ramirez replied, his gaze never leaving the road as he merged onto the freeway, heading in the direction that would finally take me home.

"Or perhaps the wrong someone's forgotten." I didn't bother mincing my words this time around.

I had nothing to lose.

Nothing more to lose, anyway.

Ramirez had walked out on me weeks ago. I didn't feel I owed him anything and certainly wasn't clear about his current intentions. Why had he brought me to the Congressman? Had he become a pawn in their game, whether by choice or convenience?

Either way you flipped that pancake, it just didn't land right.

There was one person I did trust and so I filled her in once Ramirez unceremoniously dropped me off at home. I knew I could trust her insights and that she would pose much-needed questions or considerations, regardless of what side of the fence they fell on.

"You don't sound all that surprised," I commented after

taking in her body language, or lack thereof, as I recounted the events from the time Ramirez had whisked me away to the point he had pretty much dumped me out of his truck onto my front lawn.

"About which part?" she asked, twisting the ends of her hair.

"Any of it. But even when I told you Fenton gave me the creeps, you didn't budge." Leah shrugged, so I added, "Back when we were at Charlie's party, weren't you the one saying he had some fresh ideas and displayed a lot of positive energy?"

"I also recall saying I looked forward to seeing how he did in the months ahead," she replied, her demeanor unchanged.

"And?" I motioned for her to continue.

"And I saw and now I'm over it." She chuckled when I huffed in frustration. "So yeah, after the initial shine wore off, he gave me the creeps, too."

"Now we're getting somewhere." I smacked a hand on my thigh, waking Nicoh, who had been lying on my feet and had succeeded in putting both to sleep. He emitted an exasperated huff before repositioning himself. It didn't do much to aid my situation. "Do tell."

"Nothing to tell. I thought he had some potential. And he probably still does. But he's also eager to please his party and his supporters—"

Chuckling, I raised a hand—politics were not among the items in my bag. "Let's move on to using smaller words and simpler subjects."

Leah snorted but nodded. "I basically think he'll do anything to stay in the favor of those around him."

I raised my eyebrows. "Do you think he made up the whole ambush thing?"

Leah stopped mid hair-twist and squinted. "Do you?"

I reflected for a moment before responding, "No, but I do think it gave him an opportunity to get Ramirez in his camp."

"And here you always say you just don't 'get' politics," Leah replied, using finger quotes, laughing all the while.

I waved her off. "You give me too much credit. I think Ramirez would do anything to appease Serena and if she called…" I paused, allowing Leah to take it wherever she deemed it was warranted.

She surprised me, giving her hair a rest as she sat upright. "Really? Do you think he's that much of a stooge? Or are you just wishing it on him because he walked out on you?"

"Geez, Leah, why don't you just tell me what you really think?" Perhaps it came off a bit snappish but she was poking a sharp stick into my tender parts.

She threw both hands up in surrender and waved them like a maniac. "Sorry. Sore subject. I get it. But this is *Ramirez* we're talking about. I get that he may help an old girlfriend out on occasion. But slip to the dark side for her husband's sake? I don't think so."

"What does Jere say?" I asked, noting how rapidly her eyes blinked at the mention of her beau, Jere Vargas, who like his best friend, Ramirez, was a homicide detective, in a separate jurisdiction.

"Geez, AJ! You just told me about this, how could I have asked Jere for his opinion?"

I shook my head slowly, knowing she was just sidestepping a response. "No Leah, what has Jere had to say about how Ramirez has been acting, you know, since—"

"Since he dumped you?" She'd picked up where I'd left off but I wasn't sure I appreciated the direction this conversation kept taking.

This time, I merely shook my head and sighed. "Again, with the whole dumping theme?"

Leah frowned. "Sorry, I just figured with Logan in the picture."

"Logan is a friend of Decker's. Period." I released a heavy sigh before continuing, "We were simply honoring a commitment that was made prior to her death by getting the dogs together."

"*Right.*" Leah clearly wasn't buying it, given the thickness of the sarcasm in her response. Paired with overt eye-rolling.

Three times was a bit much so I offered my own in return.

"Seriously, can we get back to it?"

"If you say so, AJ."

"I do."

She pretended to wave an imaginary wand. "All is right in the world again. AJ returns to her mopey quest."

"Whatever, Leah. Do you want to hear what I think, or not?"

She nodded. "Yes, my Queen. Exactly what is it that you want to do?"

"I want to figure out what the heck is going on and confirm whether the Congressman has gone to the dark side. I also want to confirm or deny Martin's involvement. And, I want to do it keeping Ramirez at arm's length. What do you think?"

"I think you ask a lot, my Queen," Leah nodded and smiled, before adding, "but I like the way your mind works."

CHAPTER FIVE

"But you're not surprised?"

"About which part? Keeping Ramirez at arm's length because of his association with the Congressman's wife?" When I nodded she shook her head and added, "Though I'm sure you've already realized that we could be putting ourselves in harm's way if there was something to this, we could also be impeding a law enforcement matter."

I shrugged—it was what it was—causing her to chuckle.

"If I didn't know better, I'd say I'm starting to rub off on you."

"Starting? Leah, honey…we've been doing this since we were five. I think I've absorbed all I possibly could over a decade ago."

She snickered and nodded. "Why don't I start looking into the Congressman…see what's really going on with him. If this does have to do with Gemini, is there a reason he's trying to draw Martin out? Or perhaps he's associated with someone who does? We need to figure out what they want. And who. 'Cause if they are using you to get to him, that doesn't sit well with me." She paused to release a breath and gauge my reaction. I gestured for her to continue. "You…my friend, need to track Martin the Magician down. See whether he was taking a little joy ride with our Congressman. If so, what's his gig? Do you think you can handle that?"

"I think I can manage. I have something he wants, after all," I replied, my tone smug.

"Right. The chips. Perhaps you need to revisit the info that Tony B. extracted. You mentioned that you weren't really looking for specifics but maybe once we pull some of this stuff together, it will give us a thread to work with." She ventured a glance at me, adding, "If you are up for dredging that old skeleton up, that is?"

I knew she was still a bit miffed that I had refused to reveal Tony B.'s initial feedback, no matter how many times she'd asked.

The truth of the matter was, I had been unable to process the information he'd given me, so I'd shut down, rather than have to face it. Or burden my best friend with it.

Still, I appreciated the fact she'd had the consideration to ask. When I nodded, she continued, "As for Ramirez, it's a good plan to keep him out of the way—until we figure out which horse he's betting on." She paused, biting her lip. "I do think I have a few creative ways of zoning in on his current mindset."

I put up a hand. "Leah, no." I certainly didn't want her to jeopardize her relationship with Vargas on my account.

"Don't worry. I'm not going do anything that I wouldn't normally do when I want something from the detective." She wiggled her brows and gave me a knowing grin.

"Ah, okay. That's about as much as you need to share," I replied, scrunching my face. "But for future reference, when you decide to pursue that same…avenue…try not to sound so darn happy about it, alright? It diminishes the whole 'thrill of the hunt' part."

"Noted." Leah worked hard to keep from laughing at my emphatic use of finger quotes, saluting me with her variation of a Star Trek Vulcan gesture.

"What else?" I prompted.

"With Ramirez out of the way, let's talk Logan. You kind of left him high and dry out there at the beach." The sudden shift in her tone surprised me, as did the intensity of her stare.

Any hint of silliness had melted away.

"Yeah, about Logan." I bit my lip, still not sure how to proceed with that one. "We had a bit of a chat out there—about Decker. Seems she made a final request."

I peered at my friend from beneath my bangs, not sure where I should start. Or how she would react. I reflected on Logan's advice. *"With both feet firmly planted, confident that you know what direction you're taking before you take that step,"* he had said, which was how most things in life should probably be tackled but rarely are.

As clumsy as I was, I started the best way I could...with baby steps.

When I finished relaying my conversation with Logan to Leah and how I'd—sort of—left things with him, she nodded, though her expression revealed nothing.

"Anyway, I was sort of thinking we could work on Decker's request once we figured what's going on with the Congressman, which shouldn't take too long." My voice came out a whisper, hoping my best friend hadn't thought I'd gone loco. "What do you think?"

She surprised me again, clapping her hands together like a monkey with its symbols. "Like I said before, I like the way your mind works. When do we start?"

"How does two hours ago sound, back to when I was cooling my heels with our Congressman?"

"Works for me. I always liked Michael J. Fox in those *Back to the Future* movies."

I sighed. Forget loco, if this was what I had to work with, it was gonna be a long ride.

* * *

It had been a rash of long, stressful days—ones where she and I had little rest and had been running on nothing more than adrenaline and caffeine, so I encouraged her to get some sleep but couldn't seem to take my own advice. My mind raced as I thought about Decker's request, then the Congressman's claim to have been ambushed by an unknown assailant, only to summon me by way of Ramirez, who upon finding evidence leading to me, felt it necessary to point the finger at my BioPop, Martin.

Why had Ramirez taken the leap? I wondered. Had he drawn that conclusion himself, or was the notion put into his mind by someone else? If so, for what purpose?

Ramirez was by no means a dolt but as a member of law enforcement had also failed to encourage Fenton to file a report, which surely could have helped in finding the person responsible for ambushing him. Of course, if the incident never really occurred, that was another matter entirely. And even if it had, perhaps the Congressman hadn't wanted him found in a public manner? Perhaps he wanted to personally put him on notice or draw him out into the open?

Oh Ramirez, I sighed. What have you gotten yourself into? I hoped it would be worth it, whatever it cost him in the end. For the time being, I had to believe that he was still a good guy and had only wanted to do the right thing when Serena had pulled him into the fold. I certainly didn't blame him. She had meant a great deal at one time and while she had broken his heart, he was big enough to put his feelings—whatever that entailed—aside when she'd called.

I'd tried my best to keep my composure when I laid eyes on him at Dutch Bros., but truth be told, my heart had skipped a few beats. As devastated as I was that he'd elected to walk out on me, I still missed him. And the noticeable hole that remained since his departure still wanted to be filled again with joy and hope.

Even love.

My mind skipped to Logan and did another little pitter-patter. It was the first time since Ramirez that I'd been genuinely happy and despite the sad circumstances, I had felt more than hope—I felt safe. Like I was home again.

I released another sigh, nestling that train back into the station as I pulled out the files that Tony B., my computer expert extraordinaire, had compiled and started sorting through the spreadsheet and myriads of other data relating to the Gemini project.

I didn't bother with the chips themselves, they would remain hidden in a secure location until I decided what to do with them.

For now, Tony B. had pulled together enough of what a layperson like myself could comprehend, though I knew there were also formulas, tabulations, computations, results, extraneous theories and conclusions, they were currently of no use to me. I was looking for names. One name in particular.

I thought back to the conversation I'd had with Tony B. the day he'd cracked the chip's code.

"It was pretty simple getting the data if you had both chips. Each chip contained a code needed to unlock the information on the other. You just had to do it in the right sequence. Once paired together, I was able to access the comprehensive data."

"So, one's like the table of contents and the other contains the chapters?"

"A bit more complex than that but generally speaking, you're in the ballpark. Anyway, the chips contained the

formulas for the project—as you'd expected—along with the dates, times, names of benefactors, patients and donors, including details about the offspring and their adoptive parents. Quite a dossier on your family tree, in case you're interested."

"Err...yeah, maybe later. Surely there was something...more? Something worth killing for?"

"I believe I just mentioned it."

"Come again?"

"The names, AJ. It all comes down to the list of names."

"The benefactors? The donors? The children? The adoptive parents?"

"All of them, AJ. The list is quite a doozy. You'll never guess whose names popped up."

"Do I really want to know?"

"Oh, I think you'll find it very...educational."

"Go on..."

"Two of the products of Gemini turned out to be local boys. The first is your pal, Jeremiah Vargas, and the second, Congressman Bob Fenton. And that's not even the best part— they're brothers."

Thanks to the fact that Tony B. was so proficient at his job, his efforts made short work on my end. I hadn't told Leah that the name we sought was indeed on the list, even though I knew it was. Before I opened that can of worms, I wanted to double- and triple-check. I had to be sure. It wouldn't solve any of our problems or answer any of our questions. If anything, it would add more.

I shuddered. I previously hadn't mentioned Vargas' involvement in the Gemini project, but now that Fenton had brought me into the mix, I doubted I could keep that nugget to myself for much longer.

I worried about her reaction. Would she be angry that I hadn't told her? Would she feel compelled to tell Jere of his lineage and involve him, too?

If he chose to believe her, or at least entertain her claims, the revelation would undoubtedly turn his entire existence on its head. Gemini had a funny way of doing that to people.

After that, it would only be a matter of time before those involved would ferret out his connection to Congressman Fenton and his father.

So, even though telling Leah might clear my conscience, I would also be putting the man she loved at risk.

At the end of the day, was that risk worth the truth?

It wasn't a notion I relished rehashing but now that the ambush had occurred, it was looking more and more like Martin, whatever his role, was very much involved.

Which brought up another dilemma: if he hadn't been the one in that car, would I be putting him at risk by drawing him out? Or creating a situation where I could end up being used as a pawn in order to save his life, e.g. a trade of the chips for my biological father's life?

I'd like to think I would do the right thing but as I pondered this conundrum, I honestly wasn't sure I had the answer. There was always the opposite side of the coin to consider and the possibility that Martin had been the one who had ambushed Congressman Fenton.

If so, what was his motive? Why had he come out of hiding? Again? And why now?

What message was he trying to communicate? And to whom?

If it were a message at all.

What if Martin was the one pulling the strings? Scheming to draw the remaining living players out—using me and the Congressman as pawns—in an effort to get them into the open?

Why? So he could eliminate them? Expose them?

The cynic in me went to the dark side—that he would draw them out to do his dirty work for him.

And in order to get the very thing he desired, he'd tell them what I had in my possession and then set them loose on me.

Any of the scenarios could be true, but given my history and the prickle at the back of my neck, I couldn't ignore what was in front me, no matter whose face was on the monster I was destined to battle.

CHAPTER SIX

I had fallen asleep sitting at the counter, the laptop inches from my face. Wincing at the kink in my neck as I hoisted myself to an upright position, I noticed Leah was sitting on the other side. The look on her face was undecipherable but as she stared at me with her arms crossed, I got the vibe she was less than amused. Her hair screamed of bedhead, though the half empty pot of coffee suggested she had been up for a while. I wondered how long she'd been sitting like that.

"Morning," I mumbled, pushing my own mop out of my face.

"Late night," she commented dryly.

"Just doing some research, thinking about everything Fenton told me. Or, more specifically, didn't tell me."

"Umm, hmm," she replied. "Seems to be a lot of that going around lately. I hope it's not contagious."

I tilted my head, noting that had come out a bit sarcastic. "You have something on your mind, Leah? Don't be shy."

She frowned. "Nothing shy about this chick. Just when were you planning on telling me about Jere?"

"You saw." I nodded at the laptop.

"I did," she replied. "How long have you known?"

I sighed. There was no use hiding the truth any longer. "A while."

She nodded. "Since Tony B. cracked the information on the chips."

"Yes, he's the one who told me."

"You know, I was sitting right here when he called you. You could have said something." Leah frowned.

"Would it have made a difference?"

Leah huffed, uncrossed her arms and tossed them in the air. "Gee, I don't know, AJ. How would you like it if I'd lied to you, for weeks?"

"I didn't lie," I replied, careful to keep my tone even though I could feel the anger bubbling to the surface.

She snorted. "Boy, Ramirez was right. You really are starting to sound like Martin."

"Low blow, Leah," I growled from behind clenched teeth. "I'd expect that coming from him, but not you. Do you think it's been easy being in possession of those chips? To have the knowledge of what's on them? Knowing the impact they'd have on hundreds of people's lives…their families? It weighs on me. Every. Single. Day. There's not a millisecond that goes by that I don't think about it."

She lifted her head, growled at the ceiling and huffed out a long breath before responding, "Yes, I do know and I'm sorry for my outburst. I'm just…shocked."

"It *all* shocks and horrifies me." Though my tone was calm, a shiver ran through my body. "What will you do?"

Leah clutched her coffee with both hands, as though the chill had just reached her and the mug offered her warmth. "You mean, will I tell Vargas?"

I nodded.

"I don't know." She frowned, increasing the grip on her mug as she peered at me from beneath those crazy spikes, which made her look as though she was ten. "What would you do?"

I shook my head. Now she wasn't playing fair and I told her as much.

"You realize you're asking the person who just withheld the same information from you, who you compared to her less-than-trustworthy, often missing in action BioPop, as you like to refer to Martin."

"Yeah, about that…" I waved a hand to stop her. We had been friends for too long to let a few words stand between us. She nodded. "But seriously, what would you do?"

I shook my head. It was not a question for me to answer. My situation was different. I possessed all of the names and once I opened that can of worms, all of them would come slithering out.

"If this were a story, what would your editor tell you?"

Her mouth formed an "o" as she pondered this. "That I need to gather as much info as possible, with sources that can back it up. And then, when I think I'm done, flip that story on its head and approach it from an entirely different angle."

"So, at present, do you feel as though you've collected all of that?" I asked.

"Not at all," she replied, her tone somber. "I can't take this to Vargas. I'd have nowhere to go once I'd blurted it out. He'd probably just think I'd finally taken that crazy train."

"Exactly."

"But you're not opposed to me telling him?" She stopped gripping the mug with one hand to tug at her hair—a nervous habit she'd had since childhood.

I shook my head. "It's not for me to decide…or control. Though I think your decision will be easier once you have more answers. But please know, whatever you choose to do, I support you, but until then…"

"The weight of the world will be on me," she continued my

thought. When I nodded, she added, "If you can deal with it, then so can I."

I didn't mention that the one name she had was far more personal to her than any of the rest were to me.

"So what's the game plan?" I asked.

"I think I have a few places to start collecting those bread-crumbs. And, I can do some research on our Congressman in the process." When I raised a brow she added, "Can't hurt to see if anything pops."

"Gotcha. I have a few of my own breadcrumbs to collect."

"Hmm…one of those wouldn't come in the form of the afore-mentioned BioPop, would it?" She released her stranglehold on her hair, her eyes bright.

"It would, indeed." I couldn't say I was as excited by the prospect, but I was looking forward to the challenge it presented.

"Let's get to it then," she said, slapping her legs as she hopped off the stool and trotted down the hall, swatting Nicoh on his behind as she passed.

He opened one eye a slit, glaring at her for a moment before closing it.

Leah snickered, not the least bit worried about whatever revenge he might bestow upon her later as she joyfully added, "Up and at 'em, boy. Your mama's got a plan and I'm betting you're involved."

If she was curious as to how I planned to draw Martin out, she didn't bother asking. Instead, she continued down the hall, singing to herself as she entered her bedroom and shut the door.

I hadn't bothered to shout a retort at her back because, at end of the day, when it came down to pinpointing Martin, Nicoh *was* typically part of my plan.

* * *

An hour later, I left Leah to do whatever it was she planned on doing. She had yet to emerge from her room but given the volume —and selection—of the 1980s music coming from beneath the door, the girl was on a mission and would find whatever bread-crumbs she went looking for.

I planned to do the same though I knew tracking Martin down was only half the battle. Despite his background as a scientist and his methodical, meticulous approach to every situation, the man himself was a riddle.

Snapping Nicoh's lead on, I made sure all doors were locked and that my cell phone was charged. You never knew what surprises might arise when you left the comfort of your home and entered the big, bad world.

I had a hunch and wanted to exhaust it before moving on to more aggressive means of seeking Martin out, so Nicoh and I jogged a few short blocks to one of the neighborhood parks. It was quieter than most and on a weekday morning when children were in school, empty except for the birds and other wildlife that typically inhabited it this time of year.

I passed the bench where Martin and I had first met. It had gotten a coat of paint since the last time I'd been here but still looked worn, much like the relationship I had with a man I'd barely known until recently. I guess time had its way of catching up with you and it would be the only thing that would tell us where we would be at the end of this journey.

Looping the pond, I spotted a form sitting under a shady crop-ping of trees. My heart jumped as I squinted, taking in the features and for a split-second, I thought it was a mirage. But as Nicoh and I closed in, I realized my initial impression was spot-on.

Martin.

He gave me a head-nod as we approached, whether to grant me permission to join him or simply acknowledge he had seen us,

I wasn't sure but it was too late now. Upon seeing him, Nicoh huffed and tugged, begging for me to release him.

I glanced at Martin, who chuckled and shrugged, so I set the beast free. The two reunited in an amusing bear hug, with Nicoh gracing Martin's face with a tongue bath. Martin laughed and scratched Nicoh's head and shoulders until Nicoh released him and settled all paws on the ground, while panting and resorting to a round of low "whoo-whoos."

As I reached them, I noted that Martin looked tired—there were dark, telltale circles under his eyes and his usual mop of hair was longer with more silver than I remembered, though he was still ruggedly handsome.

"Arianna." He leaned across Nicoh to give me an awkward one-armed hug.

"Martin." I hoped the shakiness hadn't reached my voice as I backed away. "Thought I might catch you here but…" I glanced toward the old bench, solitaire across the pond.

He followed my gaze and nodded. "New day. New bench."

I noticed that the one he had been sitting on was indeed, new. Its paint glistened, despite the shadows cast by the canopy of trees. I hadn't remembered seeing it there before but then again, I hadn't frequented that park as much as I used to. I could see a copper placard on the back, suggesting it had been a donation from someone in the community.

Martin diverted my attention. "It's been awhile. You look… well. Or at least better than the last time I saw you."

A shudder traveled through my body, I had been in a hospital, recovering from injuries sustained in my fight to the death with Winslow Clark. I had won that battle, but the scars still remained.

"You look good, too, Martin." I decided to sidestep any reminders of our last encounter.

When the cobwebs had finally moved out, I realized I had

witnessed Martin taking out his own arch-enemy, Winslow's father, Theodore Winslow, in a violent, ruthless manner.

Martin chuckled, rubbing a hand through his hair. "You're not a very good liar, Arianna. Just like Alison, always trying to point out the best in people and making the other person feel comfortable, despite your own discomfort with the situation."

I jumped at the mention of my biological mother's name, who had died shortly after giving birth to my sister, Victoria, and me. Victoria was also deceased, a victim of Winslow and his father's cruel game. Now, Martin and I were the only ones left standing.

Except for all those names on the disk.

Which is why we were here.

As if sensing a shift in the temperature, Martin motioned for us to walk. I re-hooked Nicoh's lead and we continued up the path.

"Surprised to find you here," I commented after a long moment.

"Are you...really?" I could feel the heat of Martin's gaze on me. Or perhaps it was the reddening of my cheeks as I reflected on his comparison between me and my biological mother.

"No. I was...hopeful, though."

From my peripheral view, I could see him nodding. I wanted to spout so many questions at him, but kept them at bay, allowing him to take the lead.

At least, for now.

"I know why you're here, seeking me out. And before you ask, yes, I was the man in the car with your Congressman Fenton. Though despite what you've likely heard, he was never in any danger. From me."

I started to speak but he raised a hand and continued walking.

"My only reason for engaging him was to warn him that his life is in danger. If I could have found an alternative way to gain access to him, I certainly would have preferred to utilize it. Unfortunately, events of late have made it difficult to approach him without raising suspicion."

I temporarily bypassed the fact he seemed to know way too much about my involvement in the situation.

"Raising suspicion? Are you serious, Martin?" I replied from behind gritted teeth. "You popped up in the backseat of the Congressman's car and nearly scared him out of his gourd."

Martin shrugged and focused his attention on the path ahead, while I continued, "Let's sidestep the fact that you broke into his vehicle and lurked there—both of which come under the 'criminal charges' umbrella"—I inserted overt finger quotes, which Martin pretended to ignore—"you could have also put his life in danger 'engaging' him in the manner you did. He could have gotten into an accident, pulled a weapon and turned the tables… whatever. So, excuse me, if I have a hard time believing you were there simply to impart a message of impending danger when you yourself could have been complicit in initiating it." I paused to catch my breath, raising a finger when Martin tried to interject.

"Explain to me, Martin, how are you trying to help our Congressman? And, please, choose your words carefully. I possess a finely-honed crapometer and if I feel as though you are being less than truthful, I will call the police and have them arrest your sorry butt. What you did was criminal, whether you believe you did anything wrong in your quest."

When he frowned and shook his head, I added, "Need I mention the name Winslow? And remind you of an abandoned building where some pretty heinous crap went down? One call, Martin. One call. And it's all over."

I was filled with a healthy dose of satisfaction when I glanced over and found Martin looking deflated—with his mouth turned down as he shoved his hands into his pockets, his gait slowing—and just as disappointed when he recovered a bit too quickly for my liking, stopping to face me, his tone stern, as though talking to a child.

"People are watching, Arianna. You. Him. The others."

"What others?" I raised my hands in frustration, gesturing around as I did.

"You know what others." This time, his voice was deep as his face morphed into a combination of frustration and anger.

I wasn't sure whether this change in demeanor was meant to generate unease or command attention but I already had his number.

"Ah, once again, you're mentioning the chips, without actually mentioning them," I kept my tone even, but wanted to belt it out into the universe. "Do me a favor, Martin, let's start being straight with one another. Okay? I'm about up to here with the cryptic mumbo-jumbo. The Congressmen thought you were a rambling crazy man, so perhaps you need to not only work on your 'approach' but your 'delivery'." Again, I implemented finger gestures for effect, using his words against him.

Martin pursed his lips and if he'd considered putting me over his knee and spanking me for speaking to him in such a manner, the notion passed as his face softened and he sighed, realizing his tactic had failed. Miserably.

"The Congressman needed to be warned that his life was in grave danger." He paused to huff out a long breath. "The consortium is trying to resurrect the Gemini project. And they plan on using the people still alive, including the Congressman, to do it."

I wasn't exactly sure what that meant but it didn't sound like a life or death scenario.

I was about to say as much when Martin added, "They intend on purifying the gene pool—by segmenting individuals who possess only the most remarkable traits—they will be able to create an unequivocally pristine race of artists, athletes, entrepreneurs, leaders, scientists, soldiers…" His voice trailed off as he stared into the distance.

"And when they've finished their harvest, what will become of these individuals?" I asked, a heaviness filling my chest as I captured the expression that spanned his face.

"All of them will be eliminated."

"And those not chosen?" I managed to squeak out.

While his expression never changed, his silence spoke volumes.

CHAPTER SEVEN

"Whoa. Whoa. Whoa."

I put my hands up in a defensive manner, causing Nicoh's ears to perk as he quickly positioned himself between us. It might have been taking it a step too far, considering he'd already investigated, but Nicoh proceeded to poke Martin in his...man parts.

"Arianna...call off your dog, please, and I will be happy to explain," Martin huffed out as Nicoh nudged him a bit too hard.

I complied, pulling Nicoh's leash lightly, alerting him that it was alright to wrap-up this particular investigation, posthaste.

Martin muttered out a "thanks" and took a moment to regain his composure before continuing, "There have been recent rumblings that some of the former members of the consortium are planning—"

I raised a hand. "Hold up. *Former members?*"

Martin shrugged. "The ones who were excommunicated, for infractions against the consortium's code of ethics."

I snickered. The consortium had a code of ethics? Now I *had* heard everything.

Martin ignored my reaction. "Anyway, rumors have it a few have gotten back together and are staging a coup, with plans of overthrowing the current regime so that they can refocus the consortium's attention on Gemini."

"But there's a possibility—if you've heard about the coup—that the current consortium members have as well and will stage a retaliation of their own. So…if there's a chance one set of baddies could take out the other set, the problem could work itself out, right?" I paused but didn't look to Martin for confirmation, before adding, "And, if that were the case, Gemini would remain safe because those who possessed the means to bring that Frankenstein back to life would have already been silenced. Permanently." I knew it was a tall order but liked the sound of its finality.

Perhaps the target on my back would be finally eliminated and the chips *could* remain where they were. Undisturbed. Forever.

Debbie Downer, aka Martin, disagreed with my assessment, given the furrow of his brow and rigid stance. Apparently, my creative brain didn't size up his more sophisticated, analytical one.

"Interesting…theory, Arianna. If it were only that simple."

I shrugged, I could concede that my ideas had been idealistic, though I wasn't sure I appreciated the way he proceeded to dumb it down, as though telling a story to a child.

"When we deal with situations like this, the monster often has many heads. You cut off one and a new one grows. There will be casualties along the way, whatever the outcome. Innocent people will die. Or worse."

I couldn't think of much worse than death but I didn't strangle the point.

"Why now?" I asked, realizing I was probably feeding into Martin's notion that I believed his rantings.

"It's the belief of those in my network that the election of your Congressman Fenton is one of the events that set things in motion," Martin replied.

I noted his mention of his network but decided to hold that

one at bay, until further needling was warranted. Right now, I was a dog with her nose to the ground.

"That makes no sense. Fenton's been in office for a while now."

"They wanted to be sure he was in a position that could be influenced. If he had turned out to be a dud, the plan wouldn't have worked as originally intended. But if it had turned out to be the case, they had plans to redirect their efforts to another subject to ensure the resurrection would work."

"Meaning?"

"While they currently believe Fenton will fit the bill, if he doesn't, they have a backup subject they are convinced will."

"What will happen to Fenton…if things don't go as planned?" I was almost afraid to ask.

"He will be eliminated. Because by that point, he will have surpassed his usefulness."

"I'm pretty sure executing a member of Congress will not go unnoticed. No one's going to let that one blow over. If anything, it could eventually draw attention to the consortium—former members or otherwise—no matter how clever or cautious they think they are," I replied, noting Martin's lack of expression, which frankly, was getting on my nerves. "Why not just allow him to go about his duties and live out his life? No one would be the wiser."

Martin shook his head, his tone somber. "As far as those who vow to overtake the consortium are concerned, if Fenton cannot serve as a tool to bring Gemini to fruition, he is no longer of any use to them."

"You do realize how sick this is?" It was time to poke him with my stick. "And now your so-called 'network' is against all of this? Isn't that a tad hypocritical, considering you were part of the original project?"

I watched Martin consume my words and witnessed the

minuscule shudder that raked his body before he managed to compose himself.

"I know you question my loyalties, daughter, and I've given you no evidence to believe otherwise, which is entirely my fault. But to have you hold me in the same esteem as these people—it wreaks havoc on my soul." He paused and had I not been so skeptical, thought I saw a bit of wetness forming in the corners of his eyes.

Could a scientist also be an actor? I wondered. Before I could give that further thought, he pressed on, his voice firm. "If you ever believed I loved your mother—Alison—then you must hear me now. These people are not to be trifled with. And while you might think me a monster for what I've done…these people are true demons…prepared to do whatever—and I mean whatever—is necessary to see their plan to fruition.

"I will stop them—with or without your help—but so help me, they will not take my only living daughter—Alison's daughter—from me. I will die to ensure that does not happen. Because a world where you no longer exist? It would no longer matter. I would have exceeded my reason to live."

Perhaps I should have been affected by his fatherly speech, if it had not been for a couple of oversights. He had placed me and the ones I loved in harm's way on more than one occasion—because he failed to come out of hiding—and I'd lost more than he had logged in his own books.

So call me a brat, but I think I had a thing or two on him where it came to loss. And, if we were still keeping track, I had way more to lose than he did by believing his crap factory.

"I agree with your assessment. These people need to be stopped. And I understand your desire, believe me, I do, but I also think that you and your network have knowledge that could benefit those of us who live and operate in the real world."

I paused for a moment and found him nodding. "Would it help

you to know that the Congressman's own father is leading the charge?" I opened my mouth but decided to let him proceed. He was, after all, extending the proverbial olive branch. And I had to take whatever twig he was offering. "At one time Robert Fenton was the spearhead of the consortium. And we believe, now that his son is in a position of power, he intends to resume the reins he once had."

"You expect me to believe that Fenton is willing to put his son's life on the line, just so he can bring this...project back to life?" I wondered if he was doing so out of loyalty to his old pal Theo, no matter how one-sided that friendship had been.

"Robert Fenton, Sr. wasn't only involved in the original project, he was at the forefront of the consortium when the project was placed on hold."

"And you believe he is willing to sacrifice his son in order for this resurrection to succeed?" I asked.

Martin nodded. "His son is merely a means to an end."

It made me sick to my stomach but I knew that it was the reality of the mindset we were dealing with.

"Even if the Congressman is fair game, surely they realize that targeting him will not go unpunished? Law enforcement will hunt them down by whatever means necessary. He *is* a public figure, after all."

"Certainly. And they just don't care." Martin frowned. "They are relying on social media, without really understanding how it works, to dispel their venom. You may have felt my approach on Fenton was low-tech and ridiculously old-school, but it served its purpose and got the job done."

"You involved me in the process," I replied, my tone dry, "dropping my business card, whether you meant to."

Martin shook his head. "It was a mere coincidence—an act of clumsiness on my part. My goal was to simply put the Congressman on notice. Period."

"So you had no idea that the Congressman's wife also happened to be Ramirez's ex and that somehow, it would funnel back to me?" My tone was not accusatory but it was curious. And cautious.

"Are you serious? In a world such as ours, where things are so randomly connected…I would never have been able to drum up that scenario in even the most perfect setting. And I am truly sorry that it trailed back to you. If anything, I want you protected from these monsters. If they caught wind of you…what you…have…"

"Ah, back to the chips again, are we?" A bit too convenient for my liking. "What if I told you they no longer existed?"

"You destroyed them?" Martin's eyes widened and I knew he had not considered that alternative.

"What if I did?" I shrugged.

Martin sighed. "Then I would say it was for the best and deal with whatever hand life gave me."

"Meaning?" He'd piqued my interest but I couldn't let him know that it had any effect. I still wasn't going to tell him where the chips were—or if they existed—regardless of the guilt trip he'd laid on me.

"They've always believed I still had them—the consortium, the network and various outliers—and had consumed their contents…"

I held up a hand. "Wait a minute. You don't…know…what's on the chips?" My tone probably came off incredulous and disbelieving, because it was.

How could this man not know what information he had collected and that until recently, my sister and I had possessed, in an effort to keep it separate, but safe?

Martin waved his hand in a calming gesture. Perhaps I had been a bit too animated for his liking. Probably a good thing he'd never raised me during my teenage years, I mused.

"I know the formulas and the original theories but I never cared about the rest—the names of the donors and the children born as a result."

"Harsh." I didn't attempt to keep the contempt or the judgment out of my voice.

Martin shrugged. "It is what it is, as you kids say. And now, given the advances that have occurred, the formulas by themselves are antiquated…worthless. All that is necessary to bring Gemini back is the DNA of any one of those children whose names are documented on those chips. And then they will have a loaded weapon at their disposal, to do whatever it is they deem necessary."

Though the thought sickened me, I nodded. "Fenton Sr. should be able to do that without destroying his son in the process."

"If he cares that much," Martin replied, frowning.

I had nowhere to go with that, so I moved on. "So, now that we know what is what, where do we go from here?"

"I think we need to be diligent, seek out whatever we can about Fenton Sr. and ascertain his plans before he's able to overthrow the consortium's current leadership. At the same time, we can't ignore their agenda. They are just as dangerous as he and his cohorts are. Combining the two is equivalent to starting a war that no one will be able to combat."

"They haven't taken in the likes of me then." I snorted. "My 'cohorts' are downright lethal." When Martin opened his mouth to comment, I added, "And we don't need to kill anyone to get our point across."

Martin was silent for so long I felt compelled to poke that stick again. "What's the matter, Martin? Got a bunch of dog hair stuck on your tongue?"

Whether that stick did the trick or he was completely gobsmacked, I wasn't sure. But then he surprised me, offering a weak smile and a thumbs-up.

"As you kids say…you go, girl."

CHAPTER EIGHT

As we concluded our walk, back at the bench where we had started, Martin and I agreed to keep in touch. I gave him my cell phone number and though he offered none in return, said he would be forthcoming with whatever information his "network" came up with on Fenton's scheme and on the consortium's plan for rebuttal and I agreed to do the same.

Hey, I didn't agree to give him the farm, just a bit of milk from the cow, when it was warranted.

Once he'd headed down the path, I settled on the bench to give Nicoh some much-needed water from my pack. As I glanced toward the spot where Martin had been seated, I noticed the dedication on the plaque.

In loving memory of Alison & Victoria...you will never be forgotten. And for Arianna...may you continue to live your life with purpose...knowing that you have been, and will always be...loved.

I secured Nicoh's lead and tucked the remainder of the water away, sucking in a sob that begged to be released.

"Come on, boy," I said to my beast, jogging in the opposite

direction, exhaling a deep breath once I'd reached the street, just beyond the park.

"Let's go home."

* * *

The house was silent when I got back and Nicoh quickly settled in and went to work chewing his foot. I checked email and followed up with clients, confirming various photo shoots, anything to avoid thinking about Martin.

Thankfully, Leah burst in, her arms filled with bags from one of my favorite Thai restaurants in Scottsdale.

"You didn't?" I clapped in delight as she dumped them on the counter. "Is it my birthday?"

She snorted. "No. I was hungry and tired of you walking around with that hang-dog expression of yours. And see? Offering you the right sustenance has already worked wonders."

I nodded, my eyes widening as she pulled a couple more treats from her bag.

"Hard cider for dinner. Tiramisu for dessert." She placed both on the counter proudly.

"Wow. You pulled out all the stops. I must be in worse shape than I thought."

Leah snorted. "Don't flatter yourself. Some of these are for me." Upon noting my forlorn expression, she quickly added, "I plan on sharing. I simply meant that I was in the mood to partake as well."

At least she hadn't said "in *a* mood."

She caught my expression. "Before I share what I've learned, tell me about your day."

Without waiting for a response, she began scooping the Panang. The mouth-watering scent of the curry and Thai spices had me yammering within seconds and by the time we'd emptied our bowls, I'd relayed the details of my outing with Martin.

"You don't seem all that surprised," I commented, noting Leah's lack of response.

She shrugged. "If he was a politician, I'd say he played the party line." When I frowned, she added, "Though as a nonpartisan, *you* did a darn good job."

"I have no idea what that's supposed to mean, but I'm guessing you're giving me a compliment, in some form?"

"Of course it is. The very fact you were able to be in Martin's presence without punching him in the throat—and don't deny you wanted to—while getting information out of him? You are a total rockstar in my book. Seriously, like David Coverdale worthy."

I blushed. She knew I couldn't deny my fascination with the wild-locked, raspy-voiced lead singer from the 1980s rock band.

"I did actually get him to spill, didn't I?" When she nodded, I added, "It did take at least three trips around that stupid pond. I thought Nicoh was going to charge in and join the ducks, he was so bored."

"Nah, the whole water on the paws thing." She chuckled.

"Yeah, there's that. Still, you're not surprised?"

"That he was willing to expound?" she asked, to which I nodded. "Not really. He didn't really give you that much intel, if you think about it. At least nothing more than we could have probably found out or ventured a guess at. We still don't know who the majority of the consortium members—current or former —are, and the claim that they're making a move still has yet to be validated. We only have Martin's word for it."

"Meaning that he could have concocted this whole thing to elicit something from me," I replied.

"It's a possibility. He could be playing on your empathy and your sense of duty to do the right thing."

"And by doing the right thing, you mean giving him the

chips." I snorted when she shrugged. "I kind of felt the same way. Perhaps all of this was a ruse."

"One thing he said did ring true," Leah replied. When I raised a brow, she added, "I came up with some very interesting information regarding Fenton Sr., which lends credibility to Martin's claims."

"Do tell," I plopped down on the sofa and she followed suit, pulling her notes from her bag.

"Well, despite the fact that you refuse to accept any knowledge of anything in the realm of politics, you do remember he was once the Governor of our state, right? Remember when we took that trip in junior high to the Capitol building? You know the one downtown with the copper top that you thought was 'pretty' but were worried who would be tasked with cleaning it once it took on a patina?"

"I sense you're toying with me to get my attention," I replied, less than amused. "And yes, I remember all of that, but what does the fact that Fenton's father used to be our Governor have anything to do with Martin's claim he was once the head of the consortium?"

Leah smiled. "Exactly. What does one have to do with the other?"

I threw my hands up in frustration. "Gah! Weren't you just saying that I was the one who sounded like Martin? Seriously, Leah, could you be any more cryptic? If I want puzzles, I'll call BioPop in to do the honors."

She ignored my quip and continued, pursing her lips as though she was quite satisfied with the dirt she had managed to dig up. Truth be told, she was pretty darn good when it came to ferreting out little-known details. One might consider her a weapon of mass destruction, if she was so inclined to release them to the wrong sort of person.

Fortunately, her moral compass would never allow that to

happen. She'd dig her own grave and bury herself in it before divulging what she knew. After what she'd been through, I can't say I blamed her. Though I admired the fact she still felt the truth warranted being brought into the light of day, when the situation called for it. This may very well have been one of those situations.

"Well, if you trace Fenton Sr. back to his not-so-humble beginnings, he happens to have attended the same university and developed quite a friendship with Theodore Winslow."

"You've got to be kidding me." I wasn't really asking a question, though I was stymied by the way these people's lives continued to intertwine and somehow always ended up leading back to me.

"Nope. They were actually roommates for a while and remained lifelong friends, before old Theo's demise—at the hands of Martin—which has never been confirmed nor denied." She winked at me but I shook my head and motioned for her to continue.

It was old news, and she and I would never be able to find evidence to corroborate what had happened that day. Martin had made sure of it. And while I believed what I had witnessed in that haze-filled moment, I would never be able to prove it. Knowing Leah believed me was good enough. And I certainly didn't want Martin breathing down my neck if he thought I would turn on him and spill the beans to law enforcement.

Ramirez had already guessed the truth but lacked the evidence, which he believed I could supply. And which had served as a catalyst for the demise of our relationship. Ramirez felt I had chosen Martin over my relationship with him—and doing the right thing—when I hadn't.

My mind simply hadn't had time to process the trauma I'd endured and when it finally did, Ramirez had already made his choice—which was to walk out the door and never look back. At the time, I wasn't in any mood or mindset to correct him, though he'd been off-base on the key factor: I never trusted Martin and to this day, still didn't.

Leah prattled away and when I finally returned to focus on the present, found my ears perking at the mention of a familiar name.

"Robert was also friends with a particular hottie by the name of Alison Anders...had quite a crush on her, but she was, unbeknownst to anyone, already betrothed to one Martin Singer. Apparently, Robert was pretty vocal when she rebuffed his affections. Had some less than kind words to say about her to anyone who would listen."

I groaned. "This just gets better and better, doesn't it? Don't tell me this has nothing to do with Gemini and everything to do with payback for unreciprocated affections? Yet another person who was infatuated with my mother, but couldn't have her because she was already secretly in love with Martin and was pregnant with his love baby...babies?"

She shook her head. "I won't because it doesn't...have everything to do with Alison, that is. Robert was also enamored with Winslow, thought him to be a genius, the next Edison or Einstein, and basically worshiped the crap out of the ground he walked on. The two were inseparable. He would have done anything for his pal and when Winslow offered to let him in on a special project, Robert jumped at the chance."

"Let me guess—by 'special project,' you mean Gemini."

"You've got it. And, coincidently, Robert had cash—his family was loaded—so when Theo whined about not having this or that, Robert happily footed the bill."

I frowned. "Martin never mentioned any of this."

"Why should he?" Leah asked. "Though, perhaps, he never really knew. Your BioPop was the real brains behind their projects. Maybe back then he trusted Theo, figured that whenever they got the things they needed, it had been on the up and up. Either that or he was stuck in his own ego at the time and just didn't care," she paused to cast a glance at me before adding, "I tend to like that notion. Seems the most plausible scenario, given everything we know about these characters."

I shrugged and motioned for her to continue. "Anyway, Robert wanted to be more than a benefactor of the project, he desperately wanted to be involved in it. Problem was, he didn't have the smarts to work on it and as far as a specimen...let's just say he was shooting blanks. Theo tried to assure his friend that all would work out and not to worry...yada...yada...that his contribution would be rewarded in some way. It would have been all good and fine, only Martin and the others were growing tired of Theo's constant placation, unaware that Robert was one of their primary contributors and Theo had made him promises he had no intention of keeping.

"Instead, Theo got Robert a date with a popular gal both had known at school—but had never given Robert the time of day. Robert and the woman hit it off after a time, eventually got married, spawned an heir...yada yada. Prior to their happily-ever-after, however, his wifey-poo had expressed an interest in the Gemini program and became a donor at Theo's insistence, which resulted in a little test-tube cherub, later named Jeremiah Vargas by his adoptive parents."

"Err...okay," I replied, noting she was oddly calm about the reporting of her beau's entrance into the world. "Not that I need you to go into nauseating detail but if Robert was shooting blanks, how did he father a child? And is he aware that his wife has other children floating around in the world?"

"He's definitely not aware of Vargas' existence. And I seriously doubt he knows the child he raised and who went on to become a Congressmen wasn't actually *his* son, either."

I tilted my head. "Another donor was used for Fenton Jr.?"

Leah looked as though she had eaten some bad sushi. "Not just another donor, AJ. The same donor. Theo threw his...specimen into the ring on both counts."

I covered my mouth, suddenly feeling the urge to vomit. "OMG. If Theo is Fenton's real father..."

"Then he and Winslow Clark were half-brothers," she replied, looking equally sick.

"And Jere—"

She put a hand up. "Please, don't say it."

I nodded. The whole thing was enough to incite an entire round of barfing.

"I don't believe it," I finally managed to whisper.

"I don't want to," she replied, a tear breaking free. "How... how can I tell Vargas what his father did...what he was?"

I moved over and gave her a firm hug. "I'm not sure but we'll figure it out...together."

"Will we?"

She had collapsed against me and suddenly my friend who was such a spark of life...always so big...so bright...looked so very small. Much like the child on the playground I had once protected against the bullies from a higher grade. I never wanted to relive that moment and certainly didn't want her to, either.

"Yes, I believe it's the least of our concerns. These things are truths we must grasp onto and eventually tackle. And we will. But right now, if there's a threat out there, one that could harm Fenton...or Vargas...or any of the children of Gemini—and we had the knowledge and didn't attempt to stop it? That loss would be on us."

She nodded. "You're right. I don't trust Martin but perhaps he has some insights, if not the resources, for handling these people. This isn't a police matter. Could you imagine explaining it to Ramirez? Or even Vargas?"

I shook my head.

"I don't like keeping things from him but right now, the truth does him no justice. We need to get to the bottom of this and head it off. If and when they need to be brought in, we'll do what's necessary. But for now, we need to take this as far down the rathole as we can, on our own." She paused to peer at me. "Am I right?"

"Right. You know I don't trust Martin either, but if we can use him to save these people, we need to do it, whatever the cost." I paused, collecting my thoughts. "But there's one thing I need you to do for me before we proceed."

She nodded. "Anything."

I hacked out a harsh laugh. "Don't be so quick to respond, my friend. You may not like it once you hear what I'm asking."

She shrugged and gestured for me to continue. Again, I laughed. Not in a friendly way.

"Martin's going to try to use those chips as leverage. At some point, it will happen." I paused and found my friend nodding. "I realize you aren't aware of their current location, but no one else knows that. When the time comes, they will attempt to use you in order to save my life. You must not waver." Her eyes widened but she did not protest. "Even though you have seen some of the content that Tony B. compiled, we are going to delete it now and you will never mention any part of it. I will destroy the laptop and all evidence at any place it has ever resided. And you will never, ever...no matter what they threaten you with, divulge anything, until this is done. Can you do that, for me?"

I almost didn't want to look at her but found her nodding earnestly when she met my eyes.

"I won't do squat for that rat Martin but I will do anything—for you," she replied. "I loved your parents, too, you know...and when they were gone, I didn't feel the pain like you did but I felt it. I think we need to do this for them and for your sister, Victoria, who never had a chance. The rest of them? They can burn in Hell."

"Let them burn in Hell," I agreed, as a tear escaped the corner of my eye.

CHAPTER NINE

"You really think Fenton Sr. never figured things out?" I asked.

"Who knows, but it probably isn't the reason he feels the need to overthrow the consortium. If anything, it has to do with Martin killing his best friend."

"Good point. The wife surely would have known, though, don't you think?"

Leah snorted. "Yeah. I'll bet she was even shacking up with Theo behind Fenton's back."

"Uh…yuck."

"Well, I hear he was quite the…stud…in those days. Certainly seems like he enjoyed making the rounds, if you know what I mean. Say…didn't Winslow have some less than congenial things to say about his mum?"

"I'm not sure I ever got the sense he knew who she was, other than what his father told him. Which hadn't been particularly nice."

Leah snorted. "Convenient. Blame the woman. After the fact. Theo certainly managed to get his spawn out into the world in multiple ways, though I doubt anyone was the wiser. Just be glad you're not related."

I shuddered, then blanched. "Please. Do not go there. My entry into this world was complicated enough."

"Sorry, was just trying to lighten the mood."

"Lighten the contents of my stomach was more like it," I grumbled. "I think we need to take a closer look at Fenton Sr., and confirm or deny Martin's claims that he's the one spearheading the takeover of the consortium. But first, we've got to figure out why he was tossed out."

"If he was even tossed out," Leah replied. "Martin could have just as easily made that part up, too, to lend credibility to his story. One thing that bothers me—if this consortium is supposed to be top secret and their activities and members are able to operate in the shadows, then how is it that Martin knows so much about their inner-workings?"

Again, I thought about what Tony B. had said, *"Turns out the benefactors had a board of directors, for lack of a better term. Anyway, the Chairman of the Board, so to speak, was also the scientist who spearheaded the consortium—someone whose name I think you're more than a little familiar with..."*

I hadn't shared that detail with Leah and felt downright guilty, after she had been so earnest in helping me. Would knowing that information help us figure out what was going on with Fenton Jr. and determine whether Fenton Sr. was trying to overtake the consortium in order to bring Gemini back to life?

Something had bothered me about that story.

"Why would Fenton Sr. need to take back control of the consortium in order to resurrect the project? Why not just gather up some of the other cronies that were ousted, maybe even some old pals of Theo's, and go direct? I mean, if he was able to regain control, wouldn't the other members rebel, or possibly cause him more trouble than he already had on the outside?"

Leah nodded. "You're right. Why would he need to overthrow the consortium? Why not just create a new one? I mean, Martin has this network thing he's always referencing, why wouldn't Fenton Sr. just do the same?"

"Why indeed. I've kind of always wondered about this network of Martin's. It's how he claimed he found out about Victoria. And knew to come help me."

"Help you...*right*," Leah mused.

"His choice of words, not mine." I shrugged. "Still. How do we know that this 'network' isn't actually the fabrication and the work of one man?"

Leah nodded. "Or that the consortium and the network are one in the same, with one puppetmaster pulling the strings—the same one who has been spinning a good yarn about Fenton Sr.'s plan to reign over the consortium."

"Leah, about that—" I started but she put up a hand and interjected.

"One thing we do know, that perhaps Martin does not, is about the triangle between Fenton, Fenton's wife and Theo. And that Jr. is not Sr.'s son. He may not have realized how close they were."

"Martin did say that bringing Gemini back would also serve as a form of revenge," I replied. "Perhaps he wasn't aware of just how personal it was."

"True. But what if Martin needs to stop Fenton Sr. for another reason. To ensure he is able to assert control over the situation, whatever that may be, without outside interference?"

"You're suggesting that Martin may be telling the truth about Fenton Sr., but that heading him off may be for a very different reason," I replied, tapping my chin.

Leah nodded. "Either way, Martin can still use it as an excuse to get those chips away from you."

"Then like we said before, we need to figure out Sr.'s involvement—starting with his backstory, including his previous involvement with the consortium."

"If there was any," she replied.

I wanted to tell her about Martin but she grabbed her phone and dialed a number.

"Bonnie, Leah. Yeah, long time no talk. You still have access to those old morgue files?"

Morgue? I mouthed.

News morgue, she mouthed back.

I nodded as she listened to whoever Bonnie was. "No, I need to go back further than that. We're talking twenty-five years and beyond? Uh, huh. Okay, good. Do you think you could get me access? Just short term. How long? Good. Let me know. Thanks."

She hung up, smiling. "Pal from the old days who owes me a favor. It should help get us started on Fenton's backstory. Bonnie will let us know when she's got what I need."

"Ah, okay? In the meantime, maybe we should start looking at Fenton Jr. and see if there's anything there. We certainly aren't going to get anything from Martin—or Ramirez—on that front," I murmured.

"You're thinking about his ex, Serena, aren't you?" I shrugged, not willing to show I was putting too much thought into that aspect of Ramirez's past, so she continued, "It is curious that she immediately thought to call Ramirez."

I glanced at her. "You think Jr. put her up to it with the intention of keeping the ambush on the down-low? Or maybe as CYA in case something went haywire?"

"Or because he knew more than he was letting on," she replied.

I raised a brow. "Boy, you really have changed your tune on the dude."

"Like I said, time would tell." She shrugged, before adding, "And as time has passed, his actions have been very…telling."

"Meaning?" I prodded.

"I don't care for some of the people he chooses to do business with or provide support to. A lot of people show a very different face to the public—especially when they want something—but behind the scenes, all bets are off."

I snorted. "It sounds like human nature, Leah."

She squinted at me. "Now who's the cynical one?" I chuckled. "Anyway, I just don't like some of the activities of the people Fenton hangs with. And before you say he may not know about their associations, he does."

"Are we talking illegal activities here? Because if you are, surely there are people who could be contacted—"

She held up a hand. "Don't you think if that were the case, I would have already done so?" I nodded my concession and she continued, "No, these people dance along the edges of the line but their little mitts are dirty from playing in the mud. One of these days they'll slip and when they cross that line, I'll be there to catch them."

"I had no idea. How long have you been working on this?" I asked.

"I've always been working on it. It's what I do," Leah replied, her tone somber.

"Okay, we need to know if there's any way Fenton Jr. is involved, other than being part of Gemini, that is."

She nodded. "Anything that would have set these people off or made him a target, other than his position."

"Do you think he knows about the consortium? Maybe Sr. even elicited his help. You said he had friends. Maybe Sr. encouraged him to get them involved."

"Interesting point. Could he have used some other means to entice him…telling him that his mother or wife were somehow in danger to ensure he was properly motivated?"

"Perhaps he didn't need motivation at all?"

Leah frowned. "I'm not sure which is worse."

"Neither am I."

"Well, that certainly puts another interesting spin on things.

Wouldn't that be something if this was just one big conspiracy to get his father back into the consortium?"

"It would mean Martin was telling the truth."

I laughed. "About that part, anyway."

"Pretty big part," she replied.

"Depends, I guess, on what his angle is. He still wants those chips. This whole thing could just be a means to an end for him."

"I think it always has been."

It was not a thought I relished. Those chips had already cost too many people too much. Lives had been destroyed. Lost. And I would be damned if I was going to let Martin or any other person put one more chink in my armor. If anything, they could put themselves in the line of fire for a change.

Then tell *me* how it feels.

CHAPTER TEN

I was busy fuming over that thought when my cell phone rang, causing me to jump. Apparently, Leah had been deep in her own weeds as she squeaked while nearly falling off her stool.

The number came in as "Unknown" but that wasn't all that surprising, as many tended to come in as blocked, unavailable or unknown these days. So much for the "smart" in smartphone. But hey, I could always talk to Siri whenever I was lonely. Leah was favoring Alexa, because Vargas had one, but I felt that chick was a little too up in my grill for my liking. I'm saying this from the perspective of someone who talks to herself. No sense confusing the poor gal, even if she was artificially intelligent.

I stared hard at the phone, willing the "Unknown" to magically convert to a number I recognized. Yeah, it never happened.

"Maybe it's Martin, using another one of his burner phones," I murmured.

"Put him on speakerphone then," Leah replied. "I want to hear what he's whimpering about this time."

"Or requesting," I grumbled.

Apparently, my best friend felt this was more likely the case, frowning as she re-situated herself back on the stool and thrummed her fingers impatiently on the counter.

I held up my index finger, indicating I needed no commentary from the peanut gallery as I engaged, for the second time in one day, with my BioPop.

Of course, I was rewarded with a series of ludicrous eye rolls. I normally would have tossed something at her head but curiosity got the better of me as I connected.

"Jonah! I need Jonah," the female voice squelched, causing me to back away from the phone as I shook my head in an effort extricate the fingernails-on-a-chalkboard greeting.

Definitely *not* Martin.

Leah looked equally appalled, noisily scooting her stool back as she put her fingers in her ears. Nicoh ran down the hall to escape the sound altogether. I could hardly blame him.

"Err. Excuse me?" I shouted into the phone. It was necessary given the distance I had put between myself and my phone.

Perhaps it wasn't the time to reminisce but I couldn't remember the last time the two of us had been separated by such a distance.

Urr…okay…that was a sad admission. Get a grip, AJ. And a life.

"I'm looking for Jonah," the voice replied, sounding less frantic but increasingly more annoyed. "Jonah Ramirez."

"Yeah, I believe I got that part." I was in no mood for pranks. Or hysterical unknown females. "Who is this?"

"Is this Arianna?" I noticed she didn't wait for an answer before adding," It's Serena. Serena Fenton."

"Um…hi. I take it you are looking for Ramirez. And that you have gotten hold of my unlisted number…somehow." I paused but it was more for effect than to elicit a response, as I added, "But I don't know why you thought he would be…here." It was not a question.

"Oh. Bob couldn't get him on his cell and well, thought that perhaps he might be with you," she replied, as though these conversations were common between us. Not so much. "I take it he's not...there?"

She didn't make mention of how she had acquired my number and frankly, it was probably a moot point, if her husband had his fingers in all kinds of things and had settled in with different types of people, as Leah had suggested. I noted she had crossed her arms, a sour expression spanning her face. It was not a good look, as the image of a creepy apple doll passed through my head and I scrunched my nose at her and waved a hand, silently suggesting she ease up on the frowny face before it stuck that way.

She snorted but complied as she noisily scooted her stool back toward the counter.

"No, Ramirez is not here. Is there anything I can help with, Serena? You seem...not to sound judgy...but kind of stressed. Are you okay?" I replied, shrugging at Leah. I didn't know the woman, other than she was Ramirez's ex, and had nowhere to take the conversation, as awkward as it already was.

A sob released over the phone. "Bob's dad died."

Leah shot me a wide-eyed looked and I managed to stutter out a few words. "Oh, my gosh, Serena. I am so sorry! What happened? I mean, if you need to contact Ramirez, perhaps you should call the station. They can dispatch the team."

"No, no, it's nothing like that. He...he"—a round of sniffles erupted over the line—"passed in his sleep. Bob's a mess..." her voice trailed off and we heard nose-blowing on the other end of the connection. "I just want to help him...and now we can't seem to track Jonah down."

I glanced at Leah, who shrugged. There was a huge discon-nect here and I didn't want to offend, especially not when Serena and her husband were suffering. Still, I needed to ask.

"The former Governor died in his sleep," I repeated. When Serena murmured sounds suggesting the affirmative, I added, "Okay, I'm not trying to be insensitive here, Serena. I am so sorry for your family's loss. But Ramirez is a homicide detective, yet you said Bob's father died in his sleep…so…"

"Oh, goodness. I thought you knew. We don't need Jonah in his official capacity as a homicide detective. He's Bob's unofficial security adviser. Bob wants to make sure this is dealt with appropriately by law enforcement and the media." This time, Ramirez's ex seemed more exasperated than panicked.

I was still missing something and she clearly felt I was holding out.

"Uh, I think we're on a different page here. Except for the night I met with your husband, I hadn't had any interaction with Ramirez…for weeks."

"Oh," she replied, her tone one of genuine surprise. If it had been me, my face would have also blossomed like a ripened cherry tomato. "I wasn't aware. I'm sorry. I don't think Bob knew either…otherwise…he probably wouldn't have been so insistent I call you."

"It's alright," I replied. "I just didn't want you to get the impression I was holding out. Truth be told, I'm in the dark here."

"I totally understand. And my apologies if I came across as accusatory." When I didn't respond, Serena continued, "Since that night, Jonah has taken a leave of absence from the department to aid Bob while he deals with the ambush business. I know he's only doing so because I asked, but Bob is still convinced that there is some unsavory element out there, ready to pounce and with all the issues that are coming up for a vote, needs to be able to focus his attention. Jonah was a temporary solution for this recent situation."

"Yet you said neither you nor Bob can reach him. That doesn't sound like Ramirez," I replied. "He's not answering his cell?"

"No. And his voicemail is full. Bob is afraid he's given him too many leads to track down and that he's so far out-of-pocket that he's not in a location where he's even able to get in touch."

"Ah, and now this has happened and he needs his ace back in the pocket, just to be sure all the angles are covered." I winced, realizing it probably came off a bit crass, given the fact her father-in-law had just passed.

Serena took it in stride. "Exactly. Only now that you haven't got a clue, we have run into a dead end. And both Bob and his mother are going to be beside themselves."

I wanted to ask what they were before, as a father and a husband had just died, but decided against it.

"I may have some other ideas about how we can track him down and get word to him." I glanced at Leah, who gave me a hard stare.

"That would be wonderful. Anything, Arianna...anything would help," Serena replied, a little too breathy for my taste, especially when she added, "See, Bob's suggestion to call you wasn't all a bust."

I murmured some benign response and I agreed to contact her with any additional information, once she provided her contact information.

I was met with a stony glare when I disconnected.

"That was interesting," I replied after an extended silence.

With Leah, anything over fifteen seconds was like Armageddon.

"Um...hmm," she replied, continuing to thrum her fingers on the counter. "I suppose you expect me to inject Vargas into this crap show?"

"Didn't say that," I replied. "If you noticed, I offered no promises."

"You did seem to get a bit chummy with the ex," she snipped, sliding off the chair and pulling a cider from the fridge. I noticed she hadn't pulled two, as she rooted in the junk drawer for a bottle opener.

"Not at all," I replied. "And for the record, we're both exes."

She paused, looking at me and nodded. "That's true. The business about it being Bob's idea to call you, were you buying that?"

I shrugged. "I don't know. To be honest, the whole thing was unsettling."

"Kind of like they weren't all that surprised the old man bought the farm and more concerned how it was handled?"

"Have a bit of respect, Leah. The man, no matter what you thought of him, is dead."

"Yeah, and with his sudden, untimely death, we've lost our primary suspect. According to Martin, anyway. Convenient." She flicked the bottle cap into the trash, took a long swig, stalked out of the room and slammed her door.

When The Kinks "Hatred" burst from under the door jamb, I looked at Nicoh, who had returned to his spot in the corner of the living room, and murmured, "If life were only that simple."

CHAPTER ELEVEN

Leah didn't emerge until the following morning. The bags under her eyes and sloth-like movements suggested she hadn't slept much better than I had. The way she manhandled the coffeemaker confirmed it, slamming the weathered carafe into position as she impatiently jabbed at the buttons, forcing the machine to gurgle to life.

"Sorry," she murmured, noting my wince, while tugging at the ends of her hair. "I wasn't angry at you last night. I was…am mad about the situation."

I nodded, gesturing for her to proceed. With Leah, there was always more to the story. And I wanted her to put it out there. To get it off her chest. To set the bad juju free. But mostly, I wanted to confirm we were still on the same page and on the same side of this…thing…whatever *it* was.

I had given her reasons to doubt me as of late and wouldn't blame her if she'd lost faith in me and decided to bail. Deep down, I knew she wouldn't, out of loyalty, but I needed to hear the words.

She nodded, frowning and she worked her hair to an inch of

itself. It was saying a lot, because her hair was pretty darn short to begin with.

"I hate being forced to retreat to square one. Our primary suspect—if Martin was indeed on the right track—has just fallen off the rails, if not fallen under them," she grumbled.

"Are we?" I asked. "Back to square one?"

Leah's head snapped in my direction, her brows raised. "What do you mean? What are the odds our supposed baddie, if it was Fenton Sr., would croak in his sleep? I mean, dying of natural causes? Why couldn't have Winslow or Theo gone down that easily?" She threw her hands up in the air. "It's not a possibility I would have considered."

Once I recovered from the shudders brought on by the mention of Winslow and his father and the images of their deaths, I ignored the insensitive nature of our conversation. I felt bad a man had died and that his family was suffering but she was right, it wasn't something we'd even remotely considered. How could you?

What if Martin was right and Fenton Sr. had been plotting to overthrow the consortium that had banished him so that he could use their resources to resurrect the Gemini project?

Would his death bring a conclusion to that scheme?

Or were there others waiting in the wings, ready to pick up where he had left off?

Would his death allow them greater power and control?

The question was—who would benefit from having the elder Fenton out of the way?

I could think of one person.

And it bothered me.

I turned to my friend, who was absently stirring sugar into her coffee. "Prior to that call from Serena—which was weird enough on its own—you stated that we had more questions than we had answers. Fenton Sr.'s death doesn't change that. He could still have been our guy but where there's one, there's always the possibility of more."

She nodded. "As in, Fenton Sr. probably hadn't acted alone. And his death…well, it was just bad timing for those he was involved with."

"Regardless, we still need whatever info your friend Bonnie turns up," I replied. "Even with Sr. out of the picture, we still need to see if Martin's theory holds water. Maybe it gives us insight into those Fenton had been working with while on the outs with the consortium."

Leah raised a hand. "Correction. Bonnie's getting me *access* to the information. I still have to do the legwork and find all the hidden nuggets."

"I think you mean we," I replied.

She shook her head. "You need to stay here while I research."

I squinted. "What do you mean?"

"When BonBon gets me that access, I will be catching a flight to Chicago, where all of this started."

I gave her a look, tilting my head at an awkward angle, causing her to chuckle.

"What? Did you think I was being cute when I referenced the morgue? It's in Chicago."

I shrugged. This time she smacked her forehead and let out a hearty laugh. It had been awhile since either of us had a reason to release one of those. Soon I was chuckling, too.

"Not all of this stuff is going to be as easy as doing a Google search, AJ. A lot of what we need has not been digitized. I need to dig into the physical files—dozens of years of boxes, which will have no particular rhyme or reason."

"That could take a while." I frowned, not pleased by the prospect I would be all by my lonesome to tackle the powers—whatever they may be—in Phoenix.

I also didn't like the fact that she would be alone. What if one of Fenton's cohorts tracked her to Chicago and backed her into a corner?

She peered at me and for a moment, I thought she was trying to read my mind. "Maybe. But I have friends who can help. And I know where to look."

"You have recruits?" This was news to me.

She waved a hand. "Of course. People owe me favors and if I need to, I'll call them in."

I groaned. "I hope you don't live to regret that. Let's not forget the last time you called in a favor." She cringed for a moment, remembering that she was recently on the receiving end of a marriage proposal.

"Whatever. I dealt with…that awkwardness…and we're still friends. He ended up marrying one of my co-workers and now they're pregnant."

I snickered. "Okay, it's so good to know you won't have another stalker for Vargas to wield his badge at. So, while you're in The Windy City, watching hockey, searching files, whatever you do…what can I do to move this thing along?"

"Well, you could find Ramirez, for one." She laughed after taking in my expression. "I'm sure Serena would appreciate it."

"Please, please, please…stay and deal with that for me? I'll totally go to Chi-Town for you. I'll be a good little worker. I promise you won't be disappointed."

She chuckled without the least bit of sympathy in her voice. "Sorry, you need to stay here. You know, to keep an eye on Martin. Plus, I think you owe Logan a call, let him know about your plans for looking into Decker's case."

"Gah, you don't ask much." This time she wiggled her eyebrows and winked.

"I know you want all of this wrapped up, even more than I do. So why fight it?"

I frowned. "Who said I'm fighting it?"

Leah snorted and pointed. "That wrinkle on your forehead when I mentioned Ramirez."

Wrinkle? I started to grab a plate to check my reflection when I caught the quirk at the corner of her mouth.

"Gotcha." She laughed. "I knew you still had a burr in your saddle where that boy is concerned. According to Vargas, it goes both ways." She paused to tap her chin. "Come to think of it, I may just need to let it slip that there's a new cowboy in town. Logan is quite the cutie."

"Leah Campbell!" I ground out between gritted teeth. "You will keep your trap shut or so help me, I'll share our junior high pics with Vargas. You know the ones where you gave yourself an unfortunate haircut and insisted on wearing silver spandex for six months straight, paired with Mary Jane's?"

Leah's mouth opened.

And closed.

"Yeah, sorry, babe, but it wasn't your best look. Or your best decade. Can't say mine was much better but Ramirez has already seen the incriminating photos from that awkward time in my life. Pretty sure you can't say the same about Vargas." I wiggled my brows and smiled.

"You are pure evil!" she squealed, throwing a roll of paper towels at my head.

I ducked just in time and laughed. "Perhaps, but you're the one making me stay here and deal with Ramirez."

"And Martin," she replied.

"Ugh, don't remind me. Let's just call it square, shall we?"

"Square as a donut is round."

Whatever that meant.

As it turned out, Leah got her access, compliments of her pal Bonnie, and was on a flight heading east a few hours later, leaving me to ponder my next steps.

Yeah, I knew which one I needed to take first, despite the fact I was fighting it.

I sifted through the contacts in my phone, selecting one that I had been tempted to delete on more than one occasion. I never knew why I hadn't but something told me that I would have remembered the number by heart, whether it resided on the list.

Ramirez picked up after two rings.

"AJ." His voice was smooth, even and without of hint of curiosity as to why I was calling.

"Serena's been looking for you," I replied, about to launch into my conversation with his ex, anything to prevent it from drifting back to myself. Or Martin.

I should have known Ramirez would skip ahead and beat me to the punchline.

"Both she and Bob caught up with me," came the reply.

Again, with no hint, of anything.

"Oh. Good, I guess. I mean, it's awful about the Congressman's father, but I'm glad you connected with them. Serena sounded pretty frantic. How are she and the rest of the family doing?"

Ramirez sighed, his first show of emotion. I released a breath as he continued, "About as well as could be expected. Shocked. Saddened. Robert was in pretty good health, both mentally and physically, so his passing came as a huge surprise. Especially to the housekeeper who found him."

"What? I thought Bob's mother found him?" I realized Serena had never actually said that, and perhaps I had just assumed at some point that it had been the case.

"No. Bob called her after-the-fact. She was out of town at the time. In Chicago." I gasped at the mention of Chicago but Ramirez continued as though he hadn't heard me. "Had to come back to learn her husband had died. Bob didn't want her to travel with that on her mind. Certainly not alone."

"That was very considerate of him. How did she take the news...is she doing okay?" I immediately kicked myself. "I mean, it would be horrible to learn your spouse died. Alone."

"Serena said she took it hard. Robert and Bob were her world. She had no other family. According to Serena, her sister had been her last living relative and when she passed—some rare form of cancer—she'd never really recovered."

"Gosh, I wasn't aware of the history." It was a filler comment. Of course, why would I have known such a detail?

Ramirez was not fazed as he expounded, which I thought was a bit odd. "According to both Serena and Bob, Jerri—that's Bob's mom—had a really hard time dealing with the loss. Of course, when you lose a twin, it's probably a lot like losing a limb. At least that's what I have been told."

I jumped, nearly knocking my stool over as I stood. "Excuse me?"

"Oh. The sister, Jeannie, I believe her name was. She and Jerri were twins."

Considering he knew that I, too, had been a twin, the casualness of his response surprised me. Could he have so easily forgotten a detail like that? He had, after all, been the lead detective on my sister's homicide.

As if sensing my discomfort, he quickly added, "God, AJ, I am so sorry. I should have realized—"

"No, no. It's fine." It wasn't, but now that the initial jolt had worn off, I was more curious about Bob's mother and her sister. "So Mrs. Fenton was a twin?" I started thinking about history and the information Leah had already found.

Something bothered me but I couldn't put my finger on it. Yet.

"Yeah, I guess so. They were very close. Robert, too. Apparently, they all grew up together. Went to school together or something or other. Like Jerri, Robert took it pretty hard when she died. He tried his best to help her recover, but she never did. It's actually kind of ironic."

"What is?" I asked, leaning into the phone.

"Jerri was in Chicago visiting her sister's grave site."

"Oh my, that is ironic…and unfortunate," I replied. "Does she go back often?"

"Yearly, on the anniversary of her sister's death." Ramirez's tone was somber.

I covered my mouth. "You're not saying…"

"Unfortunately, I am. On the day she was in Chicago to mourn her twin…"

I'm not sure how I managed to do so, considering my mounting shock, but I finished his thought, "Her husband joined her twin on the other side."

CHAPTER TWELVE

"Was the sister's death recent?" Not that it mattered but like I'd noted, this new wrinkle had piqued my curiosity.

"No. If memory serves, the sister passed before Bob was born. Or shortly after. I'm not sure which. Either way, he never knew her. Or doesn't remember her, being too young and all," Ramirez replied.

"Still, a rough situation all around," I murmured, still unable to identify what was troubling me and had my spidey senses a-twitter.

Ramirez knocked me out of my reverie. "So, did you just call to tell me that Serena was looking for me? Or was there another reason?"

Suddenly, I was starting to remember all the little things that annoyed me about him. Then again, we seemed to bring that out in one another.

"Of course, my apologies. I also wanted to touch base and see if any additional leads on the Congressman's ambush had come to light? Or any new evidence? Perhaps the Congressman even remembered something else?"

"Not a peep," he replied and while his voice didn't waver, I could sense a hint of something that didn't strike me as quite on the level.

Deception.

"Well, that's certainly disappointing, for everyone involved, including the Congressman," I responded, keeping my own tone even. "Serena said you're taking a bit of time off from the department to help him out?"

I purposely left it open-ended, hoping he would fill in a few of the oddly-shaped blanks. This time, he did not disappoint but his words were guarded.

"I am. I had a bit of extra vacation to burn and thought I would use some of it to help an old friend out."

"I didn't realize you and the Congressman were friends," I retorted, though I knew what—or more importantly, who —he'd meant.

He ignored my quip. "It's just a couple of weeks and it's not really putting me out in any way."

I thought about Leah's recent assessment of Fenton Jr. and the company he kept and snorted. "Nah, just your hard-earned reputation and integrity."

"Excuse me?" His usually calm voice turned sharp. Ah, I'd finally hit a nerve. "What is that supposed to mean?"

"According to the word on the street, Jr. has made some interesting connections and entered into some questionable business dealings since taking office. Perhaps he's picking up the areas his dad hadn't already covered."

"Hmm, by 'word on the street' you're not referencing a particular ex-investigative reporter, are you?"

I clucked my tongue. "Why Detective, you should be a bit nicer about how you choose to address your best friend's gal." In my haste to be cheeky, I also immediately regretted my misstep, having been baited into his trap.

"Oh my. So we *are* talking about one and the same," he

replied, his tone smug. "Well, perhaps she should get herself some new words or find herself a different street to hang out on."

"Offering that advice from personal experience, I see," I retorted.

I'd stung him on that one, as he released a huff. "Just what have you heard, AJ? Or more specifically, what has your cohort alluded to?"

I mouthed, "Gotcha" before responding, "Oh, just the usual talk around the water cooler. Good boy trying to make good realizes the world doesn't work that way and has to play in the Devil's playground to get something he's promised his constituents. Maybe even something that could make him a target, for say, an ambush?"

I let it hang in the air, feeling pretty confident with my onslaught. That was until Ramirez snatched it before it hit the ground.

"Interesting theory, except for the fact that the assailant not only manages to drop a business card—yours—his ramblings sounded eerily similar to someone you're quite familiar with."

"Let's cut the crap where Martin is concerned," I growled from behind teeth that were clenched so tight I could hear my dentist screaming from the golf course at his country club. "Notorious? Perhaps. But he's certainly not a father figure to me, Ramirez. I had a father. The one who raised me. And died because of me. And, for the record, Detective Ramirez, the jury's still out on Martin, whatever hole he's burying his head in these days."

"So you're still claiming you haven't talked to him." It wasn't a question and Ramirez's tone suggested he was beyond any form of amusement where our conversation was concerned.

Call me stubborn but I wasn't about to let him have his way. "Oh, I've talked to him, alright, the same day I woke up in the hospital. Alone. Just minutes prior to when you decided to walk out on me. On the whole, it wasn't a day I wanted to commemorate or add to my scrapbook, if you get my drift."

Ramirez grunted some unintelligible response before adding, "So you're maintaining that you haven't spoken one word to him since."

My heart thudded against my chest. What if he'd had people following me all this time, hoping to capture me with Martin? If they had, why hadn't they confronted us or taken Martin down?

A lump grew in my throat. What if they had gotten to him afterward? Was he in police custody, unable or unwilling to contact me?

I took a deep breath, shoved the negative thoughts down and called Ramirez's bluff. "Are you asking me in an official capacity? Because if you are, I may have to contact the department and notify them of an abuse of power of one of their off-duty detectives—and believe me, I'd be well within my rights."

"So you won't answer," came the flat response.

"I believe I just did, Detective."

Ramirez sighed. "Okay, AJ, we'll play it your way. Yes, I've heard rumblings about Fenton's bad decisions with regards to business partners and nefarious back alley dealings but have not found anything that supports it.

"Furthermore, yes, I'm helping to ensure the threat is neutralized and was tracking down a lead when Bob and Serena were unable to reach me—my voicemail was filled with their calls—while I followed the lead I was requested to follow by Bob himself. It turned out to be a dead end, but there were also tracks in the sand, ones that suggested Martin's hands were all over it.

"So, whether you've had contact with him, know this—he *is* involved. And so are you. And until you feel you can tell me what he has on you or wants from you that's making you act so crazy, please, do not call in an effort to pump me for information. You have no right to.

"If however, you are ready to come clean about Gemini, then please call me and I will do whatever I can to protect and help you, and Leah. Even Martin, if you deem it necessary. That is my promise to you, Arianna, for whatever it's worth."

I was silent so long, he uncharacteristically added, "What? Has the cat finally gotten its claws into your tongue?"

I snorted. "That's so cliché Ramirez, even coming from you. And no, the cat hasn't gotten my tongue because I've got nothing to say about any of the convoluted assumptions you've drawn, no matter how they were derived." I paused to scoff. Twice.

Ramirez waited.

"You think you know something? You don't. And neither do I. Sometimes, when you start looking for trouble, Ramirez, it eventually comes looking for you. I think someone—someone I used to believe was wise once told me that. I just wish he would follow his own advice. He may find it suits him to see the world both ways, without judgment of who is right and who is wrong.

"That's where I find myself, more and more often. Sometimes, the world does not operate in the black or white, sometimes we have to reside in the gray, with the understanding it's the shades which we choose that are what define who we are and what we stand for.

"Perhaps you find that concept foreign, and that's okay. But I can live with that. I have to. But if you can't, I get it. Just understand, at the end of the day, Jonah, you had a choice. We all do. None of us is defined by where we sit on that scale, it's who and what we stand for that truly matters. And the only thing that will be remembered when we meet our maker. Each of us has to decide…what do we want people to say about us when that day comes? What is our legacy?

"As for Martin…if it turns out he stands on the darker side of gray, I can say with one-hundred percent certainty that he can go to hell and burn. Alone. He walked out on me, just the same as you did. But I can give you a pass. You didn't feel you had a choice. And that was an honest mistake.

"Martin, on the other hand, used emotional blackmail as a tool. That was a calculated risk on his part. And he lost that bet. Good riddance I say.

"And I mean that. Lesson learned on my part. The hard way.

"For a moment, I forgot I had parents who loved me and even though I didn't have them nearly long enough, Martin helped me, in his backward way, realize that I needed to treasure every moment I had. Unlike Martin, I have known and lost true love. And before you ask, yes, I think he loved my biological mother, Alison, but at the end of the day, like Victoria and me, we were a means to an end, and the outcome, where he was concerned, would have always been the same. I am honestly glad Alison and Victoria never had to live with the burden, or guilt that they had disappointed him. I've had time to let that go.

"And I can live with that, wherever the chips fall.

"Oh, and having seen Martin in the flesh, I doubt the old man was spry enough to best our fit young Congressman, even on a good day. And besides, while Martin's name is out there, it's probably the doing of people who want to finish him off for all the crap he's pulled. You know…draw him out so they can whack him, tie blocks to his ankles and sink him in Tempe Town Lake or toss him out of one of our not-so-high-rises.

"Hey, maybe they'll even get him tanked up on Mill and leave him face-up in a pile of his own vomit in some cheap hotel on Van Buren."

This time, Ramirez snorted and I know he wanted to interject, but I continued my rant.

"So yeah, Martin Singer, aka my BioPop, may be a nuisance but he's not an idiot or a dolt, so he's not going to stick around and play whack-a-mole with his enemies. Having said that, I'm guessing he's long gone. There's nothing for him here. Nothing left, anyway. Even if I had something he wanted, he knows he'll never get it from me. Because I just don't care. I never did. And I never will.

"End of story.

"Anyway, now that I've made sure that your message has been relayed as promised to Serena, I'd really, really appreciate it if you would so kindly inform her that I am not your secretary, nor your lil' miss. Interpret that however you see fit.

"And please, for God's sake, get back to your babysitting detail. I'm sure Serena and Bob need you more right now than I do. You never know, they may even be sitting around waiting with baited breath for your call. God knows why. Perhaps it's all the hot air you tend to generate. You've got a bright future if the cop thing doesn't pan out. Lap dog suits you just fine.

"Doesn't it, Nicoh, my loyal and steadfast companion? It's so good to know that some dogs can be trusted. And are smart enough to know who—and when—to bite."

After tossing out that bit of venom, I disconnected. Finally, I sucked in some much-needed air, released it and then threw my head back and laughed. If only Leah had been here.

Though my call to Ramirez had gone badly, he had let a few key details slip—ones I knew could help Leah with her research. I called her phone and upon receiving her voicemail, figured she must still be in the air, so I left a quick message with the information Ramirez had supplied and told her to call me if she needed to discuss in further detail.

If she was short on time, it would give her more than enough ammo to hit the ground running, but I secretly hoped she'd call anyway. What can I say? I was feeling like a snit and want to share the jabs I had landed on Ramirez.

I was reliving them again when I realized my mistake—the jerk had totally baited me. While I had not confirmed I had spoken to

Martin recently, I hadn't denied it either. I also hadn't mentioned Gemini and considering it was not something that would have been at the front of his mind, it meant Fenton had brought it up. Either that, or despite his comments to the contrary, Ramirez *had* actually uncovered something when looking into the Congressman's ambush.

And while I hadn't added any details, my omission had allowed him to discern that I was aware of such information. I should have raised my own questions or filtered in some doubt. And I hadn't. I shook my head and growled, causing Nicoh to rise and move to another room.

Apparently, he wanted no part of it.

I was mentally punching myself in the face when my phone rang. I released a sigh of relief when I noted the caller—Leah.

"You will never guess who I saw at the airport!" she squealed into the phone when I answered.

"Um…Jon Bon Jovi?" Honestly, I could have listed off thousands of possibilities that would have caused this level of hysterics but it was the first one that came to mind.

She sighed, her voice only slightly calmer and the pitch now just shy of shattering glass, rather than on the other side of chart. "Oooh, I wish. It wasn't that good. Anyway, you won't believe who was getting off a flight from Chicago just as I was hopping on another that was heading back?"

I rolled my eyes. "Jerri Fenton…Bob's mom."

"What? How did you know that?" she replied in a tone that suggested I had sucked the helium right out of her balloon.

"Hello! Did you listen to my message?" I scoffed when my question was met with silence. "I didn't think so."

Finally, she released a huff. "For the record, I called you as soon as they gave the go ahead…you know, public safety and all. Anyway, I didn't bother checking because I was sure you would be highly interested. Guess I'll just keep the excitement all bottled

up next time, until I've made sure I've checked my messages."
Now she was getting downright snarky.

I sighed. "I was…am…interested." Before she could retort, I
quickly filled her in on what Ramirez had revealed.

"Interesting," she commented once I had finished. "That does
explain a few things. But not others."

"Such as?" I prompted.

"Well, for one. The widow didn't look all that distraught. In
fact, she looked…refreshed."

"Refreshed? What does that mean—that she had a facial
procedure done?"

Leah laughed. "Sorry. Let me pull out my pocket thesaurus."
She paused for a moment, clearly enjoying this way too much.
"Ah, here it is…synonyms for 'refreshed' include exhilarated,
reinvigorated, rejuvenated, replenished, revived—ooh, nix that
one, it's in bad taste, considering her husband just bought the
farm." She snorted when I released a low groan. "Choose whatever verb suits. Regardless, she didn't look all that bent about
the news."

"According to Ramirez, Bob said he elected not to tell her
until she returned. I guess he didn't want her to be upset during
the entire flight back. Maybe even wanted to deliver the news
face to face…whatever."

"Huh, that's odd. Based on a conversation I 'might' have
eavesdropped on—I heard the name Jennie—it sounded like she
already knew her."

I tilted my head. "Could it have been Jeannie?"

"Certainly…why?"

I filled her in on the other goodie Ramirez had dropped.

"You've got to be kidding me." I noticed it wasn't a question.

"I wish I was. Or maybe not. I guess it depends on whether it
leads us anywhere. Anyway, I thought it could help you in your
research, which is why I left you the message."

"Oh, it definitely will point me in a new direction, especially if it opens a fresh can of worms."

"I'm not sure how fresh canned worms would be, but I get the gist," I replied as something else popped into my head. "It could also determine whether Martin was on target or way off the range. Then again, he could be close and have just veered down the wrong path."

"Wouldn't be the first time," Leah grumbled, "and I doubt it will be the last."

"One more thing I should probably mention—Ramirez is convinced our Congressman is on the level."

This time she snorted. "Of course he is."

"It was so egregious! He actually had the gall to suggest that I was in cahoots with Martin. That we had teamed up. He even went as far as plunking Gemini into the conversation, hoping I would slip up and spill my guts."

"Oh, AJ! You didn't?"

I sighed and looking up at the ceiling. "Not exactly." I proceeded to detail my faux pas.

"Meh. Don't worry about it. He was fishing and you gave him nothing more than chum. What about the other thing you were supposed to do?"

"What other thing?" I racked my brain, wondering if something had wiggled loose. That tended to happen during conversations with Ramirez.

"Logan," Leah grumbled. "You were supposed to follow up with him."

I could feel my face redden at the mention of his name. My stuttering didn't help the situation. "Dude! I have totally been bogged down talking to Ramirez and digesting all of...this." I waved a hand around despite the fact she could not see me. "I am in no mindset nor do I have the time to see what's behind *that* curtain today."

"Chicken." She made clucking noises in my ear.

"Hardly," I retorted.

"I would think after giving Ramirez the beat down, you'd be amped for a new challenge."

"Challenge—yes. Another high wire act, not so much."

She made a scoffing noise." Maybe you're not the girl I thought you were."

"Hmm, where have I heard that before?" I tapped my chin, causing her to huff. "Besides, for once…just once…I'd like to stay off that high wire. I'm getting tired of falling into the lion's den."

CHAPTER THIRTEEN

After a spirited conversation with Leah, who was actually excited about digging into the thing she called the morgue based on the new info I had supplied, I was tempted to open my own can of worms in order to drum up my own excitement.

Yeah, I was considering a follow-up call with Serena.

Call me crazy but something told me that she held the key to some serious goodies…perhaps some even fell into the cinnamon bear range. Which was g-o-o-d. I wasn't trying to take advantage of a woman in mourning, but felt that she honestly wouldn't be opposed to sharing. I was, after all, a friend of Ramirez's and divulging any insights might serve as both a relief and a cleansing of the soul, of sorts.

However, I was also banking on the assumption that Ramirez —or her hubby—had not warned her off or instructed her not to talk to me. If anything, I was betting she had been left out in the cold on most of it.

The question was, how did I approach the Congressman's wife? I could always send flowers or have a casserole sent to their estate. Perhaps even offer to document the funeral, immortalizing

Fenton Sr. in pictures? Okay, that was creepy and frankly, not something I needed to add to my portfolio.

In the end, I felt just touching base via a phone call was the simplest and most direct route.

I dialed the number, fighting the urge to barf.

Serena immediately picked up and I was taken aback when she breathed into the phone. "Arianna, I'm so pleased to hear from you."

"Urm, you are?" To be honest, I hadn't anticipated this kind of reception.

"I know that you reached out to Jonah on our behalf. Bob and I are so grateful and touched. Of course, Bob realized that it was his own fault that he was unable to contact Jonah, due to the fact he had been busy tracking down the man who broke into Bob's car and accosted him."

Accosted? I withheld a snort but rolled my eyes, amused by the notion that Martin had gone from an ambusher to an accoster. I think he would find it humorous, too, despite the fact that he had, indeed, broken into the Congressman's car and scared the crap out of him. Always the jack-in-the-box.

Then again, those contraptions had always scared me, too.

I realized Serena was still prattling away, oblivious that the monkey in my brain had moved on to a prettier, tastier-looking banana. Yeah, I tend to get shiny object syndrome when I'm bored, stressed or procrastinating.

"Anyway, I know I owe you a debt of gratitude. And, doubly so, as I was not aware that you and Jonah had…parted ways." She released a sigh and envisioned her patting her heart, if not wiping away a stray tear.

"Um. Okay." Yeah, I was quite the conversationalist that way but really did not want to trade Ramirez stories with his ex. So I did what I do best—I changed the subject. "How are you all doing…considering? Again, I am so sorry for your loss. If there is anything I can do…"

Serena cut me off with a breathy response. "Oh, Arianna, you are just as Jonah described. Always so compassionate and giving."

I blinked. Ramirez had discussed me, with his ex? And had put me in a positive light? I certainly wasn't buying it and the adjectives he would have supplied wouldn't have been so…nice.

"Thank you for asking. Truth be told, things have been tough for all of us and especially for Bob and his mom. But the outpouring of support from the friends and the community has been simply wonderful. So many people loved and adored Robert." I noticed family had not been listed among those supporters and made a mental note to share with Leah, as I murmured some unintelligible commentary before she continued, "Anyway, all of the love, support and generosity they're receiving is making the transition so much easier for them."

Transition? Were they having the old man cryogenically frozen? If so, Martin probably could have supplied some best-practices, even though it wasn't his particular area of expertise. Oooh, maybe they were having a shaman or spirit worker come in to transport him to his next phase? Hey, I wasn't judging. I was just curious about her choice of words. Perhaps she was grasping at straws, trying to keep things positive for her family, while tackling her own emotions.

As if sensing my curiosity, she quickly added, "Goodness, you must think I'm a basket case, babbling on and on as I have."

I mentally kicked myself. Again. Last thing I needed to do was force her to shut down.

"Not at all," I replied, my tone genuine. And I was, as were the sentiments I proceeded to offer. "I think you are handling things very well, all things considered. No one pictures losing someone and when it happens, it's always a shock, no matter how it occurs. You are acting with remarkable grace and I envy that. Just remember that you need to take care of yourself first, so that you can fully be present for others when they need you the most. I've learned that lesson the hard way on more than one occasion. Maybe someday, I'll actually take my own advice." I chuckled but truthfully, there was no humor behind it.

Serena allowed me a moment of silence before responding, "I am so sorry, Arianna, Jonah told me that you had recently lost your parents. An airplane accident, I think he said."

Accident? I wanted to snort but know Ramirez had done me a huge favor by not divulging the truth. That would have been too hard and painful to explain away, especially when Serena was coming from a place that was filled with good intentions. Perhaps I hated to admit it, but it was true.

Regardless of her choice in life partner, she was by all accounts, a good and decent person. Part of me wanted to hate her whenever the comparisonitis demon reared its ugly heads—yes, that's plural heads—other times, I wanted to grip her by the shoulders, shake her until her perfectly coiffed hair looked remarkably tousled, just so I could tell her to run and never look back.

I feared that if either Martin or Leah were even remotely close to being right, she would be among the casualties of whatever war the consortium, Bob's enemies or whoever, intended upon waging.

Once again, I realized the silence had gone on for way too long—how was it I kept getting derailed? Perhaps I should have had Leah tackle this convo, but she already had so much on her plate—a lot of which had nothing to do with me and everything to do with one Jere Vargas…and the secret she was keeping from him.

"It's been a while since their passing." I finally managed to formulate a response, as trite as it was. It represented the uncomplicated side—perhaps the side I wished was true. "But I do the best I can and continue living my life. I owe it to them to represent the best version of myself, every single day. They would expect—and accept—no less. Do I miss them? Hell, yes… Does it get easier? Hell no…and don't ever let anyone tell you that you need to get over it. You don't. Need to get over it, that is. You can, however, learn to embrace and appreciate what you had with that person and respect them and yourself to live your life to the fullest. Anyone who says otherwise is lying to themselves. I don't know if that makes sense, or even helps, but it is what I firmly believe."

This time, Serena was quiet and for a moment, I thought I had offended her by being so direct. Then, I heard a tiny sob.

"Thank you. Thank you, Arianna. I needed to hear that." She blew her nose quietly, and released a breath before continuing, "Everyone in Bob's family is so strong. They don't really show—or even share—emotions or feelings. And, as a person who wears her every emotion on her sleeve—it's hard. I feel weak. Incompetent. Even unworthy sometimes of the family name."

"Hold on right there, Serena. That is just not true. If they are making you feel that way, yeah, I know it's hard but it's about them. People like you scare them, because you aren't afraid to look in the mirror. They're more afraid you'll judge them than you are of them judging you. Instead, they avoid the mirror or lie when they look in it. You hold power. The power of truth. Because the mirror doesn't frighten you. You are stronger. So, if you want to cry, then cry. If you want to express your emotions, then express 'em, even if it's not pretty. Just be true to who you are. The minute you stop doing so is the minute you stop living. You become a zombie, trudging your way through life. And that's no way to live. Perhaps I've overstepped here, but I truly believe that. Don't be afraid to be who you are."

A small sniffle erupted. "You are absolutely right. Again,

thank you." After another moment, she added, "I can't believe Jonah was bonehead enough to let you go."

I snorted, then released a bout of chuckles, causing her to giggle, too. After we'd sufficiently calmed ourselves to the point we could talk without hyperventilating, I got down to business.

"Ramirez...err, Jonah had mentioned that the Congressman's mom was out of town when his father passed."

"Oh yes, that was really unfortunate. She was in Chicago. She goes every year at this time," Serena replied.

"I understand it was to visit her sister...her grave?" When I was met with an awkward silence, I added, "Ramirez mentioned it briefly."

"Yes, she always visits on the anniversary of her death, so the timing was unfortunate. If she'd had any idea..." I could hear more sniffling and my heart went out to her.

"There's no way she could have known, Serena. Obviously, if her husband had been sick or dealing with something major, she wouldn't have gone. It was simply his time, as sad and as cliché as it sounds. From what I understand—sorry, I don't follow politics or know much about your family—but from what little I have read and heard, the Congressman's father was a force in his own right and even after his stint had ended, had stayed active with the party and his community, and was always in excellent mental and physical health. In fact, that had been one of the hot buttons of his platform, if I'm not mistaken?"

"Wow." she chuckled. "You are about as well-versed as I am. Either that, or you are a much quicker study. I didn't respond and she continued, "You're right, mental and physical health and well-being was a major part of his platform, for all ages. 'From cradle to those of a very respectable age' I believe was his tagline."

I laughed. "Yes, I think I read that. It's a good one. It just sad that he didn't get a chance to see his own twilight years."

"I know. Or I guess I should say, you never really know, do you?" she replied.

"Will the Congressman's mother be okay? It was my understanding that, except for the Congressman and her husband, she had no other family."

"That is true, once her sister passed."

"That must have been hard." I reflected on my own scenario and it had been hard, despite the fact I never knew my sister until after she had been murdered.

"I think it must be too, but..." Serena paused for a moment. "It's also hard to tell, because she never speaks about it."

"Well, I imagine losing a sibling would be painful."

"No, not that...it's that she never even mentioned having a sister."

"Come again?" I started.

"Bob only knows because his parents needed some paperwork that was located in their safe when they were on vacation and Bob's dad gave him temporary access and while Bob didn't go snooping, he was confused by his father's instructions and ended up opening a pouch that contained some of his mother's belongings. Among them were birth certificates for Jerri and her sister... a twin, born two minutes later, named Jeannie. Jerri and Jeannie —that would have been a mouthful, don't you think?"

"Indeed. But it's strange that she never mentioned having a sibling, much less a twin, to anyone," I replied.

"Oh, Bob's dad knew. They all went to school together... college, I mean. But she never said a word to Bob. Not one mention of why she took that yearly trip and until he found the papers he always thought she was going back to visit friends and spend some time by herself out of town, that kind of thing. But from the death certificate he found, also in the same pouch in the safe, he learned that she had passed shortly after he was born, so he never really would have known her, if you know what I mean."

I nodded, though she couldn't see me. "Wow. She must have been pretty young. How did she die?"

"According to the certificate, her cause of death was listed as some form of cancer, the best he could tell, something that had thirty-five syllables and sounded downright scary."

"That's just awful. It must have been hard on Bob's mother and father."

"You would think. This family holds things pretty close to the vest, though. But I'll give Bob props, he got curious once he learned about his aunt. And that his mother's only sibling had been a twin."

"Oh?" Finally, we were getting to the goods.

"Yeah, I know he felt bad betraying his parent's trust and all that, but he was compelled to learn about his history and started doing his own research. I think Jonah helped out some, too, but the details got sketchy really fast, other than to say her life…Jeannie's that is, doesn't sound like it was a very happy one."

"Was Bob able to find out anything about her cancer? It must have come on fairly quickly," I replied.

"There wasn't a shred of anything to find. In the end, Bob basically did a Google search on the cause of death listed on her certificate, which turned out to be more convoluted and confusing than the pronunciation of the disease that killed her."

"What about the coroner, physician or whoever signed her death certificate?"

"Another dead end. Bob was devastated when he learned the man who had signed the death certificate was no longer living. Bob, of course, did not want news of his inquiry getting back to his parents, especially not to his mom and to press it any further with any of the current staff might have raised a red flag."

"That is really unfortunate. It would have been nice for Bob to have some semblance of his family's history. And know where the rest of his family ended up, especially considering his father's passing."

"Oh gosh, he wouldn't even dream of bringing it up now. Whatever aspirations of finding out about his family will need to wait," Serena replied.

"Maybe one day…"

"No, no, no…Bob was adamant. He does not want to stress his mom any more. And if she were to find out that he knew..." There was a moment of silence before she added, "He is willing to wait until the timing is right."

"Meaning?"

"Goodness, I hate talking like this but after coming up short in his initial investigation, Bob said he will wait until his mother has passed, respecting her wishes to stay private as long as she is with us—which, we hope and pray, will be a very long, long time. And, when the timing is right—after a respectful period—he will seek out his family history."

"Perhaps by then, he won't have political frenemies looking over his shoulder at every turn and can do so as a private citizen. Plus, there could even be better, more comprehensive information out there that makes his search less challenging," I suggested, though I wasn't feeling it.

"I hope Bob can hold out that long." Serena sighed. "He's not a patient man."

"But he'll do it for his mother," I confirmed.

"For respect of his mother, yes," she replied. "But beyond that, nothing or no one will stop him."

I could think of a few someones. And one in particular. But instead of going down that rathole, opted to change the subject. "Gosh, Serena, I just wanted to check in and here I've monopolized so much of your time. Bob and his mother must be needing you. I'm truly sorry for that, but do appreciate your time."

She chuckled lightly. "It's nice of you to say but most days I feel like I'm just in the way. You know, the awkward duck with the big feet that everyone's tripping over?"

"I highly doubt that's the case," I replied, my tone sincere. "Bob is a lucky man. And I'm sure his mother will appreciate having genuine comfort and support from a female perspective. The guys, while they mean well, tend to overdue it."

This time she laughed. "You are so right. They do that, don't they?" She laughed again, before adding, "Can I tell you something?" Her voice was soft, as though she was unsure whether she should venture forward.

"Sure." I shrugged to myself, not sure where she was going with this. "Shoot."

"I don't know where the two of you stand. And I don't know the details. And I don't need to. But I'm secretly—well, now that I'm putting it out there, not so secretly—hoping you and Jonah can work things out. No matter the extent of your differences. I'd love to see the two of you back together." I started to speak but she cut me off.

"And before you protest, allow me to continue. I have known Jonah for most of my life. And yeah, I know I broke his heart, but I own that and have never asked him for forgiveness, only the possibility—and the opportunity—that we can be in the same space, without bringing out the worst in each of us—the resentment and anger—and the baggage. It took us a long time to get to that point…too long when you realize there are no guarantees in life and you'll never know when you get up in the morning if that will be your last sunrise. So for now, we can exist in the same world and be cordial and even have a chuckle about the old days and that works for us. It's all I can really ask of him, at least when it comes to myself. I have done too much damage to his soul.

"But you? I have never seen him light up in the way he does when he's talking about you. Oh sure, he likes to complain and tries to focus in on your stubborn, feisty and downright reckless tendencies, but he also loves your loyalty, your passion for friends and family and your zest and genuine curiosity for life. Actually, I know he loves it. And yet it scares him, because he can't protect it. It's in his bones and while he's one of the best at what he does, he's frustrated because he can't figure out a way to appease one feisty gal."

"You mean he's frustrated because he can't figure out how to tame me and get me to fit into some antiquated mold of what he thinks a woman should and shouldn't do."

Of course, after the fact, I realized that last bit had come out a bit harsher than I'd intended but Serena took it in stride.

"No, Arianna. I understand how you can draw that conclusion —he's kind of a cave man that way—but with you, I truly believe it goes deeper than that. He doesn't want to trap a wild animal, only to have it resent its environment and its captors once it realizes it will never, ever be able to return to its previous life. He also knows his choices would forever destroy its spirit. I think that's how he views a relationship with you. He couldn't bear to have you hate him because he couldn't allow you to be who you were, for fear he'd lose you."

I snorted, not intending to be unkind to her assessment, just releasing the truth, as I saw it. "He lost me anyway."

"True," she replied, not sounding the least bit incensed by my smug remark. "And to be honest, I think he believed it would be easier that way, for both of you."

This time, I allowed the anger to brim up and fester at the edges. "He left me, broken and bleeding and an emotional wreck. In a hospital," I managed to grit out from behind clenched teeth.

Ever the wild animal, I guessed.

"I don't know the details of that and I'm sorry you were alone. But I think you both suffered," she replied.

"Riiight. Yet, I was the one who was left with the scars to

prove it." I didn't mention that they were mental, physical and emotional.

I huffed out a breath and immediately regretted being so harsh on her. Even though she had good intentions—and deep down I knew she did—she was married to a man I didn't trust, one Martin had targeted for whatever reason. In the end, I didn't want or need my "stuff" being used against me, or the ones I loved. Ever again.

"Perhaps you do, but so does he."

I gave it to Serena—she was a persistent one. I could see why Ramirez had once cared deeply for her. She fought for what she believed in, especially when it came to love.

I remained silent as she continued, "I think he loves the idea of the Bond Girl who can kick butt and who holds no bones about tossing herself into the middle of something when she feels it's warranted, but I also think the thing he fears most is being alone because the person he loves most in the world has the propensity to put herself into situations where she ends up getting herself written out of the script...permanently. He simply cannot bear to lose you."

"We all lose someone at some point, "I replied. "Does that make it right to avoid trying so we don't get hurt?"

She didn't immediately respond, so I added, "I know it's deeper than that and I get it. I can't erase the things I've done or that have been done to me and I'm certainly not spending my days looking for trouble—I do have a wacky best friend and a stubborn Alaskan Malamute to look after—but sometimes we don't have a choice about what is thrown in our path. I mean, think about all the shootings, bombings, and heinous crap going on in the world. Do we change how we live because we're living in fear of the possibility of putting ourselves in harm's way? I don't think so. And I don't think Ramirez wants that either.

"At the end of the day, I think we all get that I'm not a delicate flower—and I do like to live, breath and experience life, in whatever form it presents itself. And whether Ramirez wants to believe it or not, I'm not impervious to how fragile it all is, this life we've been gifted. I've seen it in this state, first hand, more often than I care to remember. Believe me. Perhaps not to the depth Ramirez has, but a lot of the crap I've dealt with—it's been personal. And I lived. And yes, I have scars, but I still believe that people are generally good and that I am better off serving my purpose in this world than hiding because I'm afraid of the what-ifs that serve no one."

"I think the two of you just need to find a common ground. I'm not suggesting it will be easy but I think it can be done. If you still want it to," Serena replied. I noted there was not one single hint of judgment or jealousy in her tone and I gave her props for that.

"I guess only time will tell," I murmured in response.

"Sometimes time is what it takes, but don't assume it's yours to own. When your number's up…"

I snorted. "Oh, believe me, I know—been living on the edge of that cliff for the past few years."

"True. And it's not for me to judge. But there was a commonality that drew you together, was there not?" She blew out a long breath before continuing, "Find it. And use it to create understanding. It won't be easy." I grunted, settling into my own thoughts when she quietly added, "I envy you."

My eyes widened as I managed to stutter, "You…envy me?"

"You have power you aren't even aware of. And I'm not talking beauty or anything surface level. That's not what makes you special. You have a spark about you—an undeniable charisma that draws people to you—and you need to own it." After several awkward moments of silence, she added, "Hello, Arianna? Are you hearing me?"

"Yes," I replied quietly, sounding about as confident as I felt.

She chuckled. "I'm serious, even if you doubt me."

I didn't doubt her intentions. Her husband's on the other hand? Sorry, Serena, but the jury's still out.

As if sensing her message had been delivered, loud and abundantly clear, she bowed out gracefully. "Again, thank you, for everything, Arianna but I should probably get back. In the meantime, I hope you'll take what I've said, digest it and put it to good use. Wherever that takes you, is up to you. And I think in the end, you'll make the right choices about how to proceed." She disconnected without waiting for a response, either confident her message had gotten through, or not willing to accept whatever comeback I might have tossed out.

To be honest, I was a little fried on the snarky retorts and my mind had drifted to its own island. The subject of Ramirez had—and could continue to—wait. I had bigger issues to contend with.

Though my battery was nearly dead, I called Leah and reported my conversation with Serena, leaving out her suggestions where Ramirez was concerned.

"Huh…so Jr. gets into papa's safe, find some goodies and due to an untimely chain of events, is forced to wait to flush them out," she replied, once I was finished.

"Something like that," I replied. "Does any of this help?"

"Absolutely. Did Serena happen to mention the name of the person who signed Jeannie's death certificate?" I could hear her pen scratching again her trusty notepad.

"Um…no, she said the person who had signed the death certificate was no longer living and that Bob decided against pressing further, in case it raised red flags back home. Do you think it could be important?"

"Yeah, a name might be useful, perhaps even another avenue to pursue. Even though Bob couldn't get the details, he couldn't afford to open that can of worms. Meaning, he was operating on a whole other level."

"What...surface level?" I teased.

"Exactly. So if there's still meat on that bone, I can get at it."

"Gotcha, I guess I could call Serena back and see if Bob mentioned a name or a place?"

"If she had something, you never know, it might be useful. Always better to be safe than stupid," she replied.

"I think is the phrase is better to be safe than sorry."

"Just checking to see if you were still with me."

I snorted. "You're the one on Chicago time, my friend. Your brain must be singed by now."

"Don't remind me. I have to be on my A-game soon. Bonnie's friend is providing me with special off-hours access," she whispered, her tone conspiratorial. "Hopefully, I won't have anyone peering over my shoulder."

"Ahh, okay, what else can I do in the meantime?" I bit my lip, hoping she wouldn't remind me that I still had a call to Logan that was outstanding.

Thankfully, her mind was elsewhere, though I wasn't sure I found the option preferable.

"If you're up for it, maybe you could track down your BioPop again. You seem to have a knack for it. Then again, the guy has probably embedded a tracking device into Nicoh's collar and knows where we are before we do."

I frowned. "Err...creepy thought. But go on."

"First, see what he's up to and try to get a sense of where he is...physically. Mindset...I'll give you bonus points. Second, see if you can get any intel on the relationships between any of these people. He had to have known a couple of them.

"In the meantime, I'm going to continue, adding Jeannie into the mix. I'd like to know more about her cancer to see if it ties in some way." I could hear her tapping her pen on her pad. "You know, on a side note, after she managed to divulge all of that, I'm surprised that Serena didn't bring Ramirez up. She has to be curious, don't you think?"

"She did." I rolled my eyes when my friend squealed and clapped. "At the end."

"And?" I noted my friend sounded mildly amused as she goaded me along.

It was…annoying.

Still, I kept my tone even as I responded, "And, I've decided that topic ranks fairly low on my priority list."

"Good girl." She released a small chuckle. "To be honest, I'm kinda holding out hope for an AJ slash Logan reunion."

This time, I had no words. She'd gotten my goat—baaah! "Seriously, Leah? You just can't help yourself, can you?"

"Nope. Never hurts to project stuff you want to see out into the universe." Smugness did not suit her, though perhaps I was just feeling snarky.

"Whatever," I retorted. "I think I'm gonna have my hands full for a bit. Unless you have something else to tack on?"

"Nope. Just watch your back. And beware the lions…"

I guess we were continuing with the circus theme.

CHAPTER FOURTEEN

I didn't respond before she signed off. I didn't want to tell her I could feel the lions breathing down my neck. I was still walking that high wire, looking down at their salivating mugs. Perhaps I was nothing more than a snack to them but I was…fresh meat. It didn't matter that my body felt older than its years, given the stress I'd put it under in the past several months. Still. A tasty morsel of a snack.

Beware the lions.

I kept that image at the forefront as I called Serena and—thankfully—received voicemail. After the fact, she probably realized she had more advice to impart and given that she was pretty much on a roll by the time we'd signed off, I just wasn't in the mood.

Sighing, I left a brief message, asking about the death certificate and once I'd finished that task, proceeded to tap on one of the burner numbers Martin had given me. I hadn't used it for over a year and wasn't sure it still worked.

Part of me hoped it wouldn't but as I was about to jump ship, Martin picked up.

"Arianna."

"Yes, Martin. It's me. Are you…okay to talk?"

There was a moment of silence as I heard a shuffling of papers. He sounded as though he was right next door. I looked over my shoulder and shuddered.

"Of course. How can I help you?"

"First, you can tell me…where exactly, are you? You sound like you are in my guest bedroom."

"You know I can't tell you that," he replied, sounding mildly amused. "But I can assure you, if I were a guest in your home, you would know it."

Yeah, that was comforting. Not. So. Much.

"Are you…alone?" I asked, noting that I was whispering for whatever reason.

This time, he released a small chuckle. "Arianna, my daughter, despite my desire for the contrary, I find myself alone most days. And you?"

I ignored the "daughter" comment, knowing that he knew it ruffled my feathers and decided to answer honestly. "Yes. I'm by my lonesome, too. Well…Nicoh's napping…somewhere. But Leah is out and about."

"She went to Chicago, did she not?"

I think my head actually did an owl-like moment. I would probably need a chiropractor later, if not an exorcist. "Err…what?"

Another chuckle…this time a bit slower, almost sad. "You didn't think we'd allow your best friend to leave town—"

"Excuse me?"

My blood immediately started to boil and I nearly put some bad energy, as well as a bit of my sailor's mouth, out into the universe, when he added, "I simply meant to say that we would not allow your best friend to leave town…without protection. We mean her no harm but we also know that the two of you have a way of walking directly into the flame. Besides, she did contact a friend named Bonnie, did she not?"

When I failed to respond, he moved on. "She's one of ours, by way of her parents and can ensure Leah is safe. Believe me, Bonnie has been well-trained and Leah will be in good hands and will return to Phoenix, safe and sound, once her own mission is complete, whatever its nature."

I weighed my options, wondering what Leah would do.

Finally, I replied, though I frowned all the while. "Okay, yes, she went to Chicago to research Robert Fenton Sr's background. I'm sure you've heard he passed away in his sleep." I didn't wait for an answer as I plunged ahead. "We've subsequently found out —no matter how—that his wife, Jerri, was in Chicago visiting her sister's grave when he left this world."

Martin was silent for so long that I felt the need to poke that stick again.

"Did you know about the sister...Jeannie? That she was Jerri's twin?" More silence ensued. "And please, don't tell me that you had anything to do with Sr.'s departure from this life."

He finally responded, as evasive as ever. "I'm beyond confused. Are you asking me if I had anything to do with Robert's death?"

"I am. I just need to know whether you...interfered in some way. You are a former scientist with an entire set of concoctions, as well as a network behind you. Pretty sure if you wanted some old coot out of the way, you'd have the means to ensure the job was done properly." Noting his silence, I added, "I'm just jiving off our previous conversation, where you pretty much called the guy out, saying he was positioning himself to overtake the consortium in order to ensure that his plan of resurrecting the Gemini project would be brought to fruition. You also admitted to ambushing his son in an initial attempt to intervene and when that fell flat? Well, apparently, so did Fenton Sr."

"My God, Arianna, what are you suggesting?" Based upon the way he was choking out the words, I had caught Martin off-guard.

It didn't happen all that often but when it did, I'll admit—I thoroughly enjoyed it.

"Geez, Martin…after your actions, what other conclusions would you have drawn if you were me?"

Though I was amused, I remembered he was no younger than Fenton Sr. and didn't want to force him into a heart attack, so I moved the convo along.

"Anyway, you'll be pleased to know I withheld that tidbit from Ramirez when he interrogated me. And before you ask, yes, he interrogated me. He's taken leave from the department to help Jr. out, whatever that entails. From what I can tell, Bob's got him running around in circles, and I'm honestly not sure if it's on purpose. Leah doesn't like him—Jr., that is. So now it seems he's got a homicide detective on his temporary payroll, serving as a rent-a-cop."

Martin sighed before asking, "Tell me about this interrogation. Did he pull your fingernails out? Or waterboard you?"

"What?"

I rolled my eyes when I heard a chuckle. And here I thought I'd been having some fun at his expense.

"Just kidding. I'm sure you handled yourself accordingly."

"According to what?" I murmured, thinking of Serena's caged animal analogy.

He ignored my comment and moved on. "By the way, yes, I heard about Robert's untimely passing. "Did I note a sense of irritation? "It was most…unfortunate."

"Well, you did seem to think he was up to his old shenanigans in hopes of becoming the ringleader of the consortium again."

"I am confident he was doing just that. His passing…it's just very…untimely. We were so close. So, so close, to shutting them down. It's taken us such a long time to get this far and now…" Martin went silent.

Had he wanted to catch Fenton Sr. in the act? Or crush the man himself?

"People do die all by their lonesome, Martin. Not everyone has to go out kicking and screaming."

"True, still…" Martin seemed to be saying something without saying it. Did he believe that Senior had been forced along his merry, deathful way?

"Whatever. You'd prefer not to say. Did you know Robert… and Jerri…when they were a couple?"

"Oh, I've known them both for a very long time. Before they were a couple."

"So you knew Jeannie, too." It was not a question.

"Of course I knew Jeannie." Martin's response was flat.

"And that she and Jerri were twins?" I poked even though it felt accusatory, if not redundant.

"Of course I knew them and was aware that they were twins." This time, I sensed confusion in his response, if not annoyance.

"Please, Martin. Feel free to explain. No judgment here. Just curious."

"Jerri and her sister, Jeannie, and the rest of us…we were classmates."

"Are we talking kindergarten cookie-stealing classmates. High school sweethearts? Come on Martin…use you words…what do you mean by classmates?" I knew he was probably tired of my prodding but felt it was warranted.

Martin sighed. "We went to the same college."

"Uh okay, sorry to be annoying but this is like pulling teeth for me too. Can you please, please, please…just define 'we'?"

"Theodore, Alison, me….Robert, Jerri and Jeannie… There were others, too, but for the purpose of this excruciating exercise…those are the players you are concerned with."

"OMG," I snickered. "I hadn't realized this would be a Brat Pack-type scenario, before they actually existed. Life is truly stranger than fiction. I wonder, do you think Alison was a Demi Moore type? Were the twins more like Molly Ringwald? Or Ally Sheedy? I am guessing the prior but again, no judgment. As for the guys...who was Anthony Michael Hall? Judd Nelson? Emilio? Or oooh...Rob Lowe? Am betting old Theo felt he was best suited for that role."

By now I was in hysterics, wishing Leah was here so that we could clink margarita glasses while using Twizzlers as straws.

Martin waited me out but could only hold out for so long. "Um...I don't know what you mean by the Brat Pack. That doesn't sound very...hip. Or cool...as you kids say."

I covered my mouth...fighting back another snicker. "You haven't ever heard of John Hughes, have you? And before you ask, no I do not believe he was a member of your immediate group of cohorts." Or so I hoped. I didn't bother to mention that my childhood idol had recently passed.

"Mmm...no...I sense you are toying with me but pretend for a moment I know what you are talking about and that I've temporarily blacked out. Please refresh my memory."

"Okay. In your free time, research the following: *The Breakfast Club, Sixteen Candles, St. Elmos Fire, Ferris Bueller's Day Off, Weird Science*...better yet, just look up John Hughes, the director. Now, getting back to Theo, Alison, you, Robert, Jerri and Jeannie...who got along with who, who didn't, who hooked up... err, dated or whatever?"

"You know I worked with Theodore. And of course, you know about the tension there. Robert was probably the only one who thought Theodore could do no wrong and while Theodore tolerated Robert but as far as friendship was concerned, it was a one-way street. Theodore simply wasn't capable of anything more."

"Probably because he was a psychopath," I mumbled. "And the women?"

"Jerri and Jeannie were identical twins. Inseparable. In fact, they liked to play practical jokes on their friends and potential suitors. Often changing places with one another, then having a good laugh about it afterward or retelling the tale at a large social gathering, to the embarrassment of the person or persons on the receiving end of their prank."

"Geez, that must have made them unpopular," I replied, thankful not to have friends like that in my camp.

"Oddly enough, their shenanigans only helped their status with classmates and friends. In fact, they were among the most popular, well-known and sought-after girls on campus."

"Meaning they had lots of potential suitors to choose from. Were you among them?" I teased.

"I was always smitten with Alison, as you should know," Martin replied, matter-of-factly. "She was younger than the others but so, so bright and was on a full scholarship after graduating from high school early. Jerri and Jeannie, on the other hand, they were at the university because of family money, which in addition to their popularity, allowed them to have their choice of suitors."

"But you were impervious to their wily ways?" I was only half joking.

He made a clucking sound. "You know the Gabor sisters?" When I noted that I had, he continued, "It was kind of like that— attention seekers with a flair for the dramatic and an eye on the prize."

"By 'eye on the prize' do you mean they aspired to be actresses?"

"Actresses?" He chuckled. "No, no...they wanted to be wives! Mind you, I understand how you must think of my awkward phrasing."

"So, who in your group did they have their beady little eyes on?" I noticed he had side-stepped my initial question twice now and decided to approach it from another direction.

"Neither expressed interest in Robert or Theodore, at first. Of course, later Robert managed to catch Jerri's eye but he was way down on her list. The two had made the rounds with all the most viable options and he was, frankly, the last man standing."

"What about you, Martin? Did either Jerri or Jeannie fancy you? Consider you potential husband material?"

Martin scoffed. "For me, it was always Alison. Neither ever knew or gave her a moment's consideration but if you are going to continue to press me on this point, yes. Jeannie was quite... enamored with me, though I never reciprocated those feelings and had to rebuff her advances on more than one occasion, to her utter disbelief and dismay.

"Her sister was equally aghast and attempted to have me kicked out of the college, making up some ridiculous accusations about my man-handling her sister but by then, the administration was well aware of their antics and their claims were deemed unfounded and immediately put to rest. Both harbored a great deal of resentment after that and never spoke to me again."

"You don't sound too broken up about that outcome," I replied.

"I'm not...and wasn't. It was honestly a relief. The two of them were nothing but a confounded nuisance."

"And Theo, he never managed to capture either sister's eye? Based on what you've said, he had to have been seeded higher than Robert?" I winced at my choice of phrasing.

"Mmm...strangely, no. I was not aware either made advances toward Theodore. Or vice versa. He seemed to prefer work and his own ego over such frivolities."

I was getting nowhere, slowly, so I shifted the subject, "It must have been a shock when Jeannie died...being as young as

she was. How did you come to know about her death? Meaning…
who told you?"

"Theodore did."

I nearly choked trying to formulate the words. "Come again?"

"Theodore told me of Jeannie's passing." He paused for a
moment, before adding, "Yes, I am quite sure he's the one who
mentioned it."

"When was this?" I prodded.

"Oh goodness. It must have been prior to…well…you
know…my disappearance."

I didn't mention the coincidence of the timing. Instead, I
continued to push him. "What did Theo say?"

"That she died, of course."

I rolled my eyes, it was like trying to herd cats. "Did he
happen to mention the cause of death?"

"He wasn't specific, just mentioned it was some form of
cancer. Rare, I guess. Why do you ask?"

"No reason," I replied, careful to keep my tone nonchalant. It
was one thing to sound curious, another to come off as an inter-
rogator. I learned that from Leah, the hard way. "Did Theo
mention how he'd heard about Jeannie's passing?"

"Not that I remember. Where are you going with all of this,
anyway?" This time, Martin's tone seemed guarded.

"Huh? Oh nowhere. Nowhere in particular," I replied casually.
"Just curious, is all. This is all really…just so…fascinating. Like
walking down a memory lane. Just not my own."

"Hmm…right." His voice was oddly quiet…sad even.
"You're still not sure are you?"

I started. "What?"

Martin sighed. "You still haven't decided." This time, it was
not framed in a question.

"Decided what, Martin?"

"Which side I stand on?" he replied quietly.

"Does it really matter what I think?" I honestly didn't think it did but felt it warranted asking.

"It does...to me."

I nodded, despite the fact he could not see me. Or at least I believed he could not see me.

Suddenly paranoid, I peered at the ceiling vents, then at the fan, while responding, "Then you'd best be standing on the right side at the end of this, 'cause that's where I intend to be."

"How will you know?" He'd caught me off-guard, he sounded so earnest.

"Know...what, Martin?"

"That you're on the right side?" he replied. "What if there is no 'side'?"

I thought for a moment then released a breath. It was a question I'd faced before. The answer was always harder when you had to dig through the muck...and the lies.

"Then I will dig deep into my gut, muster all the courage I have and make the best decision I can—whatever serves the greater good."

"But what if it's not good...for you?" I hoped he wasn't playing me because, for once, Martin sounded lost.

"Sometimes, you can't afford to put yourself first. But you do, at the end of the day, have to stand for something," I paused for a moment to catch my breath. "Honestly, you don't need me to tell you all of this, Martin. You already know. Just like I do. Granted, I realize I've had the luxury of living a life without thinking about things like this and now that I'm faced with them, almost on a daily basis it seems, I wonder if I ever knew myself at all. I certainly can never go back to who I was...before."

"But you would sacrifice yourself...for them?" I know he meant Leah, Ramirez, Nicoh and those in the world I'd never met.

"I wouldn't even think twice about it," I replied, then added,

"It's who I am." It wasn't meant as a statement of arrogance—it was one of understanding and acceptance, of myself.

He chuckled lightly. "I wish I had your wisdom when I was your age."

"I think you did. At some point, you allowed arrogance and ego to dictate what was right and wrong. Instead of reaching down into the squishy part to figure out what really mattered, you lost your path. And your shadow side, that one waiting in the wings? It happily took over."

"Why…why did I do that?" Martin's voice rose, as though he was imploring me to explain his choices.

"It's human nature, Martin. When the world goes wonky on us, it's easier to act—often with reckless abandon—than it is to feel. Because to feel means we have to accept, not necessarily forgive, but accept so that we can move on. And, sometimes we're just not ready to move on."

"I can't…move on," he whispered. "Her life can't have so meant so little."

"Alison wouldn't have wanted you to suffer or make some of the choices you have. She was about life, making things better for future generations, not controlling the outcome. Acceptance does not equate to forgiveness—and no one is asking you to forgive… Theo, the consortium, or yourself—it's about giving yourself permission to see it for what it is and move the hell on, so that you can live your life. Our past can only hold us hostage if we let it, Martin. Don't forget it. But give yourself permission to move on. Those things we must live with are always part of us but they don't have to define us. We can…evolve."

"What if I can't accept? What if can't move on? What if my past is the only thing that will ever define me?"

"You're too smart of a man to sell yourself short," I replied. "What would Alison think? What would she be telling you? You don't have to answer that right now…think on it. Because you already know the answer and what it will take. If you truly can't do that, for Alison, your love, and for you…then I'm sorry to say it, but perhaps you should have walked off that bridge that day— it's a far better sentence than the hell you've exiled yourself to. Think about it, Martin. I'll be in touch."

And on that cheery note, I disconnected, unsure whether I would ever speak to my biological father again. It was in his hands now.

Then again, it had always been.

In the end, it always came down to choices.

CHAPTER FIFTEEN

I immediately called Leah, who answered in a sleepy tone. "Didn't expect to hear from you again tonight."

"Where are you?" I whispered.

"I'm in the morgue. Why are you whispering?"

"First, tell me how far have you gotten?"

Leah huffed. "Not as far as I would have liked. This place is a disaster, if not a fire hazard. Since we last spoke, I was able to dig up some general background stuff on Jerri and Jeannie. Taylor was their maiden name. They came from money—like bookoo bucks—and liked all of the privileges that came with it. Caused quite a scene at their university and their dad ended up having to fund a few scholarships over the years and even made an endowment to the College of Science that was so large they ended up naming an entire research facility after him—"

I had to intervene. "Leah! Shut up!"

She replied with a string of commentary that fell under the category of "needs mouth washed out with soap," but I decided to overlook it for the time being and quickly filled her in on my conversation with Martin and when I outed Bonnie, she released another round of expletives before screeching in my ear, "That little—"

I cut her off before she woke up whatever dead things were lurking in that morgue. "You can blast her later. We have issues that are of a more immediate concern."

Leah huffed, temporarily holding a can of whoop-ass at bay as she grunted for me to proceed.

"Unfortunately, I think we need to take whatever you have and call it a day. If Bonnie allowed you access because of Martin and his network, then anything you've learned likely provides them with the same intel. So even if Martin already knows some of this stuff, we're either filling in the blanks or letting him know how far we've gotten."

She released a wild yelp. "So he's had eyes on me all the time."

"I don't think we can afford to overlook that possibility," I replied, my tone somber.

"That son-of-a—" she paused, "I think I might just hate your BioPop more than I did Winslow or Theo. Do you realize what this means?"

I grunted. It had indeed cost us precious time and energy. And while Martin had created a means to keep track of us and what we knew, he had also divided us and created a diversion. The question was, for what reason? I shared my observation with Leah but it certainly didn't help alleviate her aggravation.

"I am totally calling Bonnie out! Then I'm going to ensure she's banished to the worst place in the world, wherever that currently is. What a rat!" She squealed in anger again before adding, "What in the hell is happening to this world? When did we need to start questioning everyone and their intentions? What happened to loyalty, trust and common decency?"

I was quiet for a moment before responding, "I think it still exists…somewhere."

"Well, then I want to go there—because this? It ain't working for me!"

"When are you coming home?" I replied quietly, already knowing our Chicago mission was dead in the water.

"I'll be catching the first available flight," she grumbled, "and I don't care what it costs me."

"And Bonnie?"

"God help her. She's gonna need it." And with that final growl, my best friend disconnected.

I stared at my phone, feeling more than deflated. I was sick to my stomach. Enraged. Disgusted.

And yet, I knew we'd barely scratched the tip of the iceberg… the important stuff was still hiding below the surface.

I wanted to throw up and was rising to head to the sink when I noticed I was receiving an incoming call.

At first, I thought it was Leah, with a new plan of attack but the number was one I had just dialed.

Serena.

I scrambled for the phone.

"Serena?"

"You sound harried. Did I catch you at a bad time?"

"Not at all," I replied. "I appreciate you calling me back."

"I'm not sure why, but the name of the person who signed Bob's aunt's death certificate struck a nerve. Bob seemed troubled by it, too, and even mentioned that the name sounded familiar but couldn't figure out why."

"And?" I prompted, bouncing from one foot to another. "Did he ever figure out where he'd heard it? Or how it was relevant?"

"No, he could never place it, and certainly couldn't ask his parents about it, considering how he'd obtained the information." I frowned and settled onto a stool, until she added, "Of course, in thinking back, Winslow could be considered a pretty common name."

I nearly fell as I stuttered, "Excuse me?"

"The name on the death certificate was Winslow, first initial T. Pretty random...right?" she replied, sighing.

Not so much, I thought, but kept that bit of side commentary to myself, as well as the heart-pounding that went along with it.

"It's almost so common it's amazing you even remembered it."

"I didn't."

"Uh...what?"

"No, no...I'm sorry...I tend to do that." She chuckled. "Get ahead of myself, that is."

I used my hands to prod her along, suddenly realizing she couldn't see me. "Okay...you didn't remember the name...then how—"

"Oh, I asked Bob." I slapped my forehead and bit my tongue as she continued, "Of course, he remembered right away."

"Ah," I replied, slowly, "and I suppose he was curious as to why you'd chosen that moment to bring it up."

"Nope. I told him we'd talked and you'd asked in your voice-mail. Considering how important it seemed to you, I figured I should get it cleared up straight away."

"How thoughtful of you." I tried hard to keep my tone even. So hard.

"Does it help?" she asked. "I wanted to get back to you as soon he confirmed. I'm just sorry it's so late."

"It is interesting. And I do appreciate your efforts, as well as the Congressman sharing," I replied, sounding a whole heck of a lot calmer than I felt. "But like you said, it's probably a pretty common name."

"It was odd, though."

"What was?"

"Well, when I asked Bob, Jonah was also there." That did it. I bit my lip as she prattled away. "And when Bob revealed the name, Jonah's face turned almost white. In fact, he said I probably shouldn't mention the name to you."

"That is odd," I murmured. Not so much. "Did he say why?" Please say no. Please say no, I thought.

"Not really. He was actually kind of evasive and after that, he left."

"Wow. Doesn't sound like Ramirez at all." I decided the best I could do was let it play out. "Maybe he had something else on his mind?"

"I guess," she replied, not sounding all that convinced.

"Seriously, Serena. Don't try to figure out Ramirez's brain. It'll give you nothing but a migraine."

She laughed. "You're right."

After thanking Serena and signing off, I called Leah and received voicemail, figuring she must be tracking down a flight, if not sharing a final word of thanks-not-so-much with Bonnie, settling onto the couch with paperwork I'd been trying to get back to for a week.

I must have dozed off thinking about Theo's name on the Jeannie Taylor's death certificate because I hadn't finished a single page. Rubbing my eyes, I noticed it was early—like raise the dead early—and decided rather than aggravate the kink in my neck, I'd better make my way into my bed to get a couple of decent hours of shut-eye.

I'd just gotten all comfy when I heard my cell ringing. I felt around, groaning. I looked at the caller and was about to share a few choice words with my best friend but as I answered, was met with squeals of panic.

"They're here!" I could hear muffled sounds, along with a lot of huffing and puffing.

"What? Where are you? Are you...running?" Blame it on

sleep fog but I realized if she was indeed, running, she wouldn't be able to respond to a barrage of questions.

"Yes!   Rrr...unning...   Need...to...hide!"   More   squeals ensued.

Until her phone when dead.

CHAPTER SIXTEEN

I pressed redial until my finger was numb.

What had happened to my friend?

Who had she been running from?

Was she okay?

As if her spidey senses had intervened, my phone rang again and I immediately picked up.

"Where are you?"

"In the janitor's closet," came a whispered, labored response.

"What's going on? And what can I do?" I began pacing… worried that things with Bonnie hadn't gone as well as planned and now my friend was on the run.

What had she done?

"I think I've lost them," she replied after a moment of shuffling, still whispering, her breathing only slightly more under control.

"Lost who?" My voice was higher than usual though I'd noted, I was now, for whatever reason, whispering too.

"The dudes following me from Chicago."

"From Chicago?" I blinked. Had I missed a day? I hadn't slept that long, had I? "If you're not in Chicago, where the heck are you now?"

"Hello? Haven't you been listening? I'm trapped in a freaking janitor's closet…with smelly mops, trash and other disgusting, bacteria-infested items that I don't really want to think about!"

"Help me out here, will ya? Where *exactly* is this janitor's closet?" I replied through gritted teeth, testing the boundaries of calm as I attempted to drill down to the bones of what we were dealing with.

Or at least, with Leah, rein it into the ballpark.

She scoffed, as though I had been right beside her. "Hell-o! I'm in Phoenix. At Sky Harbor International Airport," she paused but when I didn't immediately respond, continued her rant, "Alright, back it up a notch. It's clear I've lost you somewhere in the translation." I rolled my eyes.

Nothing about hiding in a janitor's closet could go without a more thorough, detailed explanation.

"Anyway, I felt a bit twingy when I got to Chicago but figured I was just being paranoid. I may have had a few too many quad lattes beforehand. You know how I get."

I nodded absently. Ornery was the best way to describe her after that dosage of caffeine, I thought to myself as she prattled on, "After that, something just felt off—tingling at the back of my neck—like somebody had eyes on me…you know the feeling?"

I murmured a yes. If she was squishy, she probably had every right to be.

"Then, once I arrived at the morgue and started digging around, I noticed that one of the dudes milling about seemed familiar. He was doing a pretty crappy job of pretending to do his own research. That's when it clicked. I realized he looked just like the dude who had been sitting at the sports bar at O'Hare, trying too hard not to look at me. And here he was, doing it again. Only this time, his pal wasn't with him."

"Okay, let me get this straight—this same guy, he was sharing space with you, in the morgue?" I was confused. Just how big was this place? I thought it was nothing more than a room with a couple of file cabinets, maybe a table and a chair or two.

As if sensing my confusion, she added, "Yeah, the morgue is much larger than the size of a say, a janitor's closet. The place is massive, so I knew beforehand there would be a chance I wouldn't be the only one there. But when I suddenly see a complete stranger…again? I get curious. And when I'm curious, I'm not focused on the task at hand."

"Geez, Leah! Why didn't you tell me about any of this sooner?"

"Tell you sooner? I was just trying to watch my back while dealing with jetlag. It's not like we've had much rest since we've gotten back from SoCal. Yeah, so much for that vacay. Having said that, had it not been for the whole thing where Bonnie turned out to be a rat fink, I think I would have rather spent my time in the morgue. Alone."

"I wouldn't repeat that to Vargas," I replied, thinking he would not be as understanding, especially if she phrased it that way.

"Morgue" referenced something entirely different in his line of work.

She scoffed. "Gah! Between your crap with Martin and Ramirez—and this new info regarding Vargas and his lineage, I honestly haven't talked to him about anything. I just left and he has no idea where I am."

"Probably best not to tell him you're in the closet," I replied, my tone dry. "So, you think you've evaded whoever it was?"

"Well, I did have to give the maintenance guy a few bucks so that he'd leave me alone." She scoffed. "Dude was pretty territorial about his mops."

"You got found out?" I covered my mouth.

"I might have shoved him in with me when I was attempting to hide."

"I'll bet that was the highlight of his day."

"Yeah...yeah, yuk it up. He's supposed to knock when the coast is clear."

"Getting back to this stalker guy. Other than the first time at the bar, you didn't recognize him?"

"No, he's pretty nondescript, blends in pretty well," she replied. "Almost too well."

"Ah, so he stood out because he seemed like he was trying not to?"

"Yeah. His pal, too."

"You think they were on your plane going both to and from Chicago?"

"On the way back for sure. It's the only flight that was coming in from Chicago at this time of the morning. I was lucky to get a seat."

"If you were barely able to secure a seat on the flight, then how did this guy—or guys—manage to get seats, too? I mean, they couldn't have known about your plans beforehand. You bailed on the morgue and completely tossed your itinerary out the window."

"Good question. And I don't like the answers swirling in my head." She released a long breath.

"So, now what?"

"Now I wait for the maintenance man."

I didn't bother mentioning that if he was called away for an emergency, it could be awhile. "Do you want me to come pick you up after you make your escape?"

"No...no sense them seeing you and trailing us both home. I'll just grab an Uber, once I'm sure it's safe."

I bit my lip. Whoever was following her likely already knew where we lived, meaning we would never really be "safe."

Suddenly antsy, I crept to the kitchen window and peered out the front. Of course, there was nothing and no one to be seen. It's not like they would be careless enough to stand out in the open, anyway. I shuddered at the thought.

"You think these were Martin's guys?" she asked. I noticed a little snark seeping into her tone.

I couldn't say I blamed her.

"Possibly, especially after the whole Bonnie thing. Seems right up his alley," I replied, thinking back to our conversation. "I mean, it didn't even give him pause to reveal they had eyes on you."

She snorted. "Still. A bit obvious for a sneak like him. Another option could be the consortium. I mean, if Martin has eyes on us, couldn't they be doing the same?" I nodded, though I didn't care for her suggestion.

"What about Fenton?" I offered, though that alternative wasn't much better.

"Like I said, the consortium, sans Sr.," she replied.

"No, I meant Jr."

Leah released a gasp. "Now there's an unsettling thought."

"Tell me about it."

"Ramirez better not have any hand in it, if you're right," she grumbled.

I was about to offer my own thoughts on that subject when I heard a muffled voice and for a moment, she dropped off. After some rustling, she was back.

"I'm free!" she squealed.

"The maintenance guy was confident the coast was clear?"

"About as well as he could be," she grunted. "I did pay him well."

"Cool. As long as you're sure." Suddenly, I was worried her stalkers had tracked her down and paid the maintenance man off even more handsomely.

"I am. See you in a few." And with that, she disconnected.

It was only then I realized I hadn't had a chance to reveal that little bombshell Serena had dropped on me.

Probably best to keep that one to myself until she arrived home in one piece. One could only tolerate so much drama in a single episode.

Those soap operas had nothing on us.

* * *

I didn't hear the Uber pull up but jumped out of my seat when the back door opened and Leah walked in, hair disheveled and usually bubbly persona traded for a slew of expletives and a seriously frowny face as she dumped over Nicoh's water bowl in an attempt to launch her bags onto the couch.

Upon catching my expression, she grunted. "Had the dude drop me a couple of blocks over, hoofed the rest of the way home."

"Probably a wise choice," I replied, giving her a firm hug. "Any lurkers along your path?" I was only half-way joking.

She gave me a sideways look. "Not that I could see, and believe me, I was looking."

"Unless, of course, one of them has taken up residence in the neighborhood." I shuddered at the thought, noting that several houses that had been for sale on the block until recently.

"Don't even go there. I just don't think I can muster the brain cells necessary to give that notion a decent amount of consideration." She plopped onto a stool and thrust her face into her hands as she propped her elbows on the counter. "Well, the last twenty-four hours have turned out to be a complete bust."

"Err...about that." I ran a hand through my hair, snagging my fingers on a few tangled strands. Guess my best friend wasn't the only one who was looking like the butt-end of a dust mop. Sighing, I continued, "Serena called back."

"Oooh, do tell." She began munching on some day-old popcorn, frowning as she did. "That's nasty."

"Sorry, didn't have time to make a new batch…it's barely past the crack of dawn, in case you hadn't noticed," I mumbled, my thoughts drifting back to the bed I had left in the lurch, only a few hours earlier…wishing it would call my name.

"Whoa…sorry, Grumpy Pants. Let's not forget, I was the one stuffed into a closet after a turbulent flight," she retorted, getting up to dump the contents of the popcorn bucket into the trash.

She was right. Her day had been far worse than mine. It was time to inject some humor. Or at least attempt to. "Hmm. A turbulent flight, huh? Just to be clear, was that from the morgue or in reference to your return trip?"

She chuckled lightly. "Both, if you really must know."

"Sorry, I really mustn't." This time we both chuckled.

"Stop procrastinating. Tell me what Serena said," she prodded.

I did and when I was finished she was silent for a long while, before responding, "I honestly don't know what to say about that. Part of me is shocked. The other part just seems too convenient, don't you think?"

"I do, especially when you factor in the rare form of cancer. Theo was a scientist. He could have made something up, for all we know."

"If not injected her with it himself." Leah shuddered. "Kind of strange that Serena just happened to remember that."

I groaned. "She didn't." When she raised a brow, I added, "She mentioned our conversation to Bob and he was the one who confirmed the name on his aunt's death certificate."

Leah slapped her forehead. "And now he knows you were asking about it."

I nodded. "And that's not the worst part. Ramirez was also there when Serena brought it up."

She released a yelp. "Gah! This is bad! How did he respond to that bit of news?"

"She said he excused himself, rather quickly…I'm paraphrasing here, but you get my drift."

She nodded. "I'll bet he did. But you haven't heard from him?"

"Nope. Not yet."

"What do you plan on telling him?"

Honestly, I hadn't contemplated that conversation and certainly wasn't looking forward to it.

"Nothing. Because we've got nothing to tell," I replied, frowning at my frustration by the truth.

"Sorry," she murmured. "I wish I could have drummed up more dirt before I was forced to skedaddle."

I waved her off. There was nothing we could do about it now. "What happened with Bonnie anyway?"

"Nothing. I never spoke to her." Leah frowned.

"Well, you were in a bit of a hurry," I replied.

"Apparently, I wasn't the only one." I tilted my head, so she added, "When I called to give BonBon a piece of my mind as I was exiting the morgue posthaste, her cell phone had been disconnected. Called her desk phone back at her office, same thing. When I contacted the main line, the service informed me she had been reassigned but couldn't say where she'd gone."

"Wow…she's been effectively…handled. Are you worried about her?"

She shook her head, pursing her lips. "Bonnie's not stupid. If she got herself into something, she did so with both feet."

"Perhaps Martin and his network had something on her, something to make her do what she did." I felt bad that she had called in a favor on my behalf and lost a friend in the process.

Leah shrugged. "Maybe so. But, like we've always said, AJ, we all make choices. And if she sold her soul to someone like Martin—no offense—then good riddance to her. She's on her own."

"Still, you need to stop beating yourself up about it," I replied, patting her on the arm. "There might be another way to approach this."

"Okay...what do you have in mind?" She leaned in.

"We've been so focused on drumming up the history surrounding all of these people but all we've yielded are historical accounts of who they were, where they lived, went to school...or died. What we don't know is the depth of the relationships between all of them, or the web that ties them all together. That's stuff you would never have found in the morgue."

Her eyes widened. "I like where you are going with this— play it out."

"Well, if you go back to the beginning. There was Martin, Theo and Robert Fenton, as far as the men were concerned and Alison, Jerri and Jeannie Taylor were the female side of the equation. All attended the same university. For now, we don't care about when, just that there was a commonality between them all. Relationships. Ties. Secrets." Leah nodded, gesturing for me to proceed.

"While Martin is secretly dating Alison, Jeannie Taylor also has a thing for him which, according to him, he rebuffs."

"Hey, I've seen pics of your bio mom, can you blame him?" Leah injected.

I shook my head, Leah was right. Alison was absolutely lovely, and from what Martin had told me, as bright as a whip, to boot.

It was just sad to think that she and Martin had to hide their relationship from their outside world. And if they had been forthcoming, would it have changed the outcome? It was a nice thought but deep down, I think the result would have been the same. With people like Theodore Winslow in the picture, there never would have been a scenario that played out with a happy ending.

As if sensing the nature of my musings, Leah prompted me to continue.

"So while Martin and Alison are off doing their thing, Robert and Theo become buds, or so Fenton thinks. Of course, we now know that the friendship was nothing more than part of Theo's ploy to get funding for his pet project. Even though Robert's following him around like a puppy dog, Theo's basically using him like a meal ticket.

"According to Martin, neither of the Taylor sisters supposedly had eyes for Robert or Theo, but Jerri later marries Robert and gives birth, not to his son, but to Theo's. Meanwhile, Theo helped spawn at least three other sons—that we know of—Winslow Clark, his twin and of course, Jere Vargas." When Leah winced, I added, "Sorry."

Again, she gestured for me to continue.

"As of right now, the identity of their mother—or mothers—remains an unknown." I paused to confirm she was still with me, to which she supplied a single head nod. "So, what if, after being rejected by Martin, Jeannie decides to go after his partner? I mean, we already know that Fenton Sr. wasn't Bob's bio dad, maybe once Jerri got preggers, Jeannie decided she needed to follow suit."

Leah scrunched her nose. "Do you think Jeannie knew that her sister was also getting hot and heavy with Theo, possibly even at the same time?" When I shrugged, she made a retching sound. "That is beyond disgusting."

"I'm just throwing spaghetti at the ceiling here. But if Theo wasn't above cheating with his best friend's girl, who's to say he wouldn't also cheat on her with her twin sister?"

Leah shook her head. "Do you think Robert knew? That Theo was really Bob's father?"

"I have no idea, but somehow it doesn't seem likely. All of it could have been a carefully crafted plan between Jerri and Theo. Maybe he allows her to keep the baby, provided she goes away quietly and never reveals the secret."

"Yeah. We already know that Theo was a master storyteller. Maybe he coached Jerri and told her what to say?"

I shrugged. "We already know he was capable of much more than that."

When she caught my eye, she squinted. "You're going somewhere with all of this. Spill it...what exactly do you have in mind?"

I shook my head and bit my lip before responding, "You're not going to like it."

"I already don't," she replied. "Might as well just tear the band-aid off."

"Well, it's been right in front of us all along—we've both known it—but we've also avoided going that route, for obvious reasons."

Leah groaned and placed her forehead on the counter. "The chips." When I nodded, she thudded her head a few times, while I grimaced. "It's not worth the risk."

"Isn't it?" I tilted my head. "We both know there's a ton of untapped info on there."

"Don't you think Tony B. would have already told you? I mean, he did delve out some pretty juicy goodies. What if that's all there was? I mean, some of it's worth lying about," she paused to glance at me, "and killing for."

I shook my head. "Not necessarily....he only pulled the stuff he thought was of interest at the time. There was a heck of a lot more there, and frankly, I told him to quit deciphering after he revealed as much as he had." Leah raised an eyebrow. "Yeah, for his own safety, ours and everyone that info will ultimately affect, I made him stop in his tracks, though I'm betting he tucked some of it away in his brain for a later day."

"Well, there are always things that are too hard to forget."

She bit a nail, clearly thinking of all the things that those chips had brought into our lives, most of them not all that positive. In fact, I couldn't put my finger on one positive thing, if my life depended upon it.

"Indeed there are. And like you said, all of them will destroy lives."

"Any chance Tony B. just destroyed the chips while he was at it?"

I shook my head. "Nope. And don't sound so hopeful about that prospect. This is our best shot and you know it. And before you ask, I'm not going to tell you where they are."

She put her hands up. "Honestly, I don't want to know."

"I can deal with that. It's for your own good."

"What about yours?" I knew she didn't really want to know the answer but felt she had to ask.

I picked at a piece of nonexistent fuzz on my t-shirt as I responded, "Let's just say I have...contingencies in place...and leave it at that."

She nodded. "Fair enough."

"Let's do this then, shall we?" After we fist-bumped, I dialed Tony B.'s number and once I relayed what I was looking for, sat through an onslaught of lectures with several expletives mixed in as he raked me up one side and down the other a few dozen times before begrudgingly agreeing.

Before I hung up he added, "If this all goes south and I'm the only one left standing, don't even think about saddling me with that dog of yours. I'd much rather go down with the ship."

CHAPTER SEVENTEEN

Though we hadn't done anything criminal, we both jumped about ten feet when there was a rapping on the window of the side door.

I glanced at Leah, who frowned. "I think the fuzz is onto us."

Praying that it wouldn't be Ramirez paying us a surprise visit did no good. Still, I allowed Leah do the honors, noting the downturn of her mouth as she peeked through the blinds before tossing the door open.

"Well, hell-o, Detective Ramirez. So nice of you to stop by and bring us lattes and donuts. Unfortunately, my pal and I were just on our way out."

She blocked him from entering but I gave a small wave and a half smile, belatedly realizing I had never bothered looking in a mirror since I'd tumbled out of bed.

Not to mention, brushed my fuzzy teeth.

Ramirez glanced from one of us to the other before nodding at the bags she had tossed on the couch.

"Seems like you just got back. Or at least one of you did. Am I interrupting something? Another trip to SoCal to check out the man candy?"

Leah snorted and rolled her eyes. "Wouldn't you like to

know? Or are you asking in an official capacity? 'Cause if you're not, we have things to do. Official things."

I gave it to Leah, she never let up where Ramirez was concerned. If there was anyone that could be more bummed at Ramirez for the way he dumped me, it was her. It was nice to know your friends had your back when it was warranted.

Ramirez sighed, perhaps rethinking his approach. "Good morning. AJ. Leah." He nodded at each of us, before adding, "May I come in?" He enunciated each word while waving the coffee tray directly in front of Leah's face.

He knew as well as I did that she was anything but immune to the scent of coffee. She tried the best she could, but her eyes gave her away as she trailed his hands while he shifted the tray perilously back and forth.

"What is that, anyway? Some sort peace offering?" She pointed at the bag of donuts while continuing to focus her sights on the tray of Dutch Bros. lattes.

He nodded, smiling as she released an exasperated huff while waving a hand, gesturing for him to enter. Ramirez carefully placed his offerings on the counter and after doling out beverages, Leah dug into the bag, pulling out a donut hole, smacking her lips in satisfaction after inhaling a half dozen while Ramirez and I watched in silence.

"Oh, don't mind me," she replied, wiping a hand across her mouth. "Please go ahead."

She nodded toward the bag but I waved it off, my stomach churning at the smell of fresh grease and sugar. Combined with the current company, it wasn't a good combo.

"You look tired, Ramirez," I said after a long moment, noting the bags settling beneath his eyes had darkened and the scruff on his face was in need of a bit of upkeep.

He'd looked tired the last time I'd seen him but on this particular occasion, he appeared not only exhausted but uncharacteristically solemn as he slumped against the counter.

It took him a moment to register my comment as he nodded, sipping his coffee slowly.

"Seems like time away from the department should be more relaxing, not less so," I murmured.

He stared at me as if really noticing me for the first time since arriving. I subconsciously patted my hair, causing him to release a weak chuckle.

"Yeah, kind of funny how that turned out. Do a favor for a friend and you end right back up in it."

"You're referencing the death of Robert Sr." When he offered a single head nod, I added, "I thought his passing was due to natural causes."

"As far as we know, it was," he replied, staring too intently at the edge of his coffee container. "Still, death is death, no matter how you play it."

I nodded. "Family's taking it pretty hard, I would assume."

"Yeah." His tone was flat, beyond instant coffee bland.

I looked at Leah, who shrugged as she peered at Ramirez. She didn't know what to make of this demeanor, either.

"We heard that Bob's mom was out of town when his father passed," she commented. "Not sure if that is a blessing or not."

"Half dozen one way...yada, yada..." Again, Ramirez just seemed off.

I couldn't take it anymore. "Listen, Ramirez, something has obviously brought you to our door at this hour. That much is clear. Having said that, you seem out of sorts, especially for you. What the heck is going on?"

He placed his coffee on the counter, pushing it away, before giving me a hard stare. "I think you know what's going on, AJ... or at the very least...who."

I met his gaze. "I'm not sure I follow," I replied, even though I was right there with him. "Please expound."

"Martin Singer." I noted his eyes squinted ever so slightly as he perused me for any change in emotion.

Leah looked from Ramirez to me and back, huffing. "Are we really back to that—again?"

"We will always be 'back to that.'" This time there was an edge to his voice. It was slight, but it was there.

And by "we," I knew he didn't mean the three of us, standing here in my kitchen.

Leah frowned. "Well then. I have nothing to say on that subject. And none of it has to do with the fact it happens to be my least favorite topic."

He glanced at her and released a snort. "Tell me about it."

She gave him an open-handed gesture to proceed.

He grunted and turned back to me. "I know you've been chatting back and forth with Serena. In fact, I happened to be there when she asked Bob to confirm the name on his aunt's death certificate. He surprised the both of us by his recall but me more so because it drummed up a name from our not-so-distant past."

I wasn't going to confess I'd talked to her after that, so I just nodded.

"You know this is going to open a can of worms, AJ. For everyone," he added.

"Yes, I can imagine it will. But what do you want me to do about it?" I raised my hands.

"Contact your father—contact Martin. Encourage him to nip it in the bud now, before any more people get hurt."

I raised a brow, my voice hinting on the shy side of snark. As if I held the world in my hands. "Meaning?"

He ground his teeth, staring at me intently before responding, "Meaning you have to give him whatever it is he's been lurking around for."

"Just how do you know he's been lurking around?" Leah interjected.

Without glancing at her, Ramirez pulled his cell phone from his back pocket, and after a moment of tapping, turned it around to face us. On the screen was a video clip of me walking Nicoh in the park, alongside us was Martin.

I shrugged. "So?"

He stopped the video and returned the phone to his pocket before responding, "So, you said you hadn't had any recent contact with him, nor had any idea where he currently was."

"That particular…outing occurred after that."

Ramirez frowned. "Whatever, AJ. Go ahead and play it that way. What I really want to know is what he wants from you. It's obviously compelling enough to keep him coming back. My guess is that it has something to do with the past. Your past."

"I don't know what you're talking about." I deadpanned. I wasn't about to give him an inch.

Of course, that's when Leah surprised me.

"I think you should tell him."

I think my head did an *Exorcist* swivel. Twice. Before I was able to face her to respond.

"What?"

"Tell him," she replied, her tone firm, as she nodded. "All of it."

"Even the part about…" I tilted my head.

She nodded, closed her eyes and left the room, leaving me in an awkward silence with my ex.

I collected my wits, released a long breath and gestured toward the stool. "Sit. Please."

My face reddened under the weight of his gaze as I formulated a coherent narrative in my head. It wasn't easy because there were so many moving parts. I couldn't even begin to know where they started much less where they led. But I knew some of it and so for the next hour, I outlined everything from the beginning, as I knew it…from the time we'd met—when I'd found the body of the girl in my dumpster, who turned out to be my twin—through to the events as of late, when Leah had escaped Chicago with a couple of thugs in close pursuit.

He was silent as I recalled all the details, patting my hand when I sniffled my way through the rough parts until I had put nearly everything on the table. There was still one more thing I needed to reveal.

Nothing like saving the worst for last.

He sat there in silence as I told him about Vargas. About halfway through, he buried his head in his hands. I'd never seen Ramirez cry—emotional sure, but never a tear—yet when he lifted his head, there was a trace of wetness at the corner of his eyes.

"Oh, God," he whispered. "Please, not Jere."

I gripped his hand and nodded, fighting to keep my own emotions at bay.

"Is he… Is it possible he could really be Theodore's…son?" He struggled to get the words out as he peered at me, his face earnest, as though begging for me to take the words back.

I wished I could. But I owed it to him more to be straight. There had already been far too many secrets and lies.

"I'm sorry, Jonah, but it's more than a possibility. I want to be sure but most likely, yes," I replied, struggling to remove the sting from the words and failing miserably, given the pain in his eyes as he fought again to keep the tears from brimming over.

"Whatever his lineage, Jere is—along with his brother Bob— definitely part of the Gemini project. Well, perhaps not part of the project itself, but one of Theo's…side endeavors." I made a face which, thankfully, Ramirez missed.

"Then he and Winslow…" Ramirez's voice trailed off as he stared at his hands.

I nodded. "Half-brothers."

"This will kill him."

"I know," I whispered, gripping his hand.

He squeezed back, his eyes meeting mine.

"How long have you known?"

I looked away. He surprised me by squeezing my hand more firmly.

"And Leah?"

I sighed and shook my head. "She just found out, a couple of days ago."

"And she's still here?"

My head jolted his direction, as my mouth dropped open and I faced him.

He shrugged, not meeting my eyes. "She's the only family you have left and yet you kept it from her."

I untangled my hand from his. "Is that what you would have done, in her position? Cut your losses and ditched?" I kept my voice low but there was a hiss of anger venting through it.

"I can't answer that."

"Why not?" I noticed my pitch had inched up a notch, as the kettle was about to bubble over.

Ramirez caught my tone and shook his head. "I can't answer...because I already ran. Wouldn't be fair of me to judge her, either way."

But you judge me? I thought to myself but said nothing. If Ramirez had expected another outburst, he'd gotten a break. I just couldn't muster the energy.

After a long moment, he broke the silence. "You look tired, too, you know." He rubbed my arm and gave me a gentle smile.

I didn't take offense at the observation. It was what it was. I nodded.

"I am...bone tired. And tired of it."

"You don't have to do it. Alone," he replied.

"Yes, I do." I sighed. "Besides, I'm not alone. I have Leah."

"What will you do?"

I blew out a long breath. "Call my tech guy and see what he can glean, then tell him to back the hell away and get out of dodge."

"Maybe you should turn it over to the police."

"No, Ramirez. It's my…burden to bear."

He shook his head. "But it isn't your life…alone that's impacted. You could be endangering him, too. And everyone whose name crops up on those chips."

"But it is my responsibility to ensure that it's handled properly and that those chips don't end up in the wrong pair of mitts."

I didn't say Martin's name specifically.

No sense adding fuel to that fire but I was guessing Ramirez had already drawn that conclusion on his own, frowning as he replied, "It's shouldn't be your burden. It must be awful to have such knowledge…to know what you've got in your possession. The impact it will have…on so many."

"It is," I whispered, shuddering. "Terrible."

"It's the reason you refuse to give it to him, isn't it?" I glanced at Ramirez and after surveying my expression, he nodded. "You don't trust him.

I shook my head from side to side slowly as a tear erupted.

"It's so hard…to know what to do."

"I think you're doing remarkably well…considering."

Another tear slid down my cheek. Oh yeah, I was doing real well, I thought as I batted it away.

"Not really. I lost everything in the process. Family. Friends. You…"

Ramirez wiped the remnants of the wetness from my cheek with his thumb, then cupped my chin so that we were facing one another. "You didn't lose me…we just…we just can't be together. Not like this."

"I know. And I understand."

"Do you?"

"No. Yes. Now is not exactly a good time for me to be focusing on a relationship anyway."

Ramirez released a sad chuckle. "You're referencing Martin as much as you are...us."

I nodded. "Regardless of what you've got on that video, I really don't trust the man. He'll be gone once he gets what he wants. Or is finally convinced I'll never hand it over."

"And since you've last talked to him, you have no idea where he currently is." It was not a question and for once, not an accusation either, which I greatly appreciated.

I shook my head. "No, but as I mentioned, we know he has eyes on us. Leah even joked that he's probably taken up residence in our neighborhood, considering all of the houses currently for sale or rent."

Ramirez frowned. "Perhaps I should look into that... discretely, of course."

I shrugged. He'd probably do it, regardless of what I wanted. It couldn't hurt.

"Will you keep me posted...whatever happens from here on out?"

"It's a two-way street, Ramirez." When he nodded, I added, "Just out of curiosity, are you going to feel compelled to report to your employer about anything I've revealed? And by employer, I mean the Congressman."

Ramirez shook his head. "I'm not technically on his payroll." His tone suggested he was less than pleased by the assumption I'd drawn. "I'm just doing a favor for an old friend."

"Some favor it's turned out to be," I replied.

"They usually end up going that way, don't they?" He chuckled but there was no humor behind it.

I nodded. Been there. Done that.

"Speaking of which, I'd best get back to it." He rose, collected his coffee and after a quick hug started for the door, when he paused. "As for Jere, I should be the one to tell him, whenever that happens. I've known him the longest."

"No!" Leah was suddenly present, her hands fisted at her sides. "You can't! Promise me, Ramirez." She strode to him and poked him in the chest. "Promise me."

Ramirez pushed her hand down and gave her a hard stare. Finally, he offered the benefit of a response. "Depends on whether I have a choice, given the nature of the situation. And the timing."

Her brows furrowed. It wasn't what she'd wanted to hear and I can't say I blamed her. And for a moment, I thought she was going to punch him in the throat. Instead, she took a step closer, standing on the tips of her toes she that she could whisper in his ear.

"There's *always* a choice, Ramirez."

She backed away, crossing her arms, challenging him to defy her.

He stared at her for a long moment before turning to leave.

Just when I thought he would depart in silence, he glanced over his shoulder.

"You keep telling yourselves that…" he paused, looking first at me and then at her, before adding, "but what you fail to remember is that choice is not always within your control."

CHAPTER EIGHTEEN

We sat in silence for a moment, each consumed by our own thoughts.

"I'm sorry," I finally whispered.

"For what?" Leah raised her head, squinting as she searched my face.

"Jere. I don't know...everything." I rubbed my hands together.

Despite the fact I was not the least bit cold, a chill was swirling, even if it was just in my head.

She shrugged. Her face, strangely, revealed nothing. "You can't apologize for what you didn't start," she replied, pausing before adding, "You had no control over what transpired...before."

I shook my head. "No, but regardless of what Ramirez just spouted, I do have control over what to do with the knowledge I am currently in possession of. Up until this point, I have done a pretty poor job of it."

Leah frowned, then waved a hand. "Hey, I urged you to tell Ramirez everything."

"Yeah, but prior to that, I made choices that perhaps I had no right to." I released a long breath and rubbed my arms, as the chill kept rising.

Leah watched me but said nothing for a while. Finally, she rose and tossed her coffee container in the trash. Stared at it. "I'm not sure what I would have done in your situation. I'd like to think I would have made the right choices, but—" She didn't get a chance to finish that thought—as the doorbell rang, causing us to look at one another in confusion—and I was left to wonder about her comment and what those choices might have been.

When it rang again, Leah smacked her forehead with her palm. "*Now* he decides to show some manners? He raps on the window of the side door at the crack of dawn the first time around —granted, he came plied with a bribe—but now rings the bell and is probably wiping his feet on the front doormat as an encore performance? That man is so confusing."

I shrugged. "Dunno. Maybe he wants the rest of his donuts back and is afraid we'll bite if he tries to take our treat away."

Leah tilted her head back and chortled. "That is true. Perhaps he's more intuitive that I give him credit for," she paused before adding, "Just for the record, he's not getting them back, no matter what level of manners he delivers."

I snorted, easing off the chair and moving toward the front door, calling over my shoulder, "Well, then perhaps he *should* ring the front door, probably a bit safer—you know, stick where the neighbors can witness everything—as to opposed to the side where we can draw him in and then make him disappear for his sins against everything sugary, buttery and deep-fried. In respect to the donut holes, of course."

"Long live the donut holes!" she called back as I pulled the door open and barely managed to withhold a gasp.

Our visitor…was not…Ramirez.

Standing in front of me was a stranger. A slight woman I placed in her mid-sixties but having been well-preserved, she could have passed from five to ten years younger under the right light.

The broad light of day, however, was forgiving to no one, though genetics and a fine surgical hand had been quite generous to the woman on my doorstep. She was impeccably dressed in a pair of ivory silk slacks and matching sweater—a little heavy for this weather in my opinion—finished off with a sensible but stylish pair of heels and a classic strand of pearls framing her neckline. Her hair was immaculately coiffed into a stylish bob the color of roasted chestnuts on a cool autumn day. Her makeup had been artfully applied and kept to a minimum, revealing skin that was remarkably smooth and satiny, except for the nearly imperceptible scar that began to the left of the bow of her lip and ended just beneath the lower on the right.

Her eyes were bright with a sparkle that was the color of sapphires, widening ever so slightly as she took me in, pressing a heavily-adorned hand to her mouth. "Oh, my goodness."

I immediately patted my hair and tugged at my t-shirt, noting the remnant of last night's dinner had somehow managed to create a trail of its own down the front. My yoga pants hadn't fared much better. And my bare feet exposed toenails that had become an unfinished experiment in testing out all of the fall colors and had resulted in a couple of freehanded designs along the way.

She recovered and quickly added, "Where are my manners—have I woken you, my dear?"

I squinted, wondering if we'd met before, given not only her congenial, motherly nature, but whatever had brought her to my doorstep on this morning.

"Um, no. You haven't woken us." Suddenly, I felt a breeze in my ear, as though my mother had appeared to remind me of my own manners. "I apologize for my appearance. How may I...we help you?"

Though I had kept my tone light, the woman's mouth turned

down, making the scar more pronounced, as she clasped her hands tightly. "Oh my. I knew I should have called but I wasn't sure, considering, you would agree to see me."

I glanced at her, tilting my head. Was I missing something?

"Ummm…" I started, not sure where to go with this.

Thankfully, Leah stepped forward and immediately grasped one of the woman's hands.

"Mrs. Fenton. I'm sorry. We should have recognized you."

The woman was so focused on Leah she failed to notice my expression—probably a combination of confusion and horror. I noted that she was careful not to stare too hard at Leah's appearance, which was a tad worse than my own.

"AJ, this is the Congressman's mother, Mrs. Fenton. My name is Leah Campbell. I believe we met at the winter formal a couple of years ago in support of the children's hospital." When I glanced at her in confusion she added, "It was a masquerade ball."

I nodded absently, though I hadn't attended, I vaguely remembered her mentioning it. Thankfully, Mrs. Fenton was able to recall the event.

"Oh yes, the reporter." She nodded and after Leah released her hand, extended it for a proper handshake.

"Yes, at the time I was an investigative reporter," Leah replied, equally surprised at the woman's memory. "Now I spend my days doing freelance research. Nothing glamorous."

"Seems to be a suitable transition," the woman replied, chuckling. "And is anything, ever, glamorous?" Her eyes left Leah and settled on me.

"Excuse my manners, Mrs. Fenton. I'm Arianna Jackson." I extended a hand and though she had taken Leah's easily, thought I saw her shudder ever so slightly before grasping my hand firmly in both of hers, her eyes never leaving mine. "Won't you come in?"

Finally, the woman snapped out of her reverie. "Are you sure that I haven't caught you at a bad time?"

It seemed a moot point but I channeled my mother and made the appropriate noises and murmured a few niceties. It was the best I could do under the circumstances and I just didn't know her well enough to divulge that pretty much every day as of late was a bad time. And that my current appearance was the least of it.

"Please, call me Jerri. It's lovely to finally meet you, Arianna. Absolutely lovely." Leah glanced at me and raised a brow.

"You, as well, Jerri. And, please, friends call me AJ." After another awkward moment, I managed to stutter out, "By all means, please, do come in."

Leah excused herself to let Nicoh roam in the backyard as I gestured for Jerri to sit in the living room, which thankfully, was in far better shape than its occupants. I'm not sure how I managed that stroke of luck, then remembered I had cleaned prior to leaving for the Los Angeles trip.

Jerri settled into a comfortable, presentable chair and nodded at Leah and Nicoh, who were playing on the other side of the glass slider door. "My, he's a…big…puppy. What…is he? It…is a he, correct?"

"Yes, Nicoh's an Alaskan Malamute. Are you familiar with the breed?" When she shook her head, I added, "Siberian Husky?" This time she nodded, to which I added, for the sake of reference, "Similar… Only bigger."

Her eyes widened. "Yes. I see that. He looks…formidable."

"Only at mealtimes," I replied, causing her to grasp her pearls.

I wondered if I was insured if the string were to break on my premises, as the result of my canine. She glanced at me, and upon taking in my grin, released a small chuckle, along with the grip on the necklace.

"We don't have pets. Robert was allergic since boyhood and therefore it was never really an option. Of course, when Bob was old enough to start asking for a puppy for his birthday, he was devastated to find out it wasn't something we were going to be able to accommodate. That's when he started begging us to let him go to friend's houses…friends that had pets."

I nodded, having grasped her meaning and she continued, "But Robert was so allergic, any contact would have sent him into a fit of wheezing, shortness of breath, tightness in his chest…it was awful. Bob even researched hypoallergenic dogs but his father was so adamant about his no pet policy, he finally gave up."

She sighed and glanced at Nicoh, who was peering back at us through the slider as Leah pulled it shut, joining us in the living room, as Jerri added, "I guess none of it matters anymore."

"We're so sorry for your loss, Mrs.—Jerri. Please extend our condolences to Bob and the rest of your family," I replied as Leah nodded and mirrored my sentiments.

Jerri patted my hand and murmured her thanks. "What makes it all that much harder is that I was out of town. Bob did his best to prevent me from enduring any stress until I returned home—he's always been so thoughtful, and protective that way—but to honest, it did little to soften the blow of returning to face an empty house."

"We understand it was…unexpected…that he passed suddenly," Leah commented.

Jerri nodded. "In his sleep. One of the staff found him after he didn't rise for his usual walk before breakfast." She paused to dab her eyes. "The man was remarkably fit for his age. Exercised in some form every day. Golfed. Played tennis. We both believe in strengthening mind, body and spirit, no matter the age but I guess sometimes it is never enough. Anyway, Bob is devastated."

"I'm sure the entire family is," I replied.

She shook her head. "It's just Bob and me. Robert's family is long gone…and mine…well, gone longer than that." She glanced out the window again, but wasn't focused on anything in particular. "Bob's the reason I'm here."

She chuckled lightly after talking in our expressions. I was somewhere between confused and surprised and Leah was probably nearing the same.

"Don't worry, you're not in trouble. You both look as though you're about to be sent to the principal's office."

I glanced at Leah. It had happened on more than one occasion for both of us when we were kids and not necessarily for the same offense, but I was always convinced that Leah's infractions were likely much worse. Of course, she viewed it much the same. It was one point on which we would never agree.

"I have a simple request." Jerri paused, tilting her head in expectation of our acknowledgment and except for the fact we didn't know what we might be asked to agree to, we both nodded for her to continue.

"I'm well aware that Bob has asked a member of local law enforcement for some assistance recently. I believe it was a Detective…Rodriguez…no, Ramirez. Bob said he was…is a friend of Serena's."

I pinched Leah's knee before she could snicker and thankfully, she was able to hold her game face…barely, without Jerri noticing.

"Anyway, at first, Bob did not inform us about his recent… encounter with an unknown assailant. Probably for the best… now. That would have sent Robert to an early grave." She thrust a hand to her mouth, shaking her head as she closed her eyes. "Oh goodness, Jerri, where has your tact gone?"

"We understood what you meant," Leah replied. "You've been through a traumatic experience…no one would blame you for a few out of place words."

Jerri opened her eyes, nodded. "Perhaps. Then again, sometimes, I'm not so sure…"

Again, she seemed to be elsewhere.

"You mentioned having a request," I prompted. "How can we help?"

Jerri turned to me. The intensity of her eyes was unnerving, especially when she proceeded to clasp both of my hands in hers.

"You've got to get him to stop." Her voice was barely above a whisper but it bore the weight of an army.

"Get who to...stop?" I realized my response sounded rather like a frog. "Detective Ramirez? Surely, you could talk to Bob about that. I have no influence over him. Has he done something to upset you?"

Leah looked equally confused, if not alarmed by the request. I noticed she had leaned away ever so slightly, just out of Jerri's reach.

Jerri's brow furrowed, realizing her mistake. "Not Detective Ramirez." She pressed her lips together then ensured she had my attention by squeezing my hands again before continuing, "I'm talking about your biological father, Martin Singer."

CHAPTER NINETEEN

As though it required clarification, she added, "I need Martin to stop whatever it is he is attempting to do."

I pulled my hands back and nearly lost my battle with the contents of my stomach as I fought to drum up a coherent, PG-rated response. I was relieved beyond words when Leah intervened.

"Sorry, I think there must be some confusion, Jerri. AJ's father's name was Richard and both he and her mother, Eileen, perished in a plane crash, a few years ago."

I gave Jerri credit—she maintained her composure as she looked from me to Leah and back again, nodding when she realized she needed a different approach.

"I did know your parents and yes, I had heard about their accident. I am so sorry for your loss. They were both lovely people. You may have been too young to remember, but your mother and I worked on several charities together—I've actually been here before, to this house.

"Oh, goodness. Eileen. She was so full of life. As was your father. Richard was a very generous, courageous man. Both were very well liked and respected in the community. You were their world and now that I've met you in person, as an adult, I can see why. They would be very proud of the woman you've become."

This time she refrained from any hand-gripping or patting, as I had tucked both around me and leveled a look that dared her to invade my private space again.

Sorry, Mom, for displaying such manners to a guest in our family home, but I could honestly care less how well she claimed to know them and if she had, doubted that she'd thought one iota about them in years.

The real thorn came from her side comment suggesting they would have been proud. It felt forced and disingenuous. My parents hadn't been gone that long and while I may have changed some in that time—we all change, after all—I was still the same person at the core. And I always would be. So, no, I didn't need this woman telling me they would have been proud. I knew they were.

Perhaps I was being a bit harsh. I realized this woman had just lost a loved one and despite the fact I was still reeling at the mention of Martin's name out of anyone's mouth besides Leah or Ramirez, I was downright seething from Jerri's reference to my parent's so-called "accident."

Yes, they had died in an unfortunate plane crash, but it had been no accident. It had been cold and calculated murder at the hands of the son of a man she'd known quite well. I owed this woman nothing, especially if she was here under false pretenses.

Maybe I should set the wild beast in my backyard loose on her after all.

As though sensing the tension swarming in the space around us, Jerri cleared her throat and continued, "I am sorry to toss this at you so randomly but time is of the essence. And while I am sorry…truly sorry about your parents, I must speak to you about your other…biological father…before it's too late."

Leah started to speak but Jerri raised her hand and gave her a look of warning. "And before you protest—or your friend inter-jects—I need to get this out. I've known who you were longer than you have."

I frowned and shook my head. For such a well put-together woman, she was certainly having a hard time spitting it out. Perhaps she should have brought her son's speechwriter along.

Jerri either ignored my look or was oblivious to it as she pressed on. "I knew Martin and your mother, Alison, a very long time ago. Quite well. Strike that. As well as anyone could get to know Alison. Not because she wasn't congenial—she most defi-nitely was—and lovely. Oh so, lovely." She pressed a hand against her cheek and sighed, glancing at me, before adding, "I don't know if Martin has mentioned it but you look so much like her. I noticed it when you opened the door. For a moment, I thought I was looking at a ghost. But then, reality settled in and knew it simply wasn't possible. You had to be Alison's daughter.

"Alison was younger than the rest of us and we ran in a different circle." She paused to chuckle and was definitely taking up time, as well as my patience. "The rest of us...Martin included...were inseparable. Yet not one of us knew about his relationship with Alison until later. Much later. And then when she...and you and your sister were gone...it was too late. Soon, Martin was gone, too. Or so we thought.

"Suddenly, here he is, in the flesh—here in Phoenix, of all places—after all of these years. I knew it the minute Bob told me of the ambush and what the man had said to him. Bob thought it was just ramblings, and to most it would have been, but when I heard what he said and learned that your business card had been left behind, it gave the message context and I knew he was back. And that the rumors had been true."

She glanced at me but I had been prepared and my face revealed nothing.

"I understand if you'd prefer not to confirm or deny any of

this. Please, just hear me out before you make your decision. Martin came back for a reason. I don't know, specifically, what it is but you must implore him, beg him…whatever you have to do…to stop.

"Tell him it's not worth it…and to go back into hiding. If he continues down this path, he won't be able to go back…this time. Believe me when I say that. And it will all be for nothing. He must understand that. His life, even if doesn't mean anything to him—his choices and his movements will impact us all. You must stop him. Your life…and the lives of everyone around you…are dependent on it."

It was quite a speech and while Jerri and I continued to stare at one another, neither of us uttered another syllable.

Finally, Leah broke the silence. "What if you're wrong about this…Martin? What if he wants the same thing you do?"

Jerri blinked but didn't break her gaze. "Perhaps he does, but his way of going about it puts us all in danger."

"Okay, I get that. He ambushed your son. Not very smart. Or well thought out. Though it did have an effect, didn't it? I mean, here you are. At our doorstep."

This time, Jerri turned her attention to Leah and gave her a hard stare. Bonus point to Leah. She took it and kept running.

"What if he's trying to prevent that very thing…the thing you are concerned about…from happening?" Jerri opened her mouth to respond but Leah held a finger up. "Even if AJ does precisely as you ask and this Martin person concedes and goes away, what's to say this threat will, too? I mean, it's already out there, is it not? Who are we to stand in this man's way if he can prevent the Armageddon from occurring?

"Because you can't prevent an end of days once it's already started."

I shook my head. "But you just said…"

Again, Jerri interjected. "It began long ago…with that project.

It's been going on, right in front of us, every single day, oblivious to everyone, except for the few of us left who know what it represents.

"Like Martin?"

"No. Martin is something else…a catalyst. His knowledge could be used to bring such devastation and destruction. Even if he means well. It is inevitable. He is the only one who can control the direction it takes."

"Why not confront him yourself?" I asked. "You seem to have a particular investment here, so why not plead your own case? Certainly, given your previous rapport, it should hold some weight?"

Jerri looked away, shaking her head. "No. Not after all this time…too much water has gone under that bridge."

I glanced at Leah, who was beyond amused and trying to keep from snorting, her hand pressed to her face. It was ironic, as Martin had supposedly taken a nose dive off the Skyway Bridge in Chicago when he faked his suicide. No, check that. Her comment was not only ironic, it was laughable.

"Alright, then let's take another path. You're asking AJ to put her neck out when you aren't willing to do the same. But what if they come after her to get to him and whatever knowledge he has?"

Jerri tilted her head. "Your choice of phrasing…is interesting. Are you suggesting this sort of thing has happened before?" She glanced at the two of us. "Just how long has he been here?"

Leah wasn't giving her an inch. "How long do *you* think he's been here?"

Jerri opened her mouth, then paused for a moment, careful with her words. "Like I mentioned, I've only recently become aware…since Bob's attack."

Liar, liar. Nothing about the way she said it, from the intensity of her gaze as she enunciated the words, to the words themselves, rang true.

Leah played it off, letting it pass. "Have you had communications with others? The people you hung with…before? Perhaps they—"

Jerri shook her head and cut her off. "Not in some time. No." I glanced at Leah, wondering if Jerri was bluffing and given the way she pursed her lips, had her own inclination as the woman continued, "Robert was insistent it was that way after we left."

"Left?" I asked.

"Chicago. School. That life. Everyone had pretty much gone their own way by that time anyway."

Or died. I thought, dryly. Except for Jerri, her husband and Theo and his spawn—if I was correct.

"Well, isn't that convenient," Leah replied.

Jerri gave her a look that could have singed what remained of her hair. I was guessing our invite to Turkey Day had been revoked.

She confirmed it when she rose and made a show of smoothing her pants. "I think I've delivered my request and it appears I've overstayed my welcome." She turned to me, started to reach for my hand and thought better of it. "All I can ask is that you consider my request. Please compel your—Martin to cease his activities, whatever they may entail."

As she turned to leave, I took a chance. "May I ask you something?"

Jerri paused and after searching my face, nodded.

"What is all of this about…really?"

My question momentarily caught her off-guard, causing her to chuckle, though it came out a bit too harsh as she closed her eyes and shook her head.

"It's what it has always been about," she replied between gritted teeth, before hissing out, "Gemini."

"What do *you* know about Gemini?" Leah called out.

Jerri stilled and leveled a glare at my best friend that could have frozen a man-made lake in the heat of an Arizona summer.

"What do *I* know about Gemini?" Jerri smirked, swiveled on her heel, tossed the door open and as she strode out, haughtily replied over her shoulder, "My dear, I *am* Gemini. That damn project? It wouldn't exist without me."

CHAPTER TWENTY

"*That* I did not expect," I commented. Leah and I had sat in silence for a good thirty seconds after Jerri made her grand exit. "What did you make of it?"

"It was a practiced story." Leah chewed a nail.

To be honest, I was surprised that I wasn't more shocked by the woman's announcement. Then again, I'd heard a lot of good exit lines in my day—several of which had been uttered in the past few months.

Leah paused from destroying her nail to add, "She definitely knew a lot more than I would have expected. Do you think Martin's aware she's onto him?"

"I honestly don't know but considering how cagey he tends to be, I think not. This could very well send him back into hiding."

She shrugged. "Isn't that what you've wanted all along—for him to go away? To crawl back into whatever hole he's been keeping himself in for twenty-five years?"

I sighed. "I did…before. Now, I just want this…whatever this is…to be over, once and for all. I don't like people…knowing…"

"About Martin?" she prompted.

I shook my head. "About me…my past. It feels…"

"Squishy?"

"Unnerving was the word I was searching for but squishy works." I chuckled but it was light on the humor. "Jerri must be pretty desperate if she sought me out, especially considering her husband just passed. You think her mind would be elsewhere."

Leah shrugged. "Perhaps she believes Martin's sudden appearance had something to do with it."

This time I tilted my head back and snorted. It felt...good.

"What, like Robert saw Martin, thought he was 'looking at a ghost,' to mirror Jerri's phrasing, and was so overcome with shock he suffered a heart attack and died?"

She snickered. "Maybe Martin was there to tuck his old pal in." When I groaned she added, "Whatever. Stranger things have happened."

"Don't remind me. I've lived through some of them."

"As have I, my friend. Now what?"

I chewed my lip. "Well, before we were interrupted by whatever *that* was"—I pointed at the door—"I had intended to follow up with Tony B., see what he was able to drum up."

"Ready for another round of tongue-lashing, are you?" She snickered. "After the brain scramble from Jerri, Tony's likely going to remind you how you will be the death of us all as long as those chips still exist. I'm surprised he even keeps a copy of the data he extracted."

"I doubt he keeps it on him. Or even onsite. He's way too paranoid for that," I replied frowning. "Either way, I can't avoid the conversation. It's the only ace we have right now. We can't trust anything coming out of Martin's mouth and Jerri's intentions may be tainted—or at the very least, skewed—to her benefit."

"So, you have a little chat with Tony B. and then what?"

"I suppose I'll have to confirm or deny some of what Jerri said and figure out the truth from all the minutiae...Martin's included." I shook my head. "There has to be more to this picture

—it just feels like we're missing part of the frame. Until then, we'll just have to take it as it comes and watch our backs."

"So pretty much like every other day," Leah murmured, before adding, "You think you'll talk to Martin again?"

I rolled my eyes. "How can I avoid it? He'll either come looking for the chips, or I'll have to hunt him down and tell him about the visit from a ghost from his own past."

"What if Martin bails on the whole thing and disappears again once he learns he's not as stealthy as he liked to believe he was?"

I shook my head. "I don't think he will. Disappear, that is. I think he'll go for a full-court press where the chips are concerned. It's the ammo he's probably been looking for and here it just conveniently pops out of the woodwork, all because he ambushes a Congressman."

"Convenient doesn't even begin to cover it." Leah snorted and glancing at me. "Will you be ready?"

"I was born ready," I replied, offering her a fist bump, after which she crossed her arms, her frame rigid as though she was preparing for battle.

"It won't be pretty."

"It doesn't need to be pretty it just needs to be finished, once and for all."

"What happens if the outcome—or the fallout—is worse than expected?"

I thought about it for a moment. "It can't be any worse than it already is."

She nodded. "I just want you to be sure. There are always choices."

"True, but at the end of the day I can only pick one."

Leah snorted. "And if all of the options suck?"

I laughed. It came out sounding more like I had a smoker's cough. "Then I'll pick the least sucky option and hope for the best."

She nodded. "That's the best sucky answer I've heard all day." I shrugged, causing her to chuckle. "I've got your back, whatever you choose."

I looked at my friend and gave her a small smile. "I appreciate that."

"One thing, though." This time, she pressed her lips into a thin line and her eyes searched mine.

"What's that?" I asked though I was almost afraid to.

"Choose wisely," she replied, her tone as serious as her expression. "We'll probably only get one shot."

I nodded. "If this plays out like I think it's going to, I'll only need one."

I dialed Tony B.'s number and left a message. Within seconds, he returned my call. Tony was interesting like that, and while I'd never met him in person, I envisioned him working inside an underground bunker on some abandoned military base in the desert, surrounded by steel-enforced walls that were six feet thick with a single entrance that was locked and booby-trapped from the inside.

I knew I wasn't his only client and considering the nature of work he was doing for me, the guy probably spent his days finding new ways to barricade himself from the world. He once told me that if I passed him on the street I would have no idea—which made me assume that he did come up for air on occasion and that he was adept at blending in—a chameleon shielding himself from the world. Then again, had I thought he was worried about me double-crossing him at some point, it could have as easily equated to a threat.

I tried not to give that too much thought, as I feared the information I'd given him just a tad more than I feared him. And, if he were to decide it was more valuable in the appropriate hands, I would be dead before I knew he'd sold me out.

"You just keep pulling me into this crap, don't you," were the first words out of Tony B.'s mouth.

I noted it was not a question and kept my piehole shut, having previously been scolded for intervening before he could unload whatever frustration he was harboring on me. It was our usual process and though I was sure his other clients were as accommodating, I figured the least I could do was allow him a forum to vent. I didn't take it personally—the guy was wound pretty tight —and his verbal vomiting likely had to do more with the quantity of energy drinks he imbibed than the work I'd asked him to perform.

"You know we're probably all going to hell for what's on those chips, right?" Again, I didn't respond. "Some people might think it's the way of the future but there are just some things— present company included—that are downright unnatural. Human genes…mutations…it's like a Petri dish of scrambled eggs…let's just whip 'em up and see what pops out." I grimaced. The imagery he was conjuring was barf-worthy. We *were* talking about human beings here.

"Anyway, as I mentioned before, your pal Jeremiah Vargas and Congressman Fenton are brothers, as in full brothers, meaning both have the same mother and father."

I rolled my eyes, having gotten the meaning from his reference to "full." I hoped he wasn't going to continue down this path because I certainly wasn't up for a lesson on the birds and the bees, given Tony B.'s style of narrative. Clinical was one thing. Antiseptic was another.

"We know that they are obviously not twins—even though his birth year matches his brother's."

I cocked my head. "What? How is that possible? You just said—"

"I know what I said, Missy, and if you'd hold onto your panties, I was getting there." I was silent long enough that Tony must have felt comfortable I was sufficiently calmed and resumed the reins. "Both Jeremiah and the Congressman have the same mother but only the latter was born the normal way...or I guess in this situation, normal is relative, but for our purposes, we mean by way of natural childbirth, so his mother brought him to term in her womb."

"What about Jere?" I asked, thoroughly confused.

"Getting there...if you could contain yourself. Geesh, you have too much Charbucks in your coffee this morning, or what?"

"Sorry, not enough coffee combined with an unexpected early morning caller."

"Tell me about it," he replied dryly and I knew he meant me. "Anyway, let's not forget the purpose of the Gemini project. Jere was a product of the other side of the equation...so getting back to our Petri dishes..." I released a retching sounded as Tony ignored me and continued, "He made his trek into our happy little universe the Easy Bake Oven way."

This time, I covered my mouth to keep from throwing up acid. I really hoped he wasn't enjoying this. If so, I would need to add "Sick Puppy" to his list of monikers.

"Kind of like Winslow and his twin, I would assume?" I managed to reply.

"There you go, jumping ahead again. Can you please let me suspend the disbelief a little bit longer?"

I made some grumbling sounds, which seemed to appease him, before adding, "It's just hard to believe Winslow Clark was the spawn of some poor woman, no matter how oozed his way into this world."

Tony merely snorted before proceeding, "Not just *some* woman, AJ. She happened to be the twin of the woman who gave birth to the Congressman and whose DNA created Jeremiah Vargas."

"Jeannie Taylor was Winslow's mother?"

"Exactly. And that's not even the best part. *All* of the little cherubs had the same father."

"Theodore Winslow," I managed to huff out as my heart thudded against my chest and threatened to erupt.

"Give that girl a pony," Tony replied, sounding mildly amused that I was finally on the same page with him. I can't say I was enjoying being in the same book. Much less page. "Man certainly got around."

"Indeed he did."

"*Did?*"

"You don't want to know," my tone was as droll as my mouth was dry. A camel would have wept.

"You're right, I don't."

"Story for another day, then." When he didn't respond, I added, "I think I mentioned that Jeannie died shortly after leaving college and according to her death certificate, it was some unpronounceable form of cancer."

"You did," he replied. "Interestingly enough, that particular type of cancer is aggressive once the symptoms manifest."

I blinked. "Wait a minute. You researched it?" I hadn't asked him to do so and while I knew Tony was thorough, hadn't expected him to venture down that particular rabbit hole. He could probably give Leah a run for her money.

I decided to keep that observation to myself, as he grunted at my comment.

"Of course I did. My research paid off, especially when I learned that Theodore Winslow had fathered all of these women's children, Petri dish or otherwise. If Jeannie would have had that cancer, then Jerri would have, too. She would have shown symptoms long before now. And yet she hasn't. Nor has her son."

He'd lost me. Not hard considering we were running through a corn maze in the dark. Or at least, I felt like I was. "Come again?"

"The cancer listed on the death certificate—it's genetic," he replied. I was thankful he didn't sound disappointed that I wasn't following.

"Any thoughts on that?"

"Are we talking hypothetically?"

I shrugged, though I knew he couldn't see me. "If it makes you feel better."

"Immeasurably so."

I wasn't sure why it mattered but he was helping me, so I couldn't question his reasons, whatever they may be. "Okay, hypothetically-speaking what are any…thoughts that might be drawn from a scenario of this nature?"

"That Jeannie ingested or was injected with enough of a dosage of something that caused a catastrophic failure of her body, shutting down her vital systems, organs…"

"Would you be able to mask it as cancer?" I asked. Wait, could you inject people with cancer? I scoffed at myself…we *were* talking about Theo here.

"You wouldn't need to. It could have been anything, it wouldn't matter what it was. Dead is dead and if no one asks or raises any questions after the fact, all the better."

I frowned. "I'm not sure I'm following you."

"Well, Theodore Winslow was the physician who signed the death certificate."

"True."

"Well, if you sign the death certificate, then take possession of the body, once you incinerate it and spread the ashes, you've pretty much got your bases covered—wouldn't you say?"

"Oh God…" It felt as though all of the air had been sucked out of my lungs.

"I don't think God had any part in this plan."

"Still, I can't help but think there was a reason Theo needed to silence Jeannie. Permanently," I murmured.

In fact, I was convinced of it. As twisted as Theo Winslow was, there was always a motive behind everything he did.

Unfortunately, it may have had less to do with Jeannie or her sister and everything to do with the man who had snapped his neck.

CHAPTER TWENTY-ONE

Tony B. concluded our business, as there were no other bombshells to drop.

At least not yet.

I felt compelled to have a little follow-up chat with Martin—to gain some further clarification—but prior to doing that, I needed to confirm something that had been bothering me.

So, before I had that one-on-one with the person I least wanted to have a conversation with, I called the one that was second on that list.

Ramirez.

I dialed his number and he picked up, to my chagrin, on the first ring. I had hoped to leave him a message but sighed, knowing this would yield results faster. Besides, it would have been childish to hang up, considering my number was in his contact list and he would have already known it was me.

"AJ, twice in one day. Don't tell me you're ready for round two?" His voice was smooth like glass, with all the sharp little edges.

"Hardly." I snorted. "And even if I was, it wouldn't be with you."

"Fair enough," he replied. "You called me. What's up?"

"That video you showed me. How long have you been following me at the Congressman's behest?"

"To my knowledge, he's not having you followed."

"Okay, then why have you taken it upon yourself to do so?" I snipped.

Ramirez sighed. "Listen, AJ. You and your pal may think the world revolves around the two of you but not everything actually is about you. I'm busy trying to help the Congressman and his family through a crisis. So, if you don't mind—"

"Hold up, Ramirez," I interjected. "Let me start over. I am very sorry for the Congressman's loss. Truly, I am. I know what it's like to lose a parent—parents—and I don't mean to come off sounding insensitive." I paused, formulating my words more carefully this time around.

"I guess what I should have come out and asked from the beginning—which I so ineloquently attempted to do—if you aren't tailing me and the Congressman isn't either, then how did you come to be in possession of the video with Martin and me?"

"Now, *that's* a better question," Ramirez replied. "And I wish I had a decent answer but honestly, I have no idea. It was sent anonymously to my phone. No message…just the video. I haven't received anything since."

"Have any thoughts about who might have sent it? Or, is there a way to track it?" I asked, my tone hopeful.

"Nope on the latter—a burner phone. On the former, I have a few thoughts but nothing to substantiate them. Besides, it would be a bit of a stretch and I'm not sure what that person or persons would have to gain."

"I'm thinking we might be thinking of the same someone or someones," I replied. "And like you, I'm trying to figure out why."

We sat in silence for a moment. It was Ramirez who spoke first.

"So, did you hear from Martin again?"

I sighed. "No. You have any more ideas about where he might be holed up?"

"I've checked into a few things but they were a wash. How about you?"

"Hmm, now that you mention it, I do have an idea." When my response was met with silence, I added, "Come on! I have a few every once in a while. Some of them are even pretty good."

Ramirez grunted before replying, "I don't suppose you'd care to share?"

"Truthfully, it's so ridiculous, it's kind of embarrassing, so I think I'll keep it to myself," I murmured.

Ramirez blew out a breath. "Fair enough. If you do decide to run it up the flagpole, do me a favor?"

"Maybe?"

He snickered, apparently not placing much stock in my response. "So it's that way now, is it?"

"Hey, it doesn't have to be any way, if you'd prefer," I retorted.

It came out a bit more snappish than I had intended. Residue, I guessed. Sometimes anger, frustration and resentment had a way of sticking in the crevices.

Once again, there was a stony silence before he responded, his tone firm but revealing nothing more. "Fine. I was just going to ask you to take Leah and Nicoh along, if you should decide to investigate this idea you have."

"Oh." Though he couldn't see me, my cheeks reddened, as I was feeling rather childish about my snarky retort. "Yeah, that's probably a good idea."

"I have a few every once in a while," he replied, without a

hint of sarcasm, despite the fact he was tossing my own words back at me. "I need to get back. Keep me posted?"

"I will. Please do the same."

Ramirez murmured something I didn't catch before disconnecting, leaving me to stare at the phone. How had we gotten to this point?

I stared at the ceiling and huffed out a long breath. I took ownership of most of it. The other part? Well, I was about to put my theory into motion.

I knocked on Leah's door and upon hearing a muffled response, entered with caution. She propped herself up on her pillow with one arm, keeping her eyes closed as I relayed my conversation with Ramirez and then outlined my plan.

She was quiet for so long after I finished I'd thought perhaps she had drifted back to sleep. I was about to repeat the last part but she finally managed a reply, her eyes still locked tight.

"I'm assuming you want to test this theory of yours out and in doing so have decided to take Ramirez's suggestion under advisement." It was not a question.

I tilted my head, surprised she wasn't up for an adventure, probably because she knew it would likely result in nothing more than an interruption of her beauty sleep. "Are you opposed?"

"To the idea? Or leaving the comfort of this bed?" When I gestured toward the prior, she stuffed her face into her pillow and released a garbled, "Nope. Just confirming." Her head popped back up. "Hey, wait, what happened with Tony B.?"

I groaned, leaning against her door jamb. "Can I fill you in on the way?"

That got her sitting straight up. "That bad?"

I shrugged, noncommittal. "You may want to pack a couple of extra poopie bags for the trip."

Leah crinkled her nose and tossed the covers away, padding to the bathroom where she shut the door with a definite thud before shouting, "You know, I could have gone all day without that visual, thank you very much. You do realize you woke me from a very nice dream where Jimmy Stewart was saving me from a dreadful plunge out of the window of the Mission San Juan Bautista."

"Like the final scene in *Vertigo*?"

"Yup, that's the one. Pretty blond…kind of looks like me?"

"Err… Okay?" I rolled my eyes. First off, my best friend probably needed some more rest. She looked more Meg Ryan than Kim Novak on any given day. Not a bad thing—just not the same thing. Second, I hated to tell her that he hadn't saved her, Jimmy that is—he's left standing, frozen, looking down at the body of the woman he believed he loved.

I shuddered just as Leah called out. "Give me twenty?"

"Sure." I backed out of the room and proceeded to my own to prepare for our adventure and whatever it brought.

After a failed attempt to tame my hair, I ended up shoving it into a ponytail and covering it with a baseball cap before pulling on jeans and a clean long sleeve t-shirt, paired with a pair of purple Chuck Taylors. No need to look too obvious, given the task at hand. Suddenly, I realized I should have relayed the same message to Leah and was mildly amused when she emerged, twenty-three minutes later, clad in an all-black ensemble. Her hair tucked under some form of cap, also black. Under closer inspection, I snorted when I realized it was a beret.

"It's not a stakeout, Leah." I pointed as she worked to tuck the wild ends of her hair under its edges. "By the way, it doesn't work like that."

She shrugged, mumbling something under her breath that sounded like a snipe about my own choice of attire.

"What?" I asked, looking down. "This is what I always wear."

"Oh…I know," she retorted. "Exactly my point."

"This coming from a chick who pulled an accessory from the play where she won the lead…in seventh grade?"

She shrugged, continuing to work her hair. "Hey, it was lucky then."

"Because you got the lead?"

She wiggled her brows. "No, because I got to play kissy face with the leading man afterward."

"Connor McClayton?" I couldn't even believe I'd drummed that name up after all these years.

"That's the one." She smirked, rubbing the hat as though the magic was still there.

"You're lucky Stella didn't find out about that."

She frowned. "Stella Stevens, the rugby player?" When I nodded, she added, "What's the Stellanator got to do with it?"

"Hell-o? She was only his girlfriend that entire year, right up until the spring dance, went she went all Stella-nation on him because Connor showing up sporting some hickeys that had not been Stella's doing—oh, my God!" A hand went to my mouth when my friend's eyes widened. "You…did…not?"

"I was twelve…and hormonal," she replied, waving a hand.

"Thirteen…"

"Whatever. Not a word…ever," she snapped, ripping the beret off her head.

"Agreed. But you have to do something for me," I replied.

"Name it." She peered at me as she tried to sound tough, but this news had thrown her for a loop and she looked a little worried.

I was having way too much fun to tell her that according to a mutual friend, the former Stellanator and her husband lived in Tulsa with their brood of boys and were expecting their first girl any day now. Having said that, I doubted she was plotting revenge against the harpy who'd snogged with her teenage crush.

"You have to put that hat back on for the duration of this mission."

Grimacing, she complied. "For the record, it's a beret."

"Like I could forget," I could barely manage to get out without snickering. "But hey, it is lucky."

This time, we both had a good chortle, loud enough to cause Nicoh to stir and come out of his hiding space to investigate.

"Are we taking the beast?" she asked after giving him a thorough once-over.

I noticed he did the same to her, leaning into her to sniff when he spied the beret, sneezing twice when he got a good whiff.

Thankfully, she was focused on me as I nodded. "I think we should. You never know when he might come in handy."

She snorted, glancing back at him as he began chasing his tail. "Yeah, I can see where *that* could be useful."

I shrugged. "As Jerri said, he *looks* formidable, so perhaps, that's something."

"Oh, it's *something* all right," she grumbled. "But just so you know, if it comes down to me or him, he's on his own."

"Are we talking about Nicoh here—or someone else?"

She released a long breath. "I'll let you know when I decide."

I laughed as I collected Nicoh, who was grumpy that I had interrupted his wild chase—which he seemed to be losing—as I attached his lead.

"Wanna hoof it?" She asked once we'd all gotten situated and stuffed the requisite accessories and snacks into our pockets.

For Nicoh, of course. It wasn't going to be that long of a trip for the humans.

I nodded. "I don't see why not. We're not going that far. Be a waste of good gas. And fresh air."

"Fresh air?" Leah scoffed. "Weren't you the one just referencing doo-doo bags?"

I shook my head and ushered them out the door.

"All right." She snorted. "Apparently, we're moving on to the next subject. So, how should we do this? I watch from a distance, you do the scaling and then let me in? Or, do you go in while I case the perimeter and listen for the sirens?"

I shook my head. "I was thinking about taking a more direct approach this time around."

Leah tilted her head. "Which is?"

"Ringing the doorbell."

"Bleck." She stuck out her tongue then pretended to gag. "That is so boring."

"Boring is good. Boring works," I replied, hoping I wouldn't live to regret it.

Of course, Leah had her own thoughts. "I'll remember to tell Ramirez you said that."

I wanted to smack her until I glanced over and saw the beret bouncing precariously on the top of her head, which brought an immense sense of satisfaction into my world.

Leah gave me a curious looked when I released a maniacal bout of laughter for no apparent reason and continued to peer at me as I managed to tone it down. Finally, I eased into a couple of tiny snorts, waving her off as she started to say something. It would have only made me start all over again.

Childish? Maybe, but perhaps we should embrace our inner child more often, especially in the face of potential danger.

We hiked up the street and crisscrossed the neighborhood until we were standing in front of the house that Randy Newman, my lawyer friend, owned. He and Nicoh's gal pal, Pandora, had moved to Dallas for a new job some time ago, but the last time we had spoken, he had indicated that he was hoping to return when his project reached its conclusion. Plus, he didn't have the heart, or the time, to sell the place.

To my knowledge, he hadn't returned since he'd accepted the new role, but given the way his yard had remained in immaculate condition, assumed he had hired a management company to maintain the property in his absence. That was the outside.

What I was curious about was on the inside of the house.

I walked directly up to the front door and rang the bell. After waiting a few moments, I went around to the back, plucked the hidey key from its spot and let myself into the back. The house should have had that musty, closed-up smell, but it didn't. In fact, it smelled as though someone had been baking. Cookies.

I alerted Leah and she joined me with Nicoh.

"Hello?" I called out, though I expected no response. Upon entering the kitchen, Nicoh immediately zoned in on the source of the baked goods—a plate of chocolate chip cookies, piled high on the counter.

"Realtor?" Leah suggested, until I pulled the fridge door open and pointed at the fresh fruits and veggies on the shelves. After peering at the date on the milk, she frowned. "Still got two weeks before it expires."

The dishwasher had a single plate, fork and glass. The trash, recently emptied. And except for a few items in the pantry and freezer, it looked as though the visitor was a light eater.

We continued moving through the house, while Nicoh sniffed at a few of Pandora's toys that had not been touched since she'd left, though there were other items that showed signs of occupancy—other than Randy's—including a small backpack with carefully folded shirts, pants, socks and boxers. Nothing was stylish, or new, but it was immaculate in the way it had been cared for. One pair of socked had been darned—as I couldn't even sew a button, I wasn't sure where I pulled that term from—and one pair of pants had been patched to cover a small tear near the back pocket.

In the bathroom, a minimum of toiletries were present—comb, toothbrush and paste, deodorant, a small shampoo and soap—also carefully arranged.

Any of the possessions could have been Martin's. Then again, they could have just as easily belonged to any other adult male. They were in effect, nondescript.

And except for the cookies, nothing suggested he expected company or spent a great deal of time here.

Leah tossed her hands up in frustration after she finished searching the last room. Nicoh settled on the floor and nosed one of Pandora's toys but wouldn't play with it, either lapsing into his former malaise or focused on the cookies on the counter.

I pulled my phone out and searched through the contacts until I found the one I sought.

To my surprise and his, Randy picked up on the first ring, sounding as though I had caught him in a hurry. And off-guard.

"Randy? It's AJ." When I was met with a resounding silence, I added, "Arianna...Jackson...from Phoenix?" More silence, followed by awkward shuffling sounds. "Your neighbor?"

"I'm so sorry, AJ. I'm hustling to a meeting. How the heck are you?"

"Good, Randy. Sounds like I've caught you at a bad time."

"I always have a quick minute for my favorite photographer. How's Nicoh?"

"Doing good. How's your girl?"

"Pandora's doing great. I was working a lot, so I got her into one of those doggie daycare resorts and they've spoiled her so much she hardly notices me when I pick her up on the weekends."

I winced. Pick her up on the weekends? One of the reasons he'd moved was so that he wouldn't have to travel as often and leave her behind.

But I wasn't here to judge. "Well, that sounds...like fun for her. How about the project?"

"Oh my goodness, it's taken on a few more heads since we last talked. Which is good from the perspective of the firm, but my workload is heavier than ever. Speaking of which, not to rush things along but what can I do you for?"

"I was walking by your house and noticed a man working in the yard—"

I glanced at Leah and she shrugged. It wasn't that big of a white lie. At least it was a starting point. No sense alerting him to the fact that someone had also taken up residence and that I had recovered his hidey key and let myself in, and was currently looking at the fresh-baked cookies on his counter.

"Oh sure, I've got a landscaping guy who comes every week. Pool guy, too. Thankfully, now, I've even got a renter to keep the inside from getting out of control and too terribly worn down on me."

"Through your management company?"

"Nope, placed an ad on one of those boards, kind of like an Airbnb, but not. Anyway, guy called back the same day. Was willing to pay cash for up to six months to start. Had my own guy—someone I've worked with in the past on other properties check him out to make sure he wasn't a creeper or a serial killer with some sort of weird cannibalistic rituals."

Nope, he pretty much falls into the mad scientist category, I thought, though I wasn't sure about any fetishes and truth be told, I didn't want to.

"So far, it's worked out real well. Guy keeps the inside maintained, gives me updates, makes sure the pool guy and landscaping guys are doing their thing...works out great for everyone."

"How long?" I asked, realizing I had zoned out. "I mean, how long has he been renting? I' be happy to stop by and say hello, welcome him to the neighborhood, that kind of thing."

"Hmm...probably a month or so after I left town." I didn't mention it but that had surpassed the six-month mark the man had originally offered up. "Yeah, Martin's been a real godsend."

"Err...Martin?" I prompted, raising a brow at Leah, who nodded.

"My tenant," Randy replied, nonchalant.

"Does Martin have a last name?" I asked.

"You still hanging with that detective, AJ, or what?" Randy chuckled. "Anders. His last name is Anders. Never met him in person but he seems like a nice guy. Certainly reliable. Plus, my guy said he checked out just fine."

I was quite sure he did. On paper, anyway.

It was interesting that he would use my biological mother's last name. Whose radar was he trying to stay off? Especially considering he had been hunkering down for as long as he had right under my nose and I hadn't known. Nor had Theo. Or Winslow. Or Jerri or her husband, for that matter.

Instead, I calmed myself before replying, "Well, that's good to hear, Randy. If I see Martin, I'll be sure to stop and introduce myself."

"That would be great, AJ. Was there anything else? I really need to run."

"No, just checking in. It was nice talking to you, too. I appreciate your time," I replied, adding just before he disconnected, "Give Pandora some scratches for us."

I paused to look at Leah, who had an undecipherable expression. "Well, that was interesting. Not all that useful, but interesting."

I nodded absently. "I'm sure you caught the last name Martin selected."

"I did," she replied, pursing her lips. "Does make you wonder how long he's been using it to hide in plain sight."

"Well, we know he's gotten away with it the entire time he's been in Phoenix."

"Certainly explains a few things. How he's always popping up right when you need him. Or knows what we're up to, pretty much the moment we decide. It's kind of creepy, if you think about it."

I glanced at her. "'Kind of creepy'? Even though he's not spying on me from right next door, I feel as though my privacy has been violated."

"On a positive note, I don't see any detailed documentation of our comings and goings," she replied, frowning before adding, "Then again, he's probably got it buried somewhere."

"I certainly wouldn't put it past him," I grumbled, heading back to the meager belongings and giving them another once-over, this time less gingerly.

Sitting cross-legged on the floor, I removed all the contents from the backpack and while Leah checked those items, I went through the various pockets and cubby holes. In the last zippered pouch, I was rewarded with something of interest.

It was a weathered photograph, folded into fours. Leah placed her searched contents on the floor and scooted next to me.

"Look—there's Theodore Winslow." She pointed at the group of individuals, poised for the shot. Though it appeared as though the image had been taken at a celebration, given the raised glasses, Theo's smile seemed forced and almost brittle as he stood at the end of the group, half-raising his own celebratory imbibement, barely above waist level. While the rest of the group smiled and laughed at the camera, possibly at something silly the photographer had said, Theo's eyes narrowed ever so slightly and glanced to something in the distance to his left, far beyond what would have been the photographer's right shoulder.

"Someone's being a party pooper," Leah murmured. "I wonder what he's looking at."

"Or who," I replied. "Seems as though the photographer's captivated everyone else's attention, including hers."

At Theo's left were the twins, Jerri and Jeannie, followed by Robert Fenton. I pointed at the twin whose smile, though no less noticeable than her sibling's, was paired with a mischievous wink at the cameraman.

"How the heck do you think they were able to tell those two apart?" Leah asked, looking back and forth between the two. "They even dressed the same."

I nodded. Both were wearing flamboyantly sequined cocktail dresses, in an alarming shade of fire engine red, creatively cut to leave a great deal of skin to peruse far above the knee, as well as to give their ample bosoms some fresh air.

"I guess no one was able to focus on their faces."

Considering the reputations both had garnered at college, I was guessing the duo used all kinds of ploys to conceal their identities, whenever it suited them.

Leah laughed and nodded at Robert. "He sure didn't seem to mind." Robert's expression was the most natural of the group, though alcohol may have had something to do with his happy-go-lucky demeanor.

Absent from the photo was Martin, and I assumed based upon prior conversations, had not been present at the festivities.

"I wonder who took the photo," Leah commented.

"Who indeed," I replied, though it was not hard to venture a guess.

"It's convenient how he always manages to slip out of things unnoticed," she murmured, and while she could have easily been referencing the photograph, it was true of Martin in any number of situations. "Though 'convenient' is not really a word that suits Martin, it is?"

I shook my head. It was not. Everything about Martin was quite calculated. Including this set-up. *Set-up*...now that was an interesting thought.

Just as I started poking at it with a stick, my cell phone rang. Ramirez.

Leah rolled her eyes after glancing at my screen. "You think the cat's out of the bag?"

"That we're sitting in our neighbor's vacated house, going through Martin's sparse belongings?" She shrugged. "I doubt it."

"You're probably right. "She sighed, before adding, "That would be double creepy."

"I doubt it would even register on the creep-meter," I commented before punching the button to answer his call.

"Where are you?" Ramirez's voice was ragged as I heard a car door slam.

I glanced at Leah, who shrugged. "Uhh…around."

"Around where, AJ? Please, for the love all things holy, just tell me!" His voice cut in and out as other muffled sounds eked their way in.

"Walking the neighborhood with Nicoh and Leah," I replied, my heart rate increasing as the sounds intensified on his end of the connection.

"Thank God," came the huffed reply.

"What in the heck is going on, Ramirez?" Leah called into the phone, her voice amping up for the shrill side. "You're freaking us out!"

"I just received another anonymous tip—a call from a blocked number," he replied, his voice choppy. "I'm gonna lose you in a second but you'd better start heading back to your house. I'll meet you there."

"What? What are you saying?" I managed to stutter out, my heart now threatening to propel itself out of my chest.

"Your house, AJ. The caller said it's on fire."

CHAPTER TWENTY-TWO

We made short work of inserting everything back into Martin's backpack but as we hustled out the door, I tucked the photo in my back pocket.

We ran all the way to the house, listening for sirens, watching for firetrucks and when we got within eyesight, stopped dead in our tracks.

There was nothing.

No sirens.

No firetrucks.

No smoke.

No Ramirez.

I started to call and tell him it was a prank and to go back to whatever he had previously been doing when Leah tugged at my arm and pointed.

The front door was wide open.

We sprinted the rest of the way, stopping short as we peered through the doorway.

Leah crinkled her nose as a waft of smoke emerged. "Something's burnt."

"Crap, the coffeemaker?" I asked but then remembered it was on a timer and had turned off long ago.

"Not unless we've been dousing our morning cup of joe with an accelerant." She pointed at an empty container of lighter fluid that had been tossed in the front bushes lining the house.

"Sloppy," I murmured, commanding Nicoh to stay put as I eased my way in, my hands fisted at shoulder height.

Leah did the same, as though we were going to pummel the intruder senseless for lighting and running. As well as littering.

"Well, I never did like that couch," I huffed, pointing at the living room accessory, which now resembled a burnt marshmallow that had accidentally slipped out of the s'more and plopped onto the ground.

"Yeah, total bummer." Leah waved at the lingering haze that filled the room and probably would latch itself onto every surface for months to come. "Especially considering it hadn't been in style since *The Brady Bunch* was on."

"We weren't even born then," I snipped, tossing the cushions and wiping soot off the coffee table with my palm. Even the syndicated versions had been run numerous times since, I thought to myself, before stopping in my tracks. "Wait, wasn't there something sitting on the couch when we left?"

I tried to retrace the past twenty-four hours as Leah looked from me to the couch and back. Suddenly the dots connected and she screamed, "My bags!" When I looked at her in confusion—it had been a long couple of days…make that weeks—she huffed. "The bags I took to Chicago!"

I raised a brow. "The ones that contained your research?"

She nodded, thrusting her hands on her hips. "Including a copy of Jeannie's death certificate."

"Well…crap."

"Seems like someone has been busy…a little tit for tat, perhaps?" She pointed at my back pocket.

"You don't think Martin—"

Before I could finish, Ramirez charged through the door. "Didn't I tell you two to wait?"

I looked at Leah and she shrugged. "No," we both said at once.

He worked his jaw, realizing that he hadn't actually directed us to stay put.

"No worries, Detective," Leah replied. "It turned out to be an accident."

When Ramirez strode over to the couch to investigate, she made a zipping gesture across her lips, then nodded toward the door and made a spraying gesture with her right hand. The lighter fluid.

I nodded and gestured for her to go.

"I'll take Nicoh around back," Leah said nonchalantly, heading in that direction.

"Wait a minute," Ramirez replied. "What happened?"

Leah shrugged. "Must have left my curling iron on the couch."

Ramirez's eyes narrowed as he perused the wisps poking out from beneath the beret. "Your curling iron?"

"Mmm…hmm," Leah replied. "Trying to tame this…mess."

She pulled the beret off her hair, allowing the static to take over, leaving Ramirez to stare, open-mouthed. If it hadn't have been for the severity of the situation I would burst out laughing, probably even fallen down, based on the look crossing his face.

"Yeah, you can see what a challenge it's been. Anyway, I must have forgotten to turn it off. And it probably got knocked off the end table when we were getting ready to leave."

"Nicoh's tail," I replied, barely about to keep my voice from shaking as my lips trembled.

"Yeah, speaking of—" she tilted her head in his direction and Ramirez waved her on.

Without having to be told twice, Leah hustled out of the house and away from his watchful eye.

"Looks like the fire was confined to this area." Ramirez peered at the couch from all angles, careful not to touch it.

"Yeah, pretty lucky, huh?" I chewed my lip, realizing there was one thing we hadn't addressed yet as part of our ruse.

"So, how'd you put it out so fast?" Ramirez asked, looking around for a fire extinguisher, effectively posing the question I'd hoped to avoid but knew was imminent.

"We didn't," I replied, swiping the surface of the end table, also covered in soot.

"Come again?" Ramirez swiveled his head in my direction.

"It was out when we got here," I replied slowly. "Maybe it just burned out?"

Ramirez shook his head. "Where are your extinguishers stored?"

"One's in the pantry, the other's in the garage." I pointed, hoping to move him in that direction so that his eyes would no longer be trained on me.

He gave me a hard stare before heading to the pantry. When he emerged with nothing, he paused to glance at me but then continued into the garage, returning with a healthy frown.

"Both holders are empty."

"Okay."

"You're sure you had extinguishers."

I noted it was not a question.

"Yup. Pretty sure. Back when the Stanton's did their handy work on"—I stopped, not wishing to reveal the security room they had retrofitted—"the house after the last fiasco."

It did make me wonder—why hadn't the alarm gone off and alerted the fire department?

Ramirez quickly drew the same conclusion and asked.

"I'm honestly not sure," I replied. "I'll definitely need to look into that."

That and the fact nothing went off when someone broke into the house to set the fire. Had I forgotten to lock up when we'd gone to Randy's?

After surveying me for a dangerously long period, Ramirez nodded just as Leah let herself in through the slider, leaving Nicoh to gaze at us longingly. When he started to paw the glass, I nipped it in the bud with a single command and he resorted to a round of low whoo-whoos before retreating into the backyard.

"Seems like you two got awfully lucky, especially considering you were out and about, walking the neighborhood, wasn't it?" Ramirez looked from me to my friend but we both offered him nothing more than a single head nod.

Squinting, he looked again at the couch, before adding, "I'd get those extinguishers replaced and have the alarm tested."

"Nothing else, Detective?" Leah asked.

I tossed her a look that should have caused the hair on the back of her neck to singe. Instead, she crossed her arms, stared him in the eye as he gave her a final once-over.

"I don't know, Leah, is there?"

"Nope, just an accident. Nothing more," she replied. "We appreciate the heads-up though. You can never be too careful."

He nodded and turned to exit, pausing to glance at her. "Yeah, next time you decide to tame your hair, leave the electric appliances out of it."

As he pulled the door shut, his gaze slid to me and I caught a glimpse of something that caused a lump to form in my throat.

Disappointment.

"What was that all about?" Leah whispered, despite the fact we'd heard his truck pull away and down the street.

I quickly filled her in.

"Wow," she replied, pulling the lighter fluid out of a plastic bag that had been tucked under her shirt. I noticed she was holding it with an oven mitt. "Grabbed it on my way out. Didn't want to muck up any potential fingerprints."

"Yeah, like we have a mobile lab in the backyard," I retorted.

"Hey, it's worth a shot. Besides, I may know someone who would be willing to help."

"Yeah, like that worked out well for us last time," I replied, nodding at the couch, now missing the bag and the research she had gleaned from Chicago before we were betrayed by her friend Bonnie.

"Hmm…true. Let me think on that."

I really didn't want to point out that we probably wouldn't have time to identify the fingerprints, if there was any before we ran out of time. Someone was definitely getting desperate. And I was starting to wonder just how involved Martin was.

I didn't think he had started the fire but his motives were intertwined with the person who had. The question was, what drove those motivations? Whether well- or ill-intentioned, there was too much at risk to assume the outcome would serve as a resolution, no matter what side the coin landed on.

Leah kicked at the couch and wiped residue from the end table, looking at me as she did.

"This isn't going to end well."

"I was thinking the same thing."

"That makes three of us," called out an unexpected voice.

We turned as Martin entered from the direction of the den, my father's former office, holding an extinguisher under each arm.

"Sorry for the mess. I did the best I could." He nodded at the couch as we stared at him, our mouths offering an invitation to any bug in the vicinity.

"What?" I managed to spit out as he placed both extinguishers on the counter and grabbed a couple of brooms and a dustpan from the pantry.

I didn't bother asking how he'd known where to find them, as Martin had already proven himself quite resourceful.

After handing me one of the brooms and Leah the dustpan, he busied himself with his own broom.

"I happened to be walking by your house"—Leah rolled her eyes at me before stooping to catch Martin's sweepings—"when I saw plumes of smoke billowing out your front door, which was wide open, though I didn't see either of you. I began calling your names as I approached, thought I heard some movement, but still you didn't respond. So I entered, saw the fire, found the extinguishers and got the fire put out as quickly as I could."

I stopped sweeping to pat him on the arm. "Thank you, Martin, for your fast work. If you hadn't been passing by—"

Martin waved a hand but his face reddened at the show of gratitude. "I'm sorry I wasn't able to save your couch. I hope it wasn't a family heirloom."

His tone was so sincere, neither Leah nor I could keep from snickering. After receiving an exasperated look from Martin, Leah dropped her dustpan, losing all of the contents, and we broke out in full-blown guffaws. Though he wasn't quite sure what to make of our outbursts, he began chuckling too.

"Did I say something humorous?" he asked, once we'd calmed and resumed our cleaning.

"Not exactly, but you did do us a favor," Leah replied and when he tilted his head, she added, "By letting it burn."

"Okay…" Martin squinted, more confused now than he was before but Leah shifted gears.

"You didn't happen to notice anything *on* the couch when you arrived, did you?"

He frowned, glancing at the singed couch, before responding, "No, I don't believe there was anything on the cushions. They were, of course, on fire by then, but I don't recall anything sitting on them. Anything sizable, that is. Why?"

"Leah's luggage from her trip to Chicago seems to be missing, including the contents of her research." I quickly relayed her findings, as Leah carefully gauged his reaction, including the details of Jeannie's death certificate.

He was quiet when I finished and appeared to be digesting what I'd told him as he slowly continued to sweep.

"Are you sure about this—the death certificate, that is?" He asked after a long moment, his brows furrowed.

"Yup," Leah replied. "It was an official copy of the document, bought and paid for."

"So you had no idea that Theo had signed it and had been responsible for having Jeannie cremated?" I asked.

Martin shook his head. "It certainly seems as though Theodore had his hands in everything right under everyone's nose, doesn't it?"

Leah snorted. "That doesn't even begin to cover half of it." When Martin glanced at her, his expression one of confusion, she proceeded to tell him that Jeannie had been Winslow and his twin's mother—yet another thing that tied her to Theo, if not made her a liability.

"Theodore killed Jeannie," Martin's whispered when she finished.

"It certainly seems that way," I replied. When he said nothing, I added, "Does that come as a surprise to you?"

Martin blew out a long breath, shaking his head slowly. "Perhaps it should, as sick as it is, but it actually makes perfect sense, knowing Theodore as I did."

"And you never knew about any of this? Or had an inclination?" Leah asked.

He glanced at her, his face pinched, as though the words pained him. "No, though I should have. I was so caught up in my own problems I missed what was right in front of me."

"It seems a lot of people did," I murmured.

He surveyed my face, before adding, "I'm guessing there's more."

It was Leah who responded. "Bob Jr. is not actually Robert's son."

"What?" Martin's eyes widened.

"Turns out our Congressman is also a spawn of Theo's," she replied. "Let's just hope he doesn't follow in his daddy's footsteps."

Martin leaned against the wall, the color draining from his face as he wiped his brow. "I...don't believe it." He turned to me. "You confirmed this?"

Realizing he meant via the information on the chips, I nodded.

"And Robert never knew." Martin wasn't really looking at either of us and though it wasn't a direct question felt it warranted an honest response.

"We don't believe so, no. Bob is likely not aware, either."

"I can't believe Jerri managed to keep it from him, or from Theodore," Martin's voice was barely a whisper.

"What makes you think Theo didn't know about his other son?" Leah asked.

Martin turned to her but wasn't really looking at her as he replied, "Both Robert Jr. and his mother are still alive, aren't they?"

Leah's lips formed a thin line as she nodded. Both of us had caught the gist, loud and clear.

"Probably a good thing the two of you took him and his son out then." Leah's attempt at humor fell flat as Martin and I offered her cold stares.

"Sorry, bad timing." She raised her hands in surrender. "Question for you, Martin?" He shrugged and gestured for her to proceed. "Why, exactly, were you lurking in the den?"

Martin blinked. "I wasn't lurking. I had just finished putting the fire out and heard voices. Rather than expose my position, I tucked into one of the rooms. When I confirmed it was the two of you, I was about to emerge but the Detective arrived and I thought it best, where all of us were concerned, if I stayed put, hoping he'd leave before I was exposed." He paused before adding, "You two did a good job of disarming him. It almost seemed like you've had practice." He garnered me with a pride-filled smile.

I looked at my shoes, kicked at the soot covering the toe, feeling the heat of his gaze as I shifted the subject. "You said you heard someone or something when you approached the house, but you never saw anyone?" He shook his head, so I added, "Did you notice anything else?" I mentioned the lighter fluid container Leah had removed from the bushes.

"Never saw that, either, but then I was pretty focused on the smoke coming from the open door and then on the fire itself."

"Fair enough," I replied. I slid a glance at Leah, who nodded once. Both of us felt he was being truthful—on that point—and that he'd had nothing to do with staging the fire, just so that he could become our savior by putting it out.

"While we're trading questions, mind if I pose one of my own?" Martin proceeded after receiving a head nod from each of us. "Nice house like this, I assume you have an alarm system, which also includes fire detection. So why didn't either engage?"

"That's a very good question," Leah murmured, glancing at me. "We certainly don't want random people in our house rummaging through our unmentionables."

Martin cleared his throat as his face turned a lovely shade of pink. "I would think not. Much less pilfering your possessions."

"Err, speaking of possessions…" I started, just as Leah rose, brushed off her jeans, and pointed to her phone.

"Yeah, I should probably contact the alarm company about that." She grabbed it and ran to her room, slamming the door.

"Thanks, pal," I murmured, facing Martin. "I need to confess.

While you were putting out the fire, we were at your—Randy's house. We looked around…"

Martin nodded. "I know." When I tilted my head, he chuckled lightly. "Unlike your system, Mr. Newman's is actually working and I was alerted the moment you entered with the key and monitored your movements on my phone." I started to interject but Martin raised a hand. "It's fine. I understand. And while you continue to distrust me, I hope you realized, in your search, I have nothing to hide. Nothing more to hide, anyway."

I shrugged but said nothing, my eyes retreating to my shoes.

"I'm curious though," he paused until I met his eyes. "Don't you girls like chocolate chip cookies?"

I chuckled. "We love them but we also have a saying…"

"What's that?" Martin asked.

"You can never eat just one. And, well, if you've ever been privy to one of our pigouts, it wouldn't have been pretty," I replied, causing Martin to laugh, hard, when I added, "Though, truth be told, you wouldn't have found any crumbs, either."

"Fair enough," he replied. "Maybe later."

I nodded, "Maybe."

"About that. I think you two should come to my—Randy's house until we can get this situation with the alarm straightened out."

"I'm sure we can get it fixed."

"Not until tomorrow, at the earliest," he replied, nodding at the clock. "It's too late to have a tech come out. Besides, we're talking one night…a few hours. It would certainly make this old man feel better, knowing you were safe…safer, anyway."

I shrugged. "Let's see what Leah finds out and go from there, okay?"

As if on cue, she tossed her bedroom door open and stormed out. "You will not believe this!"

I rolled my eyes as I gestured for her to continue. I'd believe just about anything at this point.

"They claimed we canceled our service," she huffed.

"Well, I'm sure I paid their bill last week for an entire ninety-day period, so I think they've cut us a few weeks short," I replied dryly.

Leah shrugged, frowning as she referenced her notes. "Gal said that according to their records, the person who contacted them"—she paused to grace Martin with an Oscar-worthy stink eye—"provided all of the details necessary to access and make adjustments to our services. She also said they can supply us with a printout of the conversation as proof."

"A printout?" I scoffed. "How about an actual recording of this person's voice?"

She shook her head, chewing her lip before responding, "Not possible, the conversation took place through a chat window on their site."

"You can cancel your alarm services through a chat window?" Martin looked as surprised as I was.

"It seems so," was her reply.

"So, it could have been anybody," I commented.

"Provided they had the correct information," she replied.

"How did you leave it with them?" I asked.

"They will be out tomorrow to upgrade the system, free-of-charge, and will credit you another six months, if you choose to stay with them."

"Okay, what am I getting with this upgrade? Considering the system failed when I needed it, this has got to be pretty good. Like a trip to Bali."

"No trip...though after much kerfuffling, there was an offer to put us up for the night at a hotel, if we don't feel safe staying."

Martin shook his head. "Arianna and I have already discussed a resolution for that."

Leah squinted at Martin, then at me. "What am I missing?"

"Martin has offered to provide us with accommodations until our security issues have been addressed," I managed to choke out.

Martin looked downright pleased.

I expected her to balk, but she nodded and patted his arm. "I think Martin's got a darn good idea there. Thank you, Martin. We would be pleased to accept your generous offer." I glanced at my friend, wondering when she'd been replaced with a cyborg.

I released a sigh of relief when Leah winked, just as Martin turned to collect the garbage bag.

"Then it's settled. Once we clean up here, why don't the two of you pack a quick overnight bag and a few snacks for Nicoh? I will run ahead and grab us some appropriate nourishment. You girls like cookies. How about some ice cream to go with those?" Martin not only seemed happy, he seemed human.

"Throw in a pizza or two and you've got yourself a proper slumber party, Papason." Leah chortled.

This time, I wanted to smack her and the look I shot her said as much. She merely chuckled and shrugged.

When Martin handed her the beret she had dropped when we ran into the house and said, "This looks like it belongs to you. I'd hate for it to get all sooty." I was the one who got the last laugh.

The stymied look on Leah's face, coupled with her open-mouthed expression and her sudden inability to string together enough words to form one of her classic comebacks?

That's right—priceless.

CHAPTER TWENTY-THREE

Once Martin left for Randy's house for whatever preparations he needed to make for our impromptu sleepover, Leah and I went on a quick mission to ensure the house was secure in our absence. Or at least as secure as it could be given the circumstances.

We'd just finished checking all of the windows when she turned to me. I had noted prior to this she had been uncommonly quiet.

"Thank you for not telling Martin about Jere, you know, when you were filling him in on the details about Winslow being Jeannie's son."

I paused to look at her and found her peering at me earnestly. "I didn't think it was my story to tell."

"Unfortunately, I think all of this is your story." She sighed. "It always has been."

"Still, you know what I mean," I replied, not questioning or angry with her assessment.

It was, after all, my reality.

She nodded. "I do, and I appreciate it."

"Have you…made any decisions?"

"About whether to tell him? Or when?"

"Either. Both." I shrugged.

"When I do, you'll be the second to know," she replied, pausing before adding, "unless everything goes haywire. Then you'll be the third."

Satisfied we'd the done the best we could in securing the fortress in our absence, while giving the impression we were still home, we collected Nicoh and exited through the back gate, traversing the alley that would lead us to the street. The irony did not escape me, as it was the same alley where I'd discovered the body of a young woman.

A young woman whom I had never met when she still breathed life, but had been my twin sister.

* * *

The lights were bright and welcoming as we approached Randy's house and had I not known better, it appeared Martin was hosting a party.

Starting up the steps, I turned to my best friend. "Are you sure you're up for this?"

"The man does know how to bake a mean cookie," she replied, causing me to hesitate before ringing the doorbell.

Wait—had she actually snagged one from the plate?

If she had, she had done so quite artfully, as they had been plated for a Jenga tournament.

Catching my expression, she licked the tips of her fingers and then performed a zipping motion across her mouth. As we ascended the steps and I pressed the doorbell—for probably the first time ever since I'd been coming to this house—we both had a good chuckle.

Martin opened the door, surprising us both as he sported a retro Arizona Coyotes t-shirt, jeans and tennis shoes.

"Goodness, I didn't know this was going to be a formal event," he replied...ushering us in. "After all, I was quite sure you already knew your way around." When we both appeared stuck mid-step, our mouths agape, he chuckled. "My apologies, I was simply referring to the fact that you have been Mr. Newman's neighbor for a number of years. And considering your canine pal and his were friendly, I assumed you'd had occasion to stop by and were able to bypass the formalities, such as ringing the front doorbell?"

Leah glanced at me and I nodded as we entered the home, which had miraculously, in a matter of hours, transformed from the shell of a house our pal Randy had left behind, to a welcoming, lived in and inviting abode—where music played in the background, the lighting tended our pathway into the living space and the scents emanating from the kitchen...downright enticing.

In a word...it felt...homey.

"Err...hey Martin, who's your decorator?" Leah's voice was breathy as she took in the subtle but elegant touches that he'd added in such a short span of time.

He chuckled. "It's been a long time since I've had a home. And much, much longer since I've had an occasion in which to entertain." He glanced at me. "I'll admit, Alison rubbed off on me. She was so...creative...so inspired and while she was not a homemaker...she knew how to make any space feel like home. I always admired that and have tried to take that sentiment with me, whatever my surroundings. As it turns out, this one's probably been the most promising in a long while, for many reasons."

He glanced at me and though I was feeling oddly connected to him at this moment, looked downward and scuffed my old Chucks across one another as the blush took over and I attempted to formulate words while separating them from the emotions that were in a battle.

I'd had a wonderful family who had raised and loved me as

their own even though I wasn't their flesh and blood. To have the constant reminder of what might have been...with my sister, Victoria, Martin and Alison...was not only painful. It was excruciating. Perhaps as the only two that remained of our family, that was the bond—or the burden—we shared. We were the lone survivors.

Thankfully, without a bunch of awkward throat-clearing, Leah interjected, "Well, Alison obviously had many amazing talents."

Martin broke his gaze and suddenly found himself at a loss for words and under his own flush. I mouthed a "thank you" to my best friend, who winked.

"She was...a gem." He finally composed himself, though his mind seemed elsewhere.

It gave me the opportunity to get my own game back on track. "Well, something smells divine...and not at all like takeout pizza."

Martin finally snapped back into the present, offering me a broad grin. "Why order it when you can make it?"

"You made pizza?" Leah squealed while clapping her hands.

"Well, I did used to live in Chicago." Martin offered her a shy smile and a bow. "Besides no self-respecting Chicagoan—temporary or otherwise—would order takeout...from Papa Pizza or John's Hut or whatever those places are you Arizonans tend to favor. Besides, in my time away, I've honed my cooking and baking skills and found, like science, they can be just as fulfilling."

We moved into the kitchen and stood in front of Randy's pizza oven, peering in like small children as he continued, "I've made a Greek pizza, a classic Italian pizza and of course, a few pizza bones for the pup. Also, a nice Caesar salad with fresh grated Parmigiano-Reggiano. And to start the meal, I've selected a nice red wine. And, if you're still awake after such a heavy meal, I've also made a pitcher of fresh lime-squeezed margaritas to pair with our John Hughes' movie marathon." After surveying our expressions, he apparently felt the need to add, "I assume you girls are familiar with his movies?"

We both giggled like fourth-graders and I gave him a quick wink, given our previous conversation on the subject.

Perhaps Martin was overdoing it but he, too, seemed genuinely happy as we dished out pizza and oohed and ahhed over its deliciousness and fought over pizza crusts. Even Nicoh, who was granted his own bones after his usual bowl of kibble, seemed content as he rolled on his side, whoo-whooing for Martin to give him belly scratches.

After a scrumptious bowl of spumoni—homemade and not with crappy kind of candied fruit—Martin ushered us into Randy's den-turned movie theater.

"What would you like to start with, *The Breakfast Club* or *Sixteen Candles*? I'm not sure why, but *The Great Outdoors* always makes me chuckle. Anything after that…as you kids say, 'Meh, not so much…'"

Again, we acted pretty silly, even for us. Suddenly, caught up in the moment, Leah jumped, her eyes wide. "Oh, my God. My beret. I don't want to start a Hughes-a-thon without my beret."

"Your lucky beret." I wasn't clarifying, merely mocking, but she was oblivious.

"Do you mind?" She ignored me completely and when Martin nodded, bolted out the door, not bothering to turn as she shouted, "Be back faster than you can whip up that Jiffy Pop."

Martin glanced at me, confused.

"Don't worry. This is a pretty normal occurrence." I patted his knee as I rose to let Nicoh into the backyard. "You'll learn to get used to it. I did."

He nodded and though he cued up *The Breakfast Club*,

glanced at me curiously. "I hope you don't take offense, but I always took you for more of a Cusack sort of girl, you know, instead of that Rat Pack."

I chuckled. "I think you mean Brat Pack. You should know, *Sixteen Candles* and *Say Anything* are still Hughes' movies, which Cusack is in," when Martin's brows creased, I added, "though you've got my number, I always liked him the best. I mean…how can you beat *Better Off Dead*? You know…'two dollars'?"

Martin laughed. "I do know…but seriously, I was thinking more along the lines of *Con Air*…or *Gross Pointe Blank*?"

He laughed even harder when I couldn't formulate a response and suddenly felt myself wanting that pitcher of margaritas, until he commented, "I think you have something that belongs to me."

I snorted. "So you keep telling me, Martin."

"No, not the chips," he replied. "I meant the picture you took from my pack."

"Oh," I was completely taken off-guard, feeling like the child who had stolen the pixie stick from the local store despite the fact she had money in her hot little hands. I pulled it from my back pocket and after tenderly opening it, placed it in his hands, careful not to look in his eyes as I did so. "I hope I didn't damage it."

He was silent for a long while, though I knew he was staring, I wasn't sure if it was at the world-worn photo, or at me.

"I guess I was just curious." I finally broke the silence. "About your past."

"I'm not in this photo." He nodded at it as he attempted to press out the creases. It was in pretty bad shape, though, and the four sections wouldn't play nice, each one taunting him, rising up again as he smoothed it down.

I shook my head. "I know…but you took it, didn't you?"

He didn't raise his head, his focus remaining on the snapshot of his past.

"How did you know?"

"The woman—Jeannie…" I pointed. "She's winking…at you."

Martin looked away and nodded. "It was a long time ago."

"You mentioned that she fancied you but that you rebuffed her advances." My tone bore no judgment, a fact which was not lost on Martin as he turned to face me.

"I never engaged her. Or allowed her to think otherwise."

I lifted a hand. "Martin. You do not need to explain to me. I do…understand."

"Do you…child?"

It was not uttered in a condescending way nor did I take offense.

I nodded. "It was always about Alison."

He smiled and grasped my hand. "She was…my world."

He shoved the photo away, as though it would burn him if he got too close or continued searching it to find the answers to his past.

"She was everything," he repeated, "and then…she was gone."

"You never told any of them, though"—I nodded at the photo —"because they wouldn't have understood."

He bowed his head and I continued, fearing that he would retreat into his mind if he felt the world—his child—was casting judgment upon him. "But she understood, too…didn't she? She told you it was okay to keep the secret."

Martin shuddered and a single cry erupted. For a moment, I wasn't sure who or what released it—it was almost inhuman, except for the pain it revealed. No, no inanimate object could have conjured that sound.

"She knew that evil was in the midst," he whispered, his voice shaky. "She always knew."

"Do you think the others were aware?"

He pressed his eyes closed and I wasn't sure whether it was to remember or to shut out the memories. "I...I don't know," he replied, quiet for a moment before opening his eyes and nodding. "Yes, I think near the end, some of them could have ventured a fairly accurate guess." He shook his head. "But I don't know, for sure. Time...and the monsters...play their games on one's mind."

"And once you...disappeared, you never spoke to Jerri, her sister, or even Robert, again?" I didn't bother mentioning Theo because we were both painfully aware what the answer to that question was.

"No, I had no reason to seek them out—afterward—all I wanted was to leave that life behind," he replied, almost sounding angry as he squinted and ground out the words.

I did not mention that in his escape, he had also left Victoria and me behind. It was ground we had already covered and there was no sense tearing at that wound any longer.

And despite the fact Martin's desire had been to escape that life, he hadn't.

"You should probably know, Jerri Fenton stopped by for an impromptu visit. She not only knows you are alive, she is also aware that you are the person responsible for accosting her son, the Congressman."

His eyes went wide. "What...Jerri? How? Why?"

"It was quite an...interesting visit. She begged me to reach out to you and persuade you to stop obsessing over Gemini. Basically, she was convinced you were single-handedly going to set the end of days in motion."

Martin looked at the ceiling, shaking his head. "Jerri...said this?"

I nodded. "She did, more or less. Then again, I was still getting over the shock of finding her at my doorstep, must less divulging the information—even making the request—that she did. When Leah returns, she can confirm the finer points of the conversation. She's better at remembering all the nitty-gritty details."

He waved a hand, as though he was comfortable taking me at my word. "Perhaps I shouldn't be all that surprised that she is aware I'm alive. Though it is a bit daunting and makes things considerably more challenging."

When I raised a brow, he added, "Others, including her husband, probably already did. But the fact that she would believe that I would be instrumental in bringing about the end of days?" He thrust his head into his hands. "Oh, Robert, what have you done? What did Theodore convince you to do?" After raising his head, he turned to me, his face serious. "Tell me, Arianna, what else did Jerri say?"

I nodded and filled him in on the rest of our conversation as I watched the man who would have been my father collapse on the couch when I finished.

I felt kind of bad adding, "She made quite a grand exit, claiming that the project had been named after her. And while she had said it in the singular, if it were indeed true, it likely would have included *both* Jerri and her sister."

I wondered if Jerri hadn't been a bit arrogant in her claim, though I surveyed Martin as he squinted and nodded.

"Gemini," he whispered, slumping further into his seat.

His skin had lost its flush and his eyes were focused… nowhere. Suddenly, I worried I'd forced a stroke upon him, until he commented, "It was going on right in front of me all along but I just couldn't see what I wasn't willing to accept."

"It's human nature, Martin." I leaned forward, patting him on the arm, more to see if I would get a reaction than as a gesture of comfort and fortunately it worked, as he slowly shrugged me off, frowning as though he had been caught exhibiting weakness.

After straightening his frame and perhaps a careful deliberation of his choice of words, he faced me. "Surely, there was more?"

If he hadn't been so serious, I probably would have snickered and made a snide Shirley comment but as it was, he was indeed… quite serious. So I gave him a serious response, equally careful in my framing.

"Nothing. She pretty much left after dropping the Gemini bombshell." His frown was so deep I thought it would leave permanent marks, so I drummed up a mere curious curiosity. "On a separate note, I would like to know—how the heck did you ever manage to tell Jerri and Jeannie apart?" I pointed at the picture.

"It was always a chore, especially with all their shenanigans when it came to swapping places, though according to what you previously told me about Theodore, he apparently wasn't all that discriminating when it came to the twins."

I nodded, absently, still staring at the photo. "Huh. It's not apparent here—perhaps it happened after this photo was taken—but once Jerri sustained that scar, I'm sure it made differentiating her from her sister a lot easier, even when she tried disguising it with makeup. Then again, perhaps the accident that caused it occurred after Jeannie had already passed."

Martin surprised me when he advanced on me and lifted me by my shoulders. "What scar?"

I could only stare at him, open-mouthed. When he shook me, I responded, "Err…the one that runs from the left of her top lip and ends just beneath the lower on the right. I'm pretty sure most people wouldn't even notice because it's not that visible unless she's standing right in front of you—"

This time, Martin scared me. He shook me. Hard.

"Arianna, stop. Jerri didn't have a scar."

I nodded in the direction of the photo. "Well, not there she doesn't."

Though I was shocked by his reaction, I was careful to keep

my response and my tone calm. "It's probably something that happened after you…left. You know the saying…life happens." I winced, he probably wasn't familiar with the phrase, nor would be the sort to appreciate it.

Martin shook his head, but not for the reason I had expected. "No. It happened before…I left."

"Urr, you've lost me…*what* happened?" I put a hand on his and squeezed.

The movement jarred something in him because he released his vice-like grip on my shoulders and backed away, balling his hands at his sides.

"The accident that caused the scar."

"Uh…okay…what accident?" I managed to stutter out as Martin began pacing.

Finally, he spoke, though he gripped his head and the pacing increased two-fold. "It was awful. I didn't mean to hurt her but she was so insistent on having her way as she continued her attempt at throwing herself at me. It wasn't the first time but it was, the last. As before, I repeatedly told her no, but when she continued her advances and proceeded to undress and thrust herself at me, I pushed her."

Martin paused to suck in a harsh breath as he covered his mouth, his eyes wide. "I pushed her, way too hard, causing her to stumble and as she fell, she had nothing to brace herself with. Her head…her face connected with the sample vials we had collected earlier that day and when she hit the bench and crushed the glass…oh, God, there was so much blood. I didn't mean to hurt her. I just wanted her to stop."

"Martin, it's okay." It was my turn to go to him, pull him in by the shoulders and gently shake him until he looked at me. "It was an accident. Jerri's scar…it was nothing but a horrible, senseless accident."

Martin shrugged free from me, surprising me again as he spun on his heel so that he didn't have to face me.

"No, Arianna! No!" His voice was as angry as I'd ever witnessed and still, he batted away any form of comfort. "You don't understand." His voice cracked when he added, "Jerri didn't have a scar—Jeannie did."

CHAPTER TWENTY-FOUR

I was still registering the bombshell Martin had dropped when she entered, holding a knife to my best friend's throat.

Leah's eyes were wide and mine mirrored hers once I noticed the crimson trickling down her neck. I opened my mouth but somehow couldn't form the words. My heart was speaking for me as it thudded against my chest.

Of course, no one could hear it but me.

The woman took my reaction as an opportunity to lazily lick the trail of blood. I recognized bat guano crazy when I saw it. She would slit my best friend's throat, solely for the sport of it, just to finally have access to the prize she'd sought for so long.

"You've always been a bit slow to the punchline, Marty," her voice was husky and her eyes glistened as she took him in after all of the years that had passed. She did not appear disappointed, smiling in a way that exposed too much tooth and gums.

"It's been a long time, Jeannie," Martin replied, surveying her in kind while keeping a watchful eye on the weapon she brandished. "Seems we've both risen from our graves."

"Only I evolved," she sneered.

"Did you?"

Martin inched closer as I sucked in a breath. Did I trust him with Leah's life? In the end, fear of not acting reigned and I allowed him to play his hand. He understood this woman in ways I never could.

"After all of the tricks you and your sister played, it probably wasn't that much of a stretch to take her place…permanently. She had the husband, the adoration and the social status you both always felt you were entitled to, after all."

Jeannie straightened her neck as though it was a role she was destined to play, until he added, "Tell me, was Jerri part of the punchline? Or did you let her down easy when you allowed her to die, knowing that you would be the one who would reap the spoils of everything she'd managed to acquire? Knowing you as I do, I suppose you even deemed it some sort of sacrifice."

"You're one to talk," she snapped. "Stepping out on your wife and child…children. Look how that turned out for you. Not counting your own pathetic life, you're down two, with only one left. What will you do with *that* opportunity, Marty? Sacrifice it? Or destroy it like you did the rest?"

"One would say your sacrificial count is a bit higher. When did you decide your sister was no longer of value?" Perhaps dear Jerri, now outed as Jeannie, was farsighted because both Leah and I watched in horror as Martin tested the boundaries of crazy and stepped closer to the woman who still held the blade of certain death to my friend's neck.

"No longer of value?" Jeannie tossed her head back and had a good laugh but it came from a wicked, dark place. "My sister… died because of your stupid project."

"Do tell, because I had no part of her death. I heard about her cancer after the fact and was truly sorry to hear about her passing. And yet, here you are, all these years later, acting as though you are owed something."

"Are you judging me, Marty? Because I'll have you know,

right now. You. Have. No. Right."

Unfortunately, she enunciated each word with a jab to my friend's neck, resulting in an unnerving blood draw.

"And while you are either too embarrassed to say it outright, or being downright coy, as I expect you are—yes, both my sister and I became…friendly with Theodore. The man was brilliant and together the two of you have could have changed the world, if you hadn't been so righteous and short-sided. Your betrayal cost us all and in the end, transformed him into a vengeful, maniacal monster. Had you stayed and honored your commitment, things would have turned out differently, for all of us."

"What a lovely fairytale, Jeannie," Martin replied, crossing his arms as he eyed her. "You keep telling yourself that every time you look in the mirror. Right now, let's talk about the children. Your children."

"It was part of the deal I made with Theodore. I was simply a donor. So you can't judge me for what I chose to do or not do," she replied through gritted teeth.

Martin tilted his head. "You can say that so easily, even after you learned what became of them?"

Jeannie shrugged. "It was a small price to pay."

"For what?"

"Freedom. From Theodore. From all of it. By that time, Jerri was married and taking care of a child."

"Was she already sick?" Martin shifted ever so slightly.

Leah and I—me more so that her—watched as they did their dance.

"After she had the boy, her immune system was weakened, allowing the sickness to dig in even deeper and eventually take over. It wasn't long before she knew her days were running out."

"So, the whole thing was her idea," Martin replied, his tone dour, "and despite being on her deathbed, she still had the foresight and the wherewithal to craft a plan that included you taking over her life."

"You aren't a twin, Marty," she snapped, frowning as she continued, "You couldn't possibly understand. We both just knew what had to be done."

"And Robert never knew, despite the scar." It was not a question.

Jeannie shook her head once. "Robert never knew. He wasn't really a detail man, wouldn't have noticed an imperfection on a woman's face if she'd tattooed an arrow next to it. Besides, why did it matter, really? I took care of his child. Raised him to become…what he is."

"While you allowed one of your own children to become a monster," Martin replied, her face remaining a stony mask despite the blow he'd dealt.

I looked at Leah and could tell, even though she'd lost blood, she still had fight left in her and right now, she wanted to punch Martin in the throat. I didn't blame her, considering it was her neck on the line.

"Your daughter killed him. Would you call her a monster, too?" Surprisingly, Jeannie didn't sound angry.

She was…amused.

She'd also gotten Martin's number, as he puffed up, pointing at me. "She did what she had to do, in self-defense and in defense of others."

I rolled my eyes. Of all the times Martin could choose to have my back, he thought *this* was the appropriate time?

Still, and perhaps, thankfully, Jeannie played with him. Batting him about like a cat with a bell and a string as she gave him a toothy grin, which made her scar all that more noticeable.

"Is that what you tell yourself about Theodore, Marty? That you acted in self-defense when you broke his neck? What is that like, anyway, to wield that final blow? To know that you ended a life?"

Martin chewed the inside of his jaw and I took the opportunity to step in. "You don't seem all that concerned that he killed your sister."

She looked at Martin.

Did she not know?

I shook my head. "Not Martin. Theodore. Theodore was responsible for your sister's death."

Time stopped as she eyed me.

"Surely you were aware that he signed the death certificate. You took the copy from Leah's bag."

I raised a hand when she opened her mouth and waved her off. Both Leah and Martin watched me. Leah looked hopeful. Martin…it was hard to say. We were working with less of an emotional rainbow.

I pressed on, "Or, more specifically, what became *your* death certificate. How that came about doesn't matter—part of the deal, yada, yada—but what you didn't know was that he killed her off when she became a loose end he couldn't afford to have out there. Perhaps, unlike you, she actually loved him at some point. In order to ensure she didn't become a problem down the road, he had to eliminate her."

"My sister had cancer." Jeannie shook her head, staring intently at me, as though imploring me to stop.

It was in that moment I realized that she too had been bitten by the snake that was Theodore Winslow. This would be a bitter pill to swallow.

I had to wonder if we would be here had she known the truth.

"Google it, Jeannie." I held out my phone. "That particular cancer—the one listed on the death certificate—it's hereditary. And in case you don't know what I mean by that, if she'd actually had it, *both* of you would have exhibited signs at some point. And any offspring either of you had would have it, too. You don't have it. Bob Jr., from all accounts, looks pretty darn healthy and hasn't shown any signs."

I paused to gauge her reaction before continuing. Yep, I definitely had her attention, though her expression was unreadable as her eyes bore into me.

"Theo lied about so many things along the way. You are well aware of that. So why would lying about your sister's cause of death be out of bounds?" She opened her mouth to protest but I raised a hand. "I'm not denying she was sick but it wasn't from cancer. More likely, Theo had poisoned or injected her with something that mimicked the symptoms—that's what killed her."

Jeannie squinted at me, perhaps trying to read my BS meter. "Is that true, Marty?"

Martin shifted from one leg to the other and frowned. "I don't know. I haven't seen the certificate, but I trust AJ and her friend. They have impeccable research skills, not to mention an endless stream of resources to turn to."

"If what she says is true, then why didn't Theodore kill me, too?" she asked. "He obviously knew we'd switched places..." Her voice trailed off as she looked from Martin to me and back.

It was a very good question—one for which we would never have an answer.

Unfortunately, Leah used it as an opportunity to open her piehole and ventured her own guess. "Perhaps he just never got around to it."

She was rewarded with another prick of the knife, causing her to wince.

"I think what my friend is trying to say is that perhaps your plan with your sister precluded whatever Theo had devised for you," I offered.

Jeannie tilted her head, and used the knife to gesture for me to continue.

"By swapping places, you actually solved a problem for him. Perhaps by having you and Robert in one place, he could not only keep an eye on you both, he could reach out to you whenever he needed to compel you to persuade Robert into helping him in some way."

I shouldn't have made the assumption that Robert was the stronger of the two of them. Jeannie clearly didn't appreciate it, scoffing. I raised my hands in surrender.

"Okay, that scenario could have just as easily been the other way around. Regardless, you wanted to know why he hadn't killed you, too. In the end, maybe keeping you alive gave him some leverage, especially considering your son's political clout. You would have been in a position to help Theo acquire things he needed—compliance, resources, funding, whatever—things that allowed him to achieve his goals."

I paused, noting every eye was on me and one pair in particular would have cut right through me had lasers been attached. I closed my mouth—realizing too late that I'd made a serious misstep with that last comment.

I knew it was coming but time stood still as the fury rose and finally Jeannie snapped. "My son's political clout? You killed *my* son," she seethed from behind clenched teeth, pulling Leah closer and teasing her throat with the side of the knife.

Martin interjected, "I believe we already covered that ground, Jeannie. And need I remind you that your son also killed her parents. Her sister. And his own twin—or did you forget about your other son?"

Jeannie glared at him and for a moment, I worried he'd gone too far—and that Leah would pay for it.

Instead, she raised her head and sniffed. "Is that the way you really want to play it, Marty—an eye for an eye?"

Her tone was mocking...testing him.

Martin merely shrugged. "Let's be honest, isn't that why you are here?"

"Meaning?" She squinted at him.

I, too, was curious about the rabbit hole he was taking us down.

He crossed his arms, studying her, before responding, "Alison."

Leah grimaced and I worked to keep the emotion off my face. Way to rub salt in the wound, I thought.

Thankfully, Jeannie was amused, chuckling in a way that bordered on the obnoxious side, though considering she was still waving that knife, she had long crossed that boundary into maniacal.

"Oh yes, dear, sweet Alison." She stopped mid-cackle to level a stare at Martin that would have melted a two-ton ice sculpture. "No, Marty. I don't think so."

"What?" Martin managed to eke out.

"We are talking about Alison, are we not?" Jeannie's tone had turned snotty. "She doesn't really fall into that green-eyed monster category."

"You weren't jealous of her?"

Jeannie snickered. "Jealous? Of her? Hardly..."

I was with Martin on this one. Jeannie was saying one thing but her tone and her body language were saying quite another. I decided to pick up my stick and jab at the bear, hoping curiosity would keep Jeannie from taking my friend's life.

"Fair enough. As you suggested before, she barely made it onto your radar. Still, something's not clicking for me here, Jerri...sorry, Jeannie. Perhaps you could help me connect the dots?"

She narrowed her eyes and studied me and after a moment, granted me a single head nod. I readied my stick for another poke.

"If you're not here to get revenge because Martin chose

Alison over you, then why are you here? In the years since you took your sister's place, you've had a pretty nice life…lots of money, beautiful houses all over the world, a husband who doted over you and a son who admires you and who has made you proud and will likely do so again when he and his lovely wife bring a grandchild into the world. Heck…sounds like a dream world to me."

Jeannie nodded, then glared at Martin. "It was. Until he showed up again."

Martin opened his hands to her. "Jeannie, I swear. I pose no threat to you. My intention was merely to prevent…them from allowing what happened to you and your sister to happen again."

"What happened to us?" Jeannie sneered, jabbing the knife in his direction as she enunciated each word. "As though you didn't have a hand in any of it?" When he opened his mouth but failed to respond immediately, she snorted and shook her head in disgust. "That's rich, Marty, even coming from you."

Martin looked down, quiet for a moment before responding, "I'll take ownership for what I was responsible for in the past. I may have made choices—many of them poor—including running away from the truth. But I am here now and I'll be damned if I am going to allow them to bring that monstrosity back to life."

"Just exactly who do you believe these people are—the 'them' you keep referencing?" Jeannie squinted at him, a smirk playing at the corner of her mouth. "You sound like a lonely, paranoid old goat, a conspiracy nut who's lost track of time, and his marbles."

Martin ignored her quip. "You must know who I am referencing? Robert surely mentioned the consortium?"

"Robert?" The amusement playing out in her smile was getting a full round of rides for free. Finally, she shook her head. "I think you're mistaken, Marty. The man was a cog in the machine. Come on, you're not too old to remember how Theodore treated him. You witnessed it, right alongside the rest of us. Robert couldn't have rubbed two sticks together to build a fire without direction. Right up until the day he died."

"I don't understand," Martin replied, frowning.

Jeannie laughed. "No, of course you don't. You never…got it…did you? At the end of the day, you were all pawns."

"So you are seeking revenge because I killed Theodore, your beloved what? Muse? Mentor?"

Martin was really reaching at straws. I can't say I blamed him. I still couldn't figure out what this woman was ultimately after and unfortunately, until we tapped into that well, my friend's neck —and life—were hanging by a thread.

"That's the point you missed. You all missed. Just another cog. Another tool," Jeannie replied, her mouth forming a vicious sneer.

Martin tilted his head. "But if you removed all the cogs, you got nothing but a spokeless wheel that serves no purpose—"

Jeannie cut him off. "Not all the cogs, Marty. I've still got you. And more importantly, I've got her." She jabbed the bloodied end of the knife in my direction.

As I glared at the object of my aggression, Martin continued to engage Jeannie in her cryptic conversation. "Arianna doesn't have anything you want. I do."

Watching Jeannie sneer, I shook my head. "I think you're missing the point, Marty. It was never about Gemini." Martin turned to me, his face a mix of frustration and confusion. "It was about revenge. It always was. Gemini was just used to draw you out—the threat of resurrecting it—the real prize was getting you into the ring for the final fight."

His eyes widened as he looked from me to Jeannie. "This was never about Gemini?"

Jeannie shrugged, pursing her lips. "I could care less whether it's resurrected."

You could almost see the wheels turning as Martin shifted

from one leg to the other, frowned, mused and mouthed things that only he could hear. And, if his demeanor was any indication, he seemed downright incensed about it.

In my opinion, it was about time.

Finally, when he spoke, his did so slowly, either because he was choosing his words, or still registering the chain of events in his mind. I couldn't speak for him but I was guessing it was the latter. Which meant, things could go either way.

"So...all of this," he waved his hands about, ending with a gesture toward Leah, "Was orchestrated solely for the purpose of drawing me out by threatening the very thing I love, so that you could exact your revenge?"

Jeannie studied him and sneered. "Listen to you...'threatening the thing you love'? One might believe you were actually talking about your daughter but for you, it's always been about Gemini, hasn't it?" She glanced at me, snorting as she returned her gaze to him. "Poor thing has gone through life thinking she's been just like every child. Every teenager. Every collegiate. Every young entrepreneur just trying to make her mark in this world. Not realizing, all this time, that she's always been a pawn. Because she has something you want. It comes down to you, Marty—not me."

She paused to gauge his reaction and had I been on her side, I would have given her a high five—because, based upon his expression alone—she not only scored, she'd won the round.

"So, yes, perhaps I am getting even—and it's a two-for-one deal. I end her life and destroy your chances of getting back together with the thing you love most—the illusive Gemini. One has to wonder, had she lived, could Alison compete?"

Martin worked his jaw, squinting as though he'd drawn a troubling conclusion. "You were the one who killed her, weren't you? At the hospital."

Jeannie smiled and nodded. "Yes. I ended your precious Alison, shortly after she'd given birth. Years later, I connected with my son—my real son—and ordered him to kill your daughter, Victoria. Now, I have the honor of personally killing your final living spawn right in front of you." She laughed. It was a dry, wicked sound. "How does that make you feel, Marty?"

Martin frowned. "Why? Why this? Because I told you I didn't favor you? Or accept your advances over two decades ago?"

Jeannie clucked her tongue, as though he was a simpleton. "Oh Marty, you never could see the opportunities that were standing right in front of you. I knew you were the brains behind the project. I had money, connections and together we could have ruled the world. But you lacked vision. Or, at the very least, one that did not include Alison."

"That was your objective, Jeannie. And Theo's. Unlike you, I didn't want to rule the world. I simply wanted to make it a better place."

Jeannie shook her head and chuckled. "That's a sweet notion. Kind of like world peace, but what people like you never seem to register is that there is no peace without dissension, no apathy without anarchy—"

"No light without dark," I interjected, casting a glance from Leah to Martin. "It's about balance."

It was an easy thing to throw out but I also meant for it to serve as a Hail Mary flag—we needed to figure out a way to shut this witch down—and fast. Jeannie had been given more than her fifteen minutes—and we'd been overly generous—time for her to get the hell off of our stage.

Still, I knew I needed to allow her to play out her hand. It was, after all, merely a warning that I was nearing my limit. I was going Ronda Rousey on this woman—and even given her age—knew she would be a worthy opponent—one that I would grant no free pass. Especially if she planned on ending my life and the lives of the ones I loved.

I was aware of Jeannie's gaze upon me. And I hated what I

saw in her eyes. Regardless, I needed to keep still and play my part, knowing that at the end, all would be okay.

And that victory would be tasty.

Call me an optimist.

"Your daughter is smart, Marty," she finally commented, after grazing me from head to toe.

I should have charged her an inconvenience fee, but let it slide.

Instead, I played the game and hoped that she would at the very least, entertain my offer. "Out of curiosity, call it a twin courtesy, if you like. But let's walk this through. It's only fair." Once Jeannie granted me a head nod, I continued, "Did you also view your sister as a cog? A pawn in the game we like to call life?"

Jeannie smiled and not in a kind way. "I accept your courtesy and pose one of my own. Once you knew your sister existed, how would you have responded to the same question? Knowing that after all these years, that things could have…should have been different, had alternate choices been made?" She shot Martin a nasty glare.

I shook my head, careful not to glance at him. "I honestly can't answer that. And not because I won't. But because I never met my sister when she was alive." Jeannie tilted her head, offering me an expression that forced me to grind my teeth as I added, "The first time I made my twin sister Victoria's acquaintance, she was nothing more than bone and blood, disposed of like trash in an alley dumpster."

"How did that make you feel?" I felt her eyes scouring me and knew I needed to keep it together. If I could have launched myself and wiped that smirk off her face, it still would have yielded me no satisfaction.

My sister and Alison would still be dead, along with the mother and father who loved me and raised me as their own.

So, given the circumstances, I answered as truthfully as I

could. "I felt bad for her and for the loss of her life, but felt nothing more than sadness and confusion, as I knew nothing of our bond."

This time, she squinted at me as she asked, "You never once…felt it?"

I shrugged and shook my head. "I can't say I did."

Though I had been honest, my response incensed her deeply, as she huffed like a bull while giving me her best death stare. "Then perhaps you are no better than I am."

I tilted my head. "For the record, you're the only one brandishing a weapon and holding us all at bay." Before she could speak, I took out my second stick, hoping it wouldn't fail me. "I'd say this act of yours—claiming revenge for your sister, your sons…even yourself—has been more about ego and attention-grabbing than any gesture of compassion or loyalty on your part. It's about entitlement. Yours."

"You really want to test me."

I noted her response was not framed in the form of a question, confirming Jeannie didn't understand the rules of *Jeopardy*. Yeah, perhaps I was high on smoke fumes from the burned-out couch or maybe just exhausted from lack of sleep, but something overtook me.

I yawned, pointing at her, then at Martin, before patting my mouth sleepily and responding, "Well, since you asked so nicely, actually what I really want is a good night's sleep without having either of you lording over me, especially with a steak knife."

"You are a cagey one, Arianna Jackson."

Jeannie laughed and for a moment released her hold on my friend so that she could clap. Leah was so weak she swayed and ended up clinging awkwardly to Jeannie's side.

Before I could take a step, Jeannie, still chuckling, raised a hand. "Wait. Before you make that move I know you are seriously considering taking, I think I might just have to grant you that wish."

I opened my mouth to speak and snapped it shut as Ramirez walked in, a gun in one hand and Leah's beret in the other.

"Time for Arianna and her merry band of misfits to take a knee." His tone was as serious as the gun he was pointing in my direction. "Think you dropped this, Campbell."

He handed her the tattered beret, seeming to ignore her injuries. And though she was barely able to stand, she grabbed it and leaned against the wall with a sneer Billy Idol would have been proud of. Of course, this was after thanking him by way of a few choice words that our parents would have washed our mouths out for. And while the effort did nothing to improve her weakened state, she cast a look in my direction that I couldn't decipher—it was a cross between confusion and something…else.

To be honest, I wasn't registering much at that particular moment. I was battling nausea while considering which MMA moves would inflict the greatest amount of pain in the shortest amount of time as Jeannie arched up and planted a full-mouthed kiss on Ramirez, which ended with her licking a trail of God-knows-what from the base of his mouth all the way down his neck.

Both of them watched me intently as they let this PDDDA— also known as a Public Display of Downright Disgusting Affection—play out and based on their smirks, they fully enjoyed my reaction.

In order to allow my eyes a breather, I turned my attention toward Martin, who looked about as green as the Grinch as he cast a confused glance back at me. Leah looked equally exasperated, though I knew she was in no position to offer her usual commentary or help me kick anyone's butt.

Just as I'd managed to adjust my vomit-meter, Jeannie pressed her body against Ramirez's and turned her focus to his muscled chest, stroking it seductively.

"Looks like your...friend Ramirez, is actually my friend Ramirez...twin courtesy and all." She chuckled, slid a coy smile at me before planting another firm, wet kiss on him. This time, he pulled her in tightly with his free arm and returned her affection by performing his own full mouth checkup. I fisted my hands at my sides and tried to focus my energy elsewhere while trying my best not to hurl all over Randy's hand-scraped hardwood floors.

Eeew.

"*You* were the person she was talking to on the phone, at the airport," Leah's voice crackled as she worked to form the words.

Ramirez ignored her, too busy whispering sweet nothings into Jeannie's ear.

Jeannie giggled at something Ramirez said before responding, "Yes, Jonah was kind enough to inform me that my husband had passed. He's been such a godsend."

"I thought you were hired to assist the Congressman." It was not a question so rather than respond, Ramirez chose to nibble his way down Jeannie's ear, causing her to release a small squeal.

As Martin, Leah and I barely managed to keep our gag-meters in check—Leah weakly picked fuzz off her beret, while Martin and I shifted and counted boards in the flooring. We couldn't do much else, as Ramirez still had the gun handy, thanks in no part to his multi-tasking skills.

Finally, we were given a reprieve when Jeannie managed to tear herself away from her man candy to address my comment.

"You are correct, Arianna. Bob did hire Jonah to do some security work, but what he didn't realize what that his mother had also been using his special...skill set...for several months now."

"I thought Serena recommended you?" I'd erroneously addressed Ramirez.

Apparently, his meal ticket was doing all of the talking these days.

"Oh, that," she chuckled. "Before Bob married Serena, I performed the necessary research on my soon to be daughter-in-law and therefore, was already aware of her connection to Jonah and upon perusing his dossier, realized he had some…services that would be useful and invited him into my employ.

"Then, when Bob ran into his issues, I merely had to mention how nice it would be to have someone in law enforcement—someone who was already a family friend—check into the situation. Serena, being the darling she is, was more than happy to offer up the name of the person I knew she would." Jeannie laughed and waved a hand, which I noted, was still holding the knife. "You know how these things work."

"Yes, indeed I do," I paused to glare at Ramirez. "Was Mr. Fenton aware that he had a member of our prestigious law enforcement on his payroll?"

"Of course he did." She replied, almost sounding indignant that I would suggest something inappropriate was going on. "He was friends with the police chief and when Robert needed help looking into a series of threats, the chief willingly allowed Jonah to assist us on an as-needed basis, no questions asked and no one, including Bob, was to know. Call it goodwill, whatever. In the end, it was all part of the political dog and pony show."

"More like *your* dog and pony show," I heard Leah murmur.

I was glad she was still with us but surprised Jeannie had not caught the comment as I continued, "I understand why you wouldn't want Bob to get involved. He has his own political career to look out for. Especially when his father's signing checks to secure the services of a police officer who spends most of his time servicing his wife. I don't think he'd appreciate being drawn into the scandal."

Martin glanced at me and frowned. Perhaps I had taken things a bit too personally but heck, I was human.

Apparently, Jeannie was too, as her response was to giggle. When I realized it was at Ramirez's doing, I fought the urge to punch him in the throat, instead posing a question.

"So, tell me, Ramirez, how does one look themselves in the mirror each morning, justifying the fact that while you're whispering sweet nothings into Mrs. Fenton's ear, you're also putting people's lives on the line and getting paid double to do it?"

"Simple. I don't think of this as a job." His voice was husky and his eyes bore into mine as he grabbed Jeannie with both arms —to her pure and utter delight, given the pig-like squeals—and planted a big old juicy one on her on her opened lips.

I was about to cross the boundaries of common decency and proper ladylike behavior by offering him a one-finger salute, when in mid-smooch, he winked at me.

I did a double-take.

Wait—Ramirez winked at me?

As the eggs scrambled themselves in my brain, he pulled away, leaving Jeannie breathless, her eyes closed and mouth opened like a baby bird as he maintained eye contact with me and completed his thought.

"Then again, that's not really how we roll, is it...Campbell?"

Just as Jeannie opened her eyes and her mouth went from a position where it could suck down worms to one that formed an "o", Ramirez smirked—and though his eyes never left mine, he removed the knife from her hand just as my best friend conjured every last ounce of strength to reach inside of the beret she'd been clutching, extracted a hurking pistol and shoved it into the base of Jeannie's skull.

"Screw twin courtesy. We're going gangsta-style up in this nation!"

She'd mixed some of her idioms—chalk it up to blood loss—

but I was pretty sure Jeannie got the message loud and clear, her eyes wide as she squeaked.

When Ramirez snorted and removed the gun from her hands, Leah gave him a double thumbs-up before her lids drooped and she leaned back against the wall and slumped down, mumbling something that sounded vaguely like, "That's right. Check me, you freak and I'll give you a smackdown that'll make you wish you never messed with 'dis crew." She lazily snapped her fingers, murmuring, "Check, pleeease?" before passing out.

Once Ramirez secured Jeannie amid a series of death threats, cursing and overall bad behavior, he gave me a head nod and I rushed to my friend while he called for an EMT and backup. Apparently everyone, including his commanding officer, had been on standby, awaiting his call.

Thankfully, though still unconscious, Leah was breathing. Martin surprised me by rushing over with towels, blankets and everything else he could think of, kneeling beside me as I fussed over her and cast impatient glances at Ramirez, wondering where the ambulance was, even though only a few minutes had passed.

"You did good, Kid," Martin whispered.

"You didn't do too bad yourself," I replied, patting his arm.

"I'm just glad you made it out of here this time without racking up the body count." I looked up to find Ramirez looking down at me, having handed Jeannie off to another officer. I could still hear her screeching about the handcuffs and something about wanting her face to be covered when she exited to avoid any paparazzi that might be lying in wait. I looked down at the blankets Martin had brought and snorted.

"We're gonna need something bigger than this to cover that mouth."

Both men chuckled and after we moved aside to let the EMTs do their handiwork, I expected another lecture from Ramirez but he surprised me by reaching over to Martin and clasping his hand firmly.

"Mr. Singer...or is it Dr.? Either way, it's a pleasure to finally meet you. I don't know if Arianna has mentioned me in passing but my name is Jonah Ramirez. I am...usually a homicide detective for the City of Phoenix and one day, when she and I can sort things out, I am hoping you and I can get to know one another, provide that you and she have also mended your ways. I've grown...quite fond of her and am hoping that nothing you've heard about me would sway your decision about wanting to spend a bit of time together, with either of us."

"Thank you for the offer, Detective," Martin replied, trying to keep the smile that was fighting the corner of his mouth under wraps. "I appreciate your candor but at the moment, I'd appreciate it if you would do me a courtesy," he paused, his serious tone taking the characteristically unflappable Ramirez off-guard as his eyes widened.

He nodded but his mouth was pinched as he squinted at Martin, who took one look at Ramirez and chuckled before adding, "I'd appreciate it if you would drop the Mr. Singer—and the Dr.—and just call me Martin."

Ramirez smiled and the two shook hands, just as the officer in charge approached. I bit my lip and glanced at Martin, who blew out a long breath and patted my hand. Neither of us was sure what to expect—the turn of events up to this point had been a surprise, if not more than a bit of a shocker.

"Lieutenant McElroy, this is Martin Anders. He's currently renting the property from Randy Newman. Arianna Jackson and Leah Campbell are neighbors and were visiting Mr. Anders when the suspect, Jerri Fenton, entered the home wielding a knife on Leah Campbell, who she had taken as a hostage in order to elicit compliance from Mr. Anders and Ms. Jackson."

The lieutenant listened but I noticed him glancing at me with a bit of a twinkle in his eye as he absorbed the details.

Once Ramirez finished, McElroy rubbed his chin and glanced at the three of us. "Any idea why Mrs. Fenton happened to end up at your doorstep, with a weapon in tow?"

"She did just lose her husband," I replied. "I don't know any woman, unless she wanted her husband dead, who wouldn't be distraught. Perhaps she'd been placed on medication? Hadn't been sleeping? Got confused?"

I was about to add a few more colorful ideas when the lieutenant raised his hand. "Thank you for your input, Ms. Jackson. I'll have an officer take both of your statements." I nodded, glancing at Martin, who also gave his consent.

"After that, we'll get you to the hospital so that you can check on your friend," the lieutenant added, patting me on the arm.

"Thank you. Is she—"

"Ms. Campbell is going to be just fine. Dehydrated. Dealing with the loss of blood but she'll be okay."

I nodded but bit my lip to prevent the tears from spilling over.

"One question, though." I looked up to find McElroy squinting at me. "Does your friend have any tendencies toward… violent behavior?"

My eyes widened. "Leah? She wouldn't hurt a fly. Why are you asking?"

McElroy shifted from one foot to the other and back before responding, "Well, I'm not sure how to put this, but she was making some odd comments in the ambulance, something about busting up a joint and give the ho a whirlybird or something. The EMTs thought it she was delirious from the blood loss, but then she took a turn and got downright feisty." He paused and when I gestured for him to continue, blushed as he added, "One of the EMTs is getting stitches as we speak."

I put a hand to my mouth. "Uh, chalk it up to the blood loss?"

My tone was hopeful and when he nodded, I released a sigh of relief.

"You ever see her act out like that?" McElroy asked.

I chuckled. "Only when someone makes an unsavory comment about her hair."

Before I could utter another syllable, McElroy turned on his heel and sprinted out the front door, cell phone in hand. It was saying something because despite being in moderately decent shape for a man of that age and girth, I doubted he'd done the forty-yard dash that quick since he'd been in high school.

Though he probably he couldn't hear me, I was compelled to call after him.

"Excuse me, Lieutenant? What the heck did I say?"

CHAPTER TWENTY-FIVE

Later, when the dust settled, I finally got answers to the questions that had been burning in my skull.

Okay, I was curious but truth be told, no brain matter was hurt in the process.

And, in full disclosure, I never received all of the answers I sought.

Big. Surprise.

While Leah was tended to in the hospital—opting out of various psychological tests that came highly recommended for reasons she still wasn't clear about, I joined Ramirez for coffee at a Dutch Bros. that was near the hospital and we huddled in the tiny seating area among the hipsters, newlyweds and exhausted new parents toting their strollers and people-watched.

We'd begun our third round of coffee-infused beverages, despite my declaration that I was cutting back to one a day. To be fair, I had stood out in my backyard and shouted the words earlier but no one but Nicoh and the birds had heard me, so I decided it wouldn't hurt to cheat. A little.

Besides, Nicoh was at home at the moment as the current

surroundings provided too much stimulation, I knew he wouldn't out me.

"So…you nabbed yourself an undercover gig, huh?" I asked him after all the pleasantries had been covered.

Ramirez took a sip of his coffee—black—before responding, "Yeah, we got a tip a while ago—around the time Martin showed up back in town and the thing with Theodore and his son went down—that turned us onto Robert Fenton's supposed nefarious activities, claiming he was into everything from extortion, money laundering, loan sharking, obstruction of justice and bribery."

It was quite a coincidence about the timing of the tip and I had to wonder if there was a reason—other than providing a frame of reference—that Ramirez had mentioned it, but decided to put a pin in that thought for now.

"Geez, that's almost the quintessential definition of racketeering. And after all of that, the baddie actually turned out to be his wife. Too bad Fenton had to die in order for her to get her way." When he nodded, I added, "You think he knew what was going on right under his nose?"

"Hard to say. It's hard to believe he knew nothing. But as far as having dirty hands? No, nothing pointed directly at him. Not to be disrespectful, but the man was more of a follower. Sure, he was our Governor, but it was his wife's wealth, and his own family money, that helped get him there."

I reflected on what Martin had said about the man in college and his relationship with Theo, then to Jeannie's comment about cogs.

"Once you knew his wife was the one who was behind everything, it must have been difficult being that closely tied to her. Especially having to serve as her confidante, knowing she killed her own husband, not to mention all the other things she was responsible for, probably while trying to throw his good name under the bus so that she could get away with it."

Ramirez studied his cup in silence. Even for Ramirez, it went on for far too long.

In my quest for answers, I hoped I hadn't made him uncomfortable or feel as though I was casting judgment. I realized getting close to the woman he had thought to be Jerri had been his job and I couldn't fault him for that, so I gave him a temporary pass by shifting the subject.

"How did she kill him? Everyone believed that it was natural causes, but that wasn't really the case, was it?" Ramirez's mouth twitched, ever so slightly. If you hadn't known what to look for, you wouldn't have caught it. "You held something back, something that would make her think she'd gotten away with it."

Ramirez shrugged but it was enough confirmation for me. "Not many people were aware of it—mostly immediate family and close friends—but Robert was highly allergic to animals. Specifically, dog hair."

I nodded. "She mentioned it when she came by for the impromptu visit—the one where she tried to convince me to ward Martin off." Ramirez looked down at his cup and I knew I'd touched on something, I just wasn't sure what. "Are you saying that she used his allergy as a means to kill him—with dog hair?"

"Not just dog hair. *Your* dog's hair," he replied, still not venturing at gaze in my direction.

"Nicoh's?" I blinked. "That's not possible. She wasn't in my house until after Robert had already passed."

"We don't know when or how she acquired it—you did say she was familiar with your home—she may have been watching your house—though I'm not sure how she would have managed to bypass the system."

"The alarm system," I groaned, slapping my forehead.

When Ramirez finally looked up, I told him how my service had been canceled by someone other than me or Leah.

"Once it was off, all she had to do was access the backyard.

There are a ton of Nicoh tufties floating around." Something else came to mind. "That might explain *how* she got the hair, but how did you know it was Nicoh's?"

Ramirez frowned and sighed. "From his DNA." When I gestured for him to continue, he added, "We collected samples from the warehouse—where Winslow and Theo were...allegedly killed and when Nicoh was in the animal hospital being tended to for his injuries from that...event—well, I collected some there as well for comparison."

I leaned back in my chair and crossed my arms. "So what, Nicoh's in some criminal canine database now?"

"No, I just had a hunch."

"A hunch?" I raised my brows.

"That's all I can say on that particular subject," he replied, his tone firm.

If he thought he'd closed the door on the previous topic—or on my mouth—he was sorely mistaken.

I uncrossed my arms and tapped my fingers, right in front of his cup. "Okay, so what? She stuffed Nicoh's hair in Robert's pillow, in lieu of a mint, before heading off to Chicago?"

Ramirez shook his head and sighed. "She injected him with it." *Eeew.* I feigned a barfing gesture as he continued, "She added it to his B12 shots and after he'd ingested enough of it, he basically stopped breathing."

"Didn't he have one of those pen thingies?"

"An epinephrine injector?" I nodded and motioned for him to continue. "He did but it was conveniently at the opposite end of the house. If he was unable to breathe..."

"He wouldn't have been able to make it in time," I finished his thought.

"Which is probably why we found him in the hallway," Ramirez replied.

"I thought he died in his sleep. In bed." When Ramirez

shrugged, I nodded. It had all been part of the ruse to make Jeannie think she had gotten away with it.

"You didn't know she was actually Jeannie, though, did you? That she and her sister had traded places when her sister got sick."

He shook his head. "Not until later. For the sake of everyone concerned, we're keeping that under wraps. She'll be charged and tried as Jerri Fenton. There's no need to open that can of worms. For now, anyway."

I nodded. I, along with others, would certainly appreciate that, whether they were aware of the circumstances—and the history—of Gemini, or not.

"How are Bob and Serena doing?" I asked.

"It's been a confusing time," Ramirez replied. "Especially considering that we are trying to keep Martin and the whole Gemini project angle out of it. They just can't understand how she ended up at Randy's that day."

"I take it none of my suggestions were viable."

"No, it's not that. In fact, they came to the same conclusions. It's just hard to lose your father one week and have your mother hauled off to jail for his murder the next."

"I can't begin to imagine...poor Bob," I replied, before adding, "Honestly, I think it's best he didn't find out the real truth."

Ramirez studied me for a moment. "You're talking about Theodore Winslow being his real father." When I nodded, he added, "I wouldn't want to live with that knowledge either."

I couldn't say I blamed him.

"By the way, how did you manage to show up when you did?" I asked after a moment of awkward silence.

Ramirez squinted, focusing on his cup. "I was already in the area."

"Following Jeannie?"

He shrugged. "That, and keeping an eye on you."

When I opened my mouth to retort, he raised a hand.

"Let's be serious for a minute, AJ. That incident with the fire made no sense. I suspected it was Martin who had put it out and kept thinking about your suspicions he was nearby. I was stopping by to chat about it and low and behold, Leah shows up, like a bat out of hell. I watch her grab the beret and head back out. She had just reached Randy's and was about to go around to the side door when Jerri…err, Jeannie, snagged her at knifepoint and forced her into the house. In the struggle, Leah dropped the beret."

I nodded. "Jeannie had probably followed us and had been waiting for a moment to strike. Leah's insistence upon retrieving the beret provided the optimal scenario…she knew she would return, so she just bided her time, lying in wait, until she could pounce. Only she didn't realize you had followed Leah and the beret…"

"Provided me with an opportunity," he concluded.

"So you waited and listened as we drew the story—and her confession—out, but how did you know that the gun in the beret would work?"

"Because I knew what you would do in the same situation."

I blushed, knowing he was right.

Ramirez, thankfully, was the one who changed the subject this time around. "How are you and Martin doing?"

I gave him the so-so gesture with my hand. "Eh, he's backed off on the whole Gemini thing, claims he wants us to get to know one another."

"But you think the moratorium on Gemini is temporary, which makes his intentions…questionable." Ramirez knew me well enough that he didn't need to pose a question. Or prod.

I sighed. "I do."

"What will you do?"

"Probably the same thing you chose to do—when it came to

telling Jere about his background—keep the details close. Until you can't. Only with Gemini, it seems like I'm never really in control, it has a way of popping up everywhere I turn...revealing its own details. If that makes any sense?"

"It does," Ramirez replied. "Speaking of our pal, Jere. Funny how he and his biological mother, Jerri, had the same name, don't you think?"

I nodded. I had made that connection a while ago. "You know how I feel about coincidences."

Ramirez laughed. "Indeed I do—perhaps you should have been a cop." I slid a look at him that could have cut glass, causing him to laugh two-fold. "Forget I said that. Ditto goes for your best friend." It was my turn to chuckle. "How's Campbell doing, anyway?

"Well, other than the repeated recommendations for a full psychological workup, she'll be fine."

Ramirez snorted. "Yeah, that EMT is still pretty freaked out."

"After what he said to her...he should be." When I caught his frown, I added, "Seriously, Ramirez, we are talking about Leah here."

He nodded and chuckled before turning serious. "So, really, how are things?"

I shrugged. "Time will tell."

"Are you referring to her decision to break up with Jere? Or the state of her friendship with you?"

I slumped into my chair, played with the straw in my latte before responding, "Probably both." I was silent for a moment before adding, "Someone once told me that there would always be a price to pay."

"He was either an idiot or the smartest person in the world for saying it." I looked up and found Ramirez staring back. A small, sad smile framed his mouth.

"Probably both." He shook his head and chuckled as I

collected my beverage and got up to leave. "I'll see ya around, Ramirez."

I offered him a little finger-wave before striding off in an effortless glide into my version of an Arizona sunset, which just happened to be at 10 am. Hey—don't judge. We can all dream about our perfect exits.

But most days, we live in the real world.

He'd probably thought I that was far enough away when he released a sigh and murmured, "If your track record is any indication, Ajax, I'm sure I will."

EPILOGUE

Two weeks later…

Leah's suitcases were packed and waiting at the door.

"You don't have to go." I handed her the ticket, but couldn't bring myself to make eye contact.

"I do. And we both know it," she replied, her voice lacking any luster.

After all of these years, I couldn't remember the last time I'd felt this crappy—the perpetual pit in my stomach, the pangs of anxiety and of course, there were the tears. These days, they seemed to appear more and more frequently.

"When will you be back?"

She sighed. "I don't know. But I will be okay."

"I know you will."

Though she claimed she was heading to Los Angeles to help the Stantons with an investigation, she'd packed all of her belongings, sold her vehicle and bought a one-way ticket.

"This isn't about you, AJ," she replied after a moment.

I glanced at her, frowning. We both hated the whole "isn't you, it's me" cliché. Apparently, my facial expressions hadn't improved and though it wasn't emerging from a place of joy, we both chuckled, replying in sync, "Yes it is."

"I just need to feel—"

"Safe," I replied, finishing her thought, to which she nodded.

We were silent—too silent—until she finally added, "That was cool of Ramirez...with the cop."

I nodded, knowing that she was referencing Ramirez's effort to keep Martin's true identity under wraps when everything with Jeannie went down.

"I also appreciate the fact that you didn't divulge the details to Jeannie or Martin...about Jere."

I glanced at her. "I said I wouldn't."

"Ramirez assured me of the same, despite the fact he's probably kicking himself for making that promise—always wanting to be the dude to ride in and save the day." She mimicked a guy holding his hat while riding a horse.

"He's kind of like that." I laughed.

"You two been talking?" she asked.

"Not since you were released from the hospital."

She squinted at me. "Do you...want to?"

I shrugged. "I'd rather have him as a friend than an enemy."

"Wise choice."

We both chuckled lightly and when the laughter fell away, I still felt there was something I needed to address. "I heard you broke it off with Jere..." When she tilted her head, I added, "Ramirez told me."

She rolled her eyes and after a moment responded, "It didn't feel right...there being a secret between us."

"I'm sorry."

"Don't be."

"Will you ever tell him?" Perhaps I had no right asking but I was curious. I wasn't entirely sure what I would do in her shoes.

She shrugged. "If I do, you be the first to know."

"Second."

"Right. Second." She laughed, this time, it sounded heartfelt, which gave me hope. "In the meantime, I have a parting gift."

I quirked an eyebrow. "Shouldn't I be giving you one?"

She released a snort. "Perhaps you should review my offering first."

She extended her hand, passing me a slip of paper with what appeared to be a phone number.

When I glanced at her in confusion, she continued, "It's about time you started working on Decker's request."

Before I could protest, she added, "It's the name of the woman who used to babysit for Decker while her mother and father were at work." I tilted my head, surely there was more. My friend did not disappoint. "But that's not what makes her interesting...at least not entirely. She also used to do housekeeping for Mrs. Edwards. On the night Decker's mom was murdered, she saw a man enter the apartment, shortly after dark, and emerge twenty-eight minutes later, covered in blood."

"Terrence Edwards," I replied, my eyes wide. "But twenty-eight minutes? How could she be so exact...and why didn't she come forward at the time?"

"Because Decker wasn't the only witness to the atrocities her mother endured."

"No..." I whispered, my mouth dry.

My heart thumped against my chest when the Uber driver honked.

As Leah collected her suitcases, she glanced over her shoulder to reveal the remainder of this parting gift.

"The woman's young daughter had spent the evening, playing in the apartment of her best friend, who lived across the hall, on the same floor. That best friend..."

"Decker…" I whispered, as my own bestie nodded and walked out the door.

~ The End ~

ABOUT HARLEY

Harley Christensen lives in Phoenix, Arizona with her significant other and their mischievous motley crew of rescue dogs (aka the "kids").

When not at her laptop, Christensen is an avid hockey fan and lover of all things margarita. It's also rumored she's never met a green chile or jalapeño she didn't like, regardless of whether it liked her back.

For more information on the author and her books, please visit her at www.mischievousmalamute.com.

OTHER BOOKS BY HARLEY

Mischievous Malamute Mystery Series
Book 1 ~ Gemini Rising
Book 2 ~ Beyond Revenge
Book 3 ~ Blood of Gemini
Book 4 ~ Deadly Current
Book 5 ~ Gemini Lost
Book 6 ~ COMING SOON!

Six Seasons Suspense Series
Book 1 ~ First Fall
Book 2 ~ Winter Storm